SPEAK OF THE ...

First Edition
© Paul Coates

No part of this publication may be reproduced or transmitted in any form or by any means, electronic or mechanical, including photocopy, recording, or any information storage or retrieval system, without permission in writing from the publisher.

This is a work of fiction. Names, characters, places and incidents either are the product of the author's imagination or are used fictitiously. Any resemblance to actual persons, living or dead, businesses, companies, events, or locales is entirely co-incidental.

ISBN: 978-0-6455637-4-0

TABLE OF CONTENTS

"The greatest trick the devil ever pulled was convincing the world that he didn't exist."

Verbal Kint in the film,
'The usual suspects.' 1995.

1
SO BEGINS ANOTHER WEARY DAY.

Unremarkable is an adjective that sits easily with Martin Hazel, being a perfect descriptor of his life. Members of the opposite sex (Martin is unremarkably heterosexual of course) have been known to describe him as 'not bad looking.' His job is neither exciting nor well paid, but equally there were plenty of people in London, let alone the world, working in jobs even less exciting and less well paid. If Martin's family had a coat of arms, the inscription underneath the blazon would be 'It could have been worse'. He lives alone in a small flat in an unremarkable part of north London. His girlfriend, Maureen, was described by Martin's mother, when she was introduced three and a half years ago, as a 'nice' girl. When his mother used that four letter word, it came with a whole basket full of judgements.

Let us now begin the tale of how someone whose painfully mundane and uneventful life transmuted from the unremarkable to the extraordinary.

His alarm clock, set at a tone and volume which is not too harsh to the ear, nudges him from his slumber. Groggily, he reaches across to press 'cancel' and automatically picks up his mobile phone. There are no messages for him so he replaces it on his bedside cabinet. The cabinet itself, a metaphor for Martin's life, was bought from IKEA in an end of season sale, being the last of a discontinued range. Reluctantly he leaves the warm sanctuary of his duvet and shivers. The central heating is on the blink so he runs to the bathroom and jumps in the shower. Basking in the warmth of the water, he takes longer than necessary. One slice of toast and an instant coffee later, he leaves his flat. The workday begins in earnest.

Walking fast, but not too fast, Martin hunches his shoulders, a futile subconscious action to avoid getting wet. Under the grey sky, he dodges the low hanging umbrellas of fellow commuters and weaves past the slower ones until he reaches the sanctuary of the small station concourse. His short walk to Finchley Central station has left him damp. A swipe of his travel card and he is on the platform standing at his usual spot which is where the doors of the second last carriage will open. In forty-five minutes, this carriage will come to a halt in the prime position for an efficient exit from his destination station. He has the routine down to a tee.

Standing close to him, but not too close, is a short bald man with a briefcase which looks devoid of files or papers. It probably has his packed lunch nestled in the bottom. They don't speak, they never speak, but for five days a week they stand near each other to get the 7.05, both boarding the second last carriage. They occasionally exchange a glance which for London commuters serves as a "Good morning'. The train terminates at Morden. Neither man has ever been to Morden because they both alight at Embankment on their way to work

Trundling into the station at an apologetic pace, the train reluctantly draws to a halt and the doors open. No-one gets off, no-one ever does at this time of day in Finchley central. It's not exactly a dream destination, more a place that commuters travel through. The carriage is half empty and Martin, standing in his prime waiting position, boards first. He has a clear and unencumbered path to his favourite seat. Most days his seat is unoccupied and this is one of those days. With a satisfied smile, he claims his prize and settles in. Popping in his ear buds he selects a play list. One of his favourite bands, Madness, fills his ears. Suggs sombrely sings about the bleakness of daily life. It's too close to home, so he switches off the music and digs out a paperback from his coat pocket. The plot so far is boring, but he is only at chapter three and is doggedly persisting with it, having already committed two journeys to the turgid storyline.

Keeping half an eye on the stops, Martin's mood raises slightly when he sees that Archway is next. His attention is wrested away from the novel and a bubble of expectancy grows inside him. Adrenalin tickles his insides, as the doors of the carriage slide open. The group of standing passengers shuffle backwards and sideways to make way for boarding commuters. Surreptitious glances from Martin try to seek out a familiar face but she is not there and a sharp pang of disappointment bursts his bubble of anticipation. Before settling back into his novel, his eyes meet those of the bald man sitting opposite and they both instantly avert their gaze back to their reading material. Surely, 'baldy man' could not have been waiting for the same woman. How dare he? Not that Martin knows the woman, nor has ever spoken to her, but she occasionally exchanges glances with him, and a couple of weeks ago he is sure he received a hesitant smile. Or at least he thought she was smiling at him. Love remains unrequited for another day.

For the rest of the journey Martin stares into his book seeing the words on the page but not reading them.

Twenty more minutes pass before the train arrives at the Embankment. The doors slide open, he disembarks slightly ahead of 'baldy man' and briskly walks through the tunnel directly opposite the carriage doors, then onto the escalator and through the station exit. Still grey, still raining, he walks fast, but not too fast, shoulders hunched, dodging the occasional umbrella and eventually enters a non-descript soulless building.

In the elevator he nods to a colleague as they ride up to the third floor but avoids any verbal exchange feeling self-conscious due to the presence of other passengers in the lift. He nods again as he exits, leaving his colleague to ride up to the fifth floor.

Acknowledging the smattering of other early starters as he strides through the open plan office, he gives an involuntary sigh when he spots his boss reading the newspaper in a private office at the end. Martin's desk is in the open plan area, in plain sight of his boss. The instant he logs on and taps in his password, his boss materialises beside him. A polite attention-grabbing cough prompts Martin to look up at a smiling face.

"Morning Mister Hazel, how are we today?"

"Fine, Mister Herring. Nice to see you back from your holidays. Did you have a good time?" asks Martin with the same level of faux formality. It's an office 'in' joke. Herring seems to find addressing each other as 'Mister' highly amusing and Martin plays along when he is in the mood.

Despite Martin's greeting, it wasn't particularly nice to see Herring back from his holidays, quite the opposite. As for whether Herring had had a good time, Martin couldn't give the proverbial toss.

His friend Ben describes Herring as a bit of a 'knob'. He often voices the opinion that Herring worked his way up by kissing the nether regions of his superiors. Martin isn't inclined to disagree.

A deep intake of breath precedes Herring's response to Martin's polite inquiry regarding the vacation. This indicates that he wants to discuss his holiday before moving on to work matters.

"The Maldives are amazing. And the food, oh the food, incredible. The ocean, amazing. Absolutely pristine. The location is so exclusive as well, you get a better class of person there if you know what I mean. Expensive mind you, and a bit of a stretch even on a manager's salary but the other half appreciated it and

I'm now well and truly in her good books. Major brownie points for Assistant Manager Herring."

"Sounds great," replies Martin, in a tone devoid of any enthusiasm.

"Speaking of holidays, I just signed off your leave for this December. Where were you thinking of going?"

"Dunno, not decided yet," lies Martin. Maureen had found a bargain deal in Lanzarote which wasn't surprising given the weather and the empty bars at that time of the year. He has limited interest and enthusiasm at the prospect but puts on a brave face when Maureen talks about it.

"But enough about the jet setting life of senior management," says Herring, sarcastically. The self-deprecation is disingenuous. "Let's move onto business matters, Mister Hazel. I was just wondering about the state of play of the McKinnons report. I thought you said it would be ready for me on my return."

"'Fraid not, they've been slow in providing the information we requested, so this held up the data analysis exercise," lies Martin. "I'll check my emails. I've almost finished, just need a couple of things clarified by their accounts department."

Unconvinced, Herring says, "In that case you'd better give them a good nudge. We don't need them complaining about missed deadlines if they are not pulling their weight and keeping their side of the bargain. Do we?"

Ignoring Herring's overtly crafted expression of scepticism, punctuated by a raised eyebrow on hearing his excuse, Martin agrees to get on to it.

"Please do," responds Herring with a slightly curt tone to underline who is in charge, before he turns and marches back to his office.

Having overheard the conversation, Ben sidles over. Ensuring that Herring has closed his office door, he leans across Martin's desk.

"What a tosser, Maldives my arse. What's his problem? Anyway, I thought you told me that you'd done the report already."

"Yep, I have. I just need to top and tail it. To be honest the job was so boring that I couldn't be bothered finishing it and moved onto something else. I swear he gives me the shit stuff on purpose."

"Whaddya mean. Do you reckon he still holds a grudge from the Christmas party? Wasn't your fault his bird draped herself over you. She was pissed as a fart."

"So, what are you saying?" chuckles Martin. "A woman has to be inebriated to fancy me?"

"Probably, but just trying to be supportive mate," laughs Ben.

"I'd be a liar if I denied that being managed by someone younger than me winds me up ... especially with his attitude."

By lunchtime he finishes the McKinnons report and emails it to Herring who waves through his office window and gives him the thumbs up. An action that makes Martin cringe.

Desperate to escape the suffocating atmosphere of the office, Martin pops over to Mario's Sandwich Bar to grab some lunch. Breathing in the fresh air, he looks up to the sky which has turned from light to dark grey and unhelpfully deposits some heavy droplets onto his head. No culinary risks are taken when he orders lunch and he selects one of the two sandwich options he chooses week in, week out. Today is prawn with lettuce and thousand island dressing on brown bread. Tomorrow, he will mix it up with his other favoured option, minted lamb on a white roll. He wanders back to the office in the rain with his slightly damp paper bag, sits down at his desk and peels it apart. Staring at the BBC football website which fills his screen, he chews mechanically whilst sipping on a cup of tea. To cap off an uninspiring morning he reads the report of his team's loss on Sunday.

Post lunch, the hours drag like a ship's anchor through heavy mud. If he had been abducted, chained to a chair and tortured mercilessly, Martin could not have told his captors what happened during the afternoon in any sort of detail. In between two departmental meetings, which he attends in body if not mind, he sits at his desk staring at the computer screen. He might have still been there for half the evening had Ben not tapped him on the shoulder on his way out with a cheery 'goodbye'. In his boredom induced torpor, he packs up and absently responds to Herring who also wishes him a good evening as he passes Martin on his way out.

On his journey to the tube station, he jogs by commuters in his eagerness to get home. Above him the sky has turned from dark grey to black as the winter evening takes hold. Wrapped in the comforting warmth of the tube station, he makes his way to the platform and places himself in the best position for boarding and alighting. Wind rushes through the tunnel heralding the arrival of the train but he does not take it because its destination is on the end of the Edgware branch. Three minutes later his train arrives, bound for High Barnet, and the doors open exactly where he has placed himself. He enters the carriage that will deposit him directly at the exit of the Finchley Central station in forty-five minutes. Squeezing himself into the standing area of a crowded train, he wriggles and reaches awkwardly into his pocket. Ear buds in place he loses himself in the music. The Jam are playing 'Down in the tube station at midnight'.

An uneventful journey takes a slight turn three stops from home. Doors slide open and the carriage empties sufficiently for all those standing to have a more comfortable amount of personal space. Through the gap of the open doors, he watches the crowd move towards the exit tunnel like a swarm of tightly packed bees. His attention is drawn to the back of the pack by the familiar sight of the blond bob of his unrequited love. She must have been in the carriage next to him. So close yet so far. That familiar pang of disappointment churns in his stomach.

Back in the flat the microwave pings. Extracting the tray of food, a Tesco's meal for one, he fumbles it onto the plate and pulls off the cellophane cover. Acquiring a slight burn from the escaping steam, Martin swears as he settles into his armchair to watch the seven o'clock news. His mobile phones buzzes. Recognising the caller, he places the meal on a side table and answers.

"Hi Maureen, what's up?"

"Well, that's a nice response, isn't it. Am I interrupting something?"

"No love, sorry, it's been a long day and I've only just got back and having a bite to eat."

"Don't be a silly Billy. I'm only joking Martin. I was just calling to say I'm tired and to be honest I can't face coming over this evening. Hope you understand."

Not only does Martin understand but he's relieved. Careful to craft the tone of his response with the right mix of concern and disappointment, he gives understanding murmurs during her explanation before he has space to reply.

"That's okay love, I totally get it, we've both got busy lives at the moment and you must be exhausted. We can do it another night."

"Thanks for your understanding, Martin. I'm going to watch a bit of telly. Something trashy and mindless, then I'm off to bed. Love you and I'll call tomorrow."

Without any degree of enthusiasm, Martin picks up his food and methodically works his way through an unremarkable meal. It was an unremarkable end to another unremarkable day.

2
IT'S A REPEAT AND
IT'S GETTING OLD.

Tuesday. Alarm. Duvet exodus. Shivering. Warm shower. Instant coffee. Toast. Exits flat. Raining. Hunched shoulders. Through barrier. On the platform standing in his usual spot.

Hearing the squeak of electricity, Martin looks expectantly up the line and is rewarded by the sight of the train rumbling towards the platform. The 7.05 is six minutes late. There is no sign of 'baldy man'. Either he got the 6.56 or he's also running late. The doors slide open, Martin boards and moves swiftly into his usual seat, which is unoccupied for the second consecutive day. A good week so far. Ear buds in, the Red-Hot Chilli Peppers beat out a rhythm. Once settled, he surveys the carriage.

Baldy man's normal seat is occupied by a younger man with gelled black hair swept into a rakish side parting. Martin unintentionally catches his eye, and, with a tinge of embarrassment, offers up a self-conscious semi-smile. Confidently, the young man returns the smile, his grey eyes sparkling with mischief. Appraising the man's couture - sharp black suit, white shirt, light blue silk tie - Martin decides he's probably a stockbroker going for the bohemian look. Maybe even a jazz fan, sporting a neat, close trimmed, jet-black goatee beard. A modern-day, sharper version of Acker Bilk.

Feeling the need to justify averting his eyes, Martin digs out his book and tries to read. Four days in and there is no sign of the story coming to life. Reading the words does little to elucidate any discernible plot. He may as well be looking at blank pages. Instinctively he glances up when Archway arrives. It's been over a week since he's shared a carriage with Unrequited love and was losing hope until last night, when he spotted her briefly on the platform during his journey home. The doors slide open and the standing crowd, in the centre of the carriage, shuffle to let in new passengers. Surreptitious glances, but no luck today. He looks down the carriage. Perhaps she entered through the doors further down, but still no sign. Once again, he catches the eye of the stockbroker, who returns a smile. This time the smile seems to have more meaning. Almost a 'knowing' smile. But, of course, the stockbroker cannot possibly know about his Unrequited love. Slightly embarrassed, Martin ducks his head back down into the sanctuary of his book, where it stays for the rest of his journey.

In a soulless monotone, the driver announces that the next station is Embankment where passengers can change for the District, Circle and Bakerloo lines. Martin closes his book and returns it to his coat pocket. Rising from his seat as the doors open, he notices that Mister Goatee beard is no longer there. Probably got off at Charing Cross.

Approaching his desk, Martin looks through the window of Herring's office. Instinctively Herring looks up, noting his arrival, then lifts his wrist to check his watch before gracing Martin with an ambiguous expression. It's somewhere between a knowing grin and an admonishment. This slightly irritates Martin. Granted, he's arrived a few minutes later than normal but it's still relatively early. Waving and smiling back at Herring, he is thinking *'fuck you'*.

"You okay?" asks Ben, who sidles up unnoticed.

"Yeah, sure. Just a bit later than normal because the trains were running late." Nodding over to Herring's office, he adds, "Though that dickhead seems to have a bit of a problem."

"Ignore him Marto, he's still basking in the glory of getting promotion before he's out of nappies."

"Assistant manager my arse, he couldn't manage a piss up in a brewery," says Martin, feeling a little more bitter about the situation than usual.

"Speaking of breweries, I'm at a loose end tonight, fancy having a couple at the Ship and Shovell after work, to lubricate your way home?"

Momentarily Martin considers the offer before accepting. He needs little persuasion to pop into their works local. Tuesday is near enough to a mid-week drink and frankly he's already bored out of his mind with his current assignments. What's more, the week ahead doesn't show any likely signs of improvement.

Buoyed by the prospect of an evening drink, Martin is surprised at his productivity and makes inroads into his latest mind-numbing project. At lunchtime he celebrates his progress with minted lamb in a white roll from Mario's Sandwich Bar. The afternoon passes much quicker than the previous day and he finishes the first draft of his report two days ahead of schedule. Leaning back in his chair with a feeling of satisfaction, he puts his hands behind his head and closes his eyes.

"No time for dozing Mister Hazel."

Where the hell did Herring appear from? Martin's eyes snap open and he swivels round in his chair to face his boss. "Just cogitating Mister Herring. Just cogitating."

"Can't have you doing that in work hours, you'll get arrested."

Forcing out a strained laugh, Martin nods and gives a thumbs up to acknowledge the joke. Not that it could rightfully lay claim to being humorous.

"Anyway, Mister Hazel, whilst the workers are dozing, the managers are strategizing. I'm off to the monthly managers' meeting and won't be back. So, I'll see you tomorrow."

Following Herring's progress to the exit past Ben's desk, Martin suppresses a chuckle when he catches his friend making the "wanker" gesture. He gives Ben a salute and turns back to face his screen. In the bottom right-hand corner, the time stamp reads 15.47. Courtesy of his own brief stint as acting manager, Martin knows that the monthly managers' meeting mostly involves 'team building' in a local wine bar. At least this means he will not be bumping into Herring in the Ship and Shovell. Five working days a week is plenty sufficient to have the pleasure of his company, without it leaking into social hours.

Notification of an unread message pops up on his screen. He opens it and a GIF of a robustly built man drinking a pint of beer pops up. "Let's go" is typed underneath. He looks over to see Ben at his desk miming the beer drinking motion. Martin returns the favour with the same mime. Twenty minutes later they're in the pub drinking real, not mimed, beer.

"Are you still looking for a transfer" asks Ben once he has placed their second round on the table.

"Dunno, maybe I'll get out altogether. It's not exactly like I've got a stellar career ahead of me here, is it?"

"Yer can't go mate. I'd miss you too much."

Blowing Ben a kiss, Martin jokes, "Darling, a man must do what a man must do. Parting is such sweet sorrow. It may end up with me having to make a choice of either ending our love affair or ending Herring's life."

"I'd opt for Herring's life. Have you applied for anything?"

"Not yet, I'm struggling to decide what to do. Mind you, I've been thinking about several options. One or two might involve moving out of London and what, with my mates all here and Maureen of course, I'm not …"

Martin stops in his tracks realising that Ben's attention has wandered.

"Ben, mate, wakey, wakey. Am I boring you?" Still getting no reaction, Martin gives his friend a hefty nudge, which does the trick.

Leaning in conspiratorially, Ben says, "Sorry mate, what were yer saying? I got distracted. Check out those babes over there." Ben points to a table in the corner. Martin nearly chokes on his beer. Oblivious of his friend's reaction, Ben continues to stare. "They are both a bit tasty mate, especially that blond one."

Composing himself, Martin says, "Er, yeah mate, not bad at all."

"Not bad! Not bad! I know you're in love with Maureen but c'mon. She's gorgeous mate."

"Yeah, fair enough, but stop making it so obvious, you'll get us arrested for stalking," replies Martin, staring in disbelief at his unrequited love.

Stomach churning, several questions rush around his brain. *How come he'd never seen her in the pub before? Does she work near here? Is she a regular?*

Unrequited love and her friend are deep in conversation throughout the evening. It looks like a serious heart to heart session. Ben talks incessantly, barely drawing breath, but Martin just nods mechanically to give the impression he is listening, although most of his attention is drawn across the room.

At one point he thinks Unrequited love glances over to their table and is half convinced that she recognises him and smiles, but then he decides he's fooling himself. Ben on the other hand has well and truly moved on to discussing football and his planned holiday to Ibiza. Over the last wo weeks, he's been trying to persuade Martin to join him. Martin has repeatedly declined, refusing to budge believing that Maureen would give him grief for even suggesting it. A boy's holiday in Ibiza would be a bridge too far for Maureen. Sanctioning such a trip with Ben, unsupervised, is an unlikely outcome, should Martin ever broach the topic with her. Scantily clad party girls on MDMA and alcohol, she would think not.

Three pints in, the beer takes hold of his bladder. Martin is forced to answer the call of nature and goes to the toilet. When he returns, he feels a mixture of disappointment and relief. Unrequited love and her friend have left the pub. Whilst Ben regaled him with Ibiza holiday plans, Martin had inwardly developed a more imminent plan of his own and it is not anything to do with Ibiza. It's about Unrequited love. He had half resolved to leave the pub when she did, in the hope that they would both be catching the same train. Fate has outwitted him; she has done the proverbial runner. He works it all through in his mind.

Who the hell is he kidding, there's no way he has the guts to do anything even if she'd stayed. What was he thinking he would do? Approach her on the train, chat her up, ask her out? Get real. On second thoughts, maybe there's still a chance. Maybe, if he leaves now, he might catch her up. She can't be far ahead. If I'm going to do it, I need to go now.

Reality kicks in.

A raised voice steals Martin from his musings.

"One for the road?" asks Ben, rhetorically.

"Eh! What? Yeah, go on," replies Martin, submitting to the inevitable.

An hour later he's sitting on the train home with a pleasant alcohol infused buzz. Three stops away from Finchley Central, Martin notices a familiar figure six seats further up the carriage on the opposite side. Mister Goatee beard throws out something between a grin and a smile. More of a grin than a smile. Strangely, he hadn't noticed him when he got on the train nor had he seen him board during the journey. Concluding that he must have dozed off at some point – it would not have been the first time he had a beer nap on the way home after an evening's drinking - Martin smiles back. Looking around, a peculiar feeling of uneasiness begins to come over him which grows when he realises that they are the only two people occupying the carriage. Checking his watch, he sees that it is only 7.42pm. Not exactly the last train, so unusual not to have the carriage at least half full at this time of the evening.

Not wishing to make a fool of himself, he decides against any attempt to make conversation. It's a winter mid-week evening in London. In the capital strangers don't engage and make conversation, unless they've connected on Tinder or Grindr or something similar. Martin has never been on either, although he could not speak for Mister Goatee beard. His best option is to employ the standard metropolitan social avoidance strategy. Keep your head down and pretend you're reading a book or watching something on your mobile phone. Adopting this approach, he feels more at ease, although the train seems to idle along and time runs slowly. When the welcome sign of Finchley Central finally appears, Martin jumps up to exit as quickly as he can. Scanning the carriage when the train pulls to a halt, he finds that he's the sole occupant. His fellow passenger must have got off earlier which he would have thought that he'd have noticed. It all felt very strange.

Perplexed he makes his way out of the station and sets a brisk pace all the way home. With the sense of being followed, he occasionally looks behind him. The streets are deserted, it is a dark winter night and he is a few bevvies to the good. Allowing himself one last look over his shoulder as he slips in the key to the door of his flat, he smiles, ridiculing his own paranoia. Scared of shadows. Pathetic behaviour for a grown man.

3
IS SHE REALLY GONNA TAKE HIM HOME TONIGHT?

Wednesday. Alarm. Duvet exodus. Shivering. Warm shower. Instant coffee. Toast. Exits flat. Raining. Hunched shoulders. Through barrier. Usual position on the platform. Train on time. Work. Herring being a dickhead. Prawn sandwich. Little work done in the afternoon. Agrees to a beer, just the one, in the Ship and Shovell.

They sit at the same table as the previous night. It's Ben's favourite table. He tells Martin that it's the prime hunting spot. Martin sets the beers down and slumps on the chair opposite his friend.

After an exploratory first sip, Martin asks, "Hunting what?"

Ben tuts, "C'mon mate, you know. The best spot to check out the chicks. To hunt down any available talent."

"You're aware that the 1970s is around fifty years ago. I don't think words like 'chicks' and 'talent' to describe women are used anymore unless you're on a night out with your dad."

"Each to their own Marto, each to their own."

"Tell me, exactly how many chicks have you picked up sitting at this table? I suspect less than one."

"Now, now. No need to be sarcastic. You may have pulled up the drawbridge and settled for Maureen but there are still some stallions running wild."

"For fucks sake Ben. Talk about a staggering degree of self-delusion. Who are the stallions? No don't tell me, Jacko, Dave and you. Team Ibiza, the threesome otherwise known as Stud muffin, Playboy and Tiger."

Laughing, Ben says, "Actually they are not bad names, I might tell the boys. Which one should I be? ... Tiger?"

"How about Love Nugget? Talking of talent hunting, how's the planning for your Ibiza trip going?"

"Pretty good, all the details are mostly settled. We've hired a flat and it has four bedrooms".

"But there's only three of you."

Ben gives a meaningful look, followed by a nod of encouragement.

"No way mate," says Martin.

"Why not, are you that afraid of Maureen? Under the thumb or what. Jesus Christ, you're not married, not even engaged for fucks sake. Seek her permission if it's needed. You'll have the best time of your life, which, in your case, wouldn't take much."

"Cheeky bugger," replies Martin, thinking to himself that Ben probably has a very good point and is not far off the mark.

Ben gives the lowdown of the timing and itinerary of the boys' trip, urging his friend to join the group. Worn down, Martin agrees reluctantly to test the water with Maureen.

Looking over Martin's shoulder, Ben's eyes widen in surprise. Reflexively, Martin starts to turn but freezes when Ben hisses an order not to look.

"Wassup?" asks Martin.

Grinning lasciviously, Ben whispers, "It's that blond, mate. The one last night."

With an involuntary shiver of excitement, Martin resists the temptation to turn round. Instead, he leans forward. "Is she with her mate?"

"You could say that. She's with a mate, but not the one from last night. A new one by the look of it."

"How do you know it's a new mate."

"Because it's a 'he' not a 'she'. For the record, the man's got style. I saw him move in smooth as a baby's bottom. He was walking past when she dropped her phone and he stopped to pick it up. He said something that made her laugh. Couldn't hear what it was but it did the trick. The smooth bastard moved in and sat next to her. They seem to have struck up a bit of a conversation."

Martin's heart sinks and he can't resist furtively turning round to survey the scene. But he's unable to get a clear view without twisting and craning his neck, so he says, "Right, I'm off to the toilet so I can check it out."

"Go Tiger," says Ben, smirking.

Intending to rely on peripheral vision, Martin walks with a slightly stiff gait, determined not to look directly to where they're sitting. It proves unsatisfactory. Against his better judgement, he succumbs and turns to get a better view. Initially he focuses on the blond woman and he feels a nervy squirm in his stomach when he recognises her. It is, without doubt, Unrequited love. Although he is now staring in her direction, she doesn't notice him. She's busy looking down, pressing and swiping the screen of her mobile phone. It looks suspiciously like she might be keying in the number of her new companion. Once Martin can tear his eyes away from the vision of beauty, he focusses on the man talking to her. His heart literally misses a beat. Her male companion is staring directly at him and worse still, gives a smile and a nod of recognition. To his horror, Martin locks eyes with Mister Goatee beard. Returning Goatees' nod with a slightly awkward head twitch, Martin briskly walks across the room into the sanctuary of the toilets.

Standing alone, Martin unzips himself and gives an involuntary groan as he feeds his last pint directly into the urinal. The low hum of the music from the bar leaks underneath the restroom door. It becomes much louder when it opens and another customer enters. Following standard male public toilet etiquette, Martin keeps his eyes firmly focussed on the urinal and goes about his private business. In his peripheral vision, he senses a large figure standing beside him.

Why the hell does he have to stand this close, there's loads of sodding space, thinks Martin.

"Hello," says the large figure who is now urinating next to him. He is sufficiently close and generates enough power to run the risk of spraying Martin with urine as it bounces off the steel wall of the urinal. Caught between a rock and a hard place, Martin responds but, stoically, he keeps his eyes firmly forward to convey through clear body language, that he is not looking down at the other man's penis. Hearing the greeting, Martin's faces the dilemma of being rude and offending the stranger by remaining silent or breaking the unwritten code of not looking directly at any other users. Breaking the code, he looks across but resolutely keeps eye contact.

Must not look down. Must not look down. Thinks Martin, successfully following his own private instruction.

"You probably don't recognise me. I was on the same train as you last night."

With an unwavering gaze, he meets the clear grey eyes of Mister Goatee beard. Martin is mortified. "Eh! Oh! Yeah! I remember you. Er. Nice to meet you," he replies, weakly.

"Nice to meet you too, my friend. Obviously, we won't shake hands as we both have our hands full," chuckles Mister Goatee beard.

"Yeah right," is all Martin can offer in response. Despite moving his head mechanically back from the position of eye contact to the tiles directly in front of his forehead, Martin's peripheral vision lets him down. He cannot fail to notice that what Mister Goatee beard has in his hand, is very large. Much larger than what Martin is holding.

As if to accentuate and draw further attention to his penis, Goatee gives it a vigorous shake before shoving it inside his suit trousers. Martin's mind filled with a visual metaphor of trying to force an oversized fluffy pillow into a newly washed pillowcase, that had shrunk in the dryer.

"Well, see you around."

Martin's interpretation of those four words is that the man who uttered them clearly has a justifiable superiority complex in the love tackle department.

Walking back from the toilet, Martin's eye is caught once more by Mister Goatee beard who is gives him a friendly wave. He waves back and notices that he is no longer with Unrequited love. The only thought that enters his mind is, *'Thank God'*.

During Martin's absence, Ben has replenished the round.

"Just got one for the road," says Ben cheerfully, adding, "What were you doing mate? You were ages?"

"Just pissing and having a heart to heart with old Goatee beard over there. Thank God the blond has buggered off."

"Whaddya mean?" asks Ben, then takes a long pull of his pint.

"I don't know what he keeps in his trousers but I suspect you need a license for it. It's a bloody offensive weapon. If that gets anywhere near the blond bombshell then, if I ever did make a move, she's in for a major disappointment. It is fucking huge."

"How do you know?"

"Mate, he was stood right next to me, it was impossible to miss it and he wasn't going out of his way to be discreet."

"How big?"

"How big! I don't know. I didn't have a fucking tape measure on me. What's more, if on the off chance I did carry one, I'm hardly going to say, 'excuse me would you mind if I measure your baloney pony before you put it back in the stable'."

"No need to get testy," replies Ben.

"Changing the subject, has Blondie buggered off?"

"Yeah, she left pretty much when King Dong got up to have a pee and bestow you with an almighty inferiority complex."

"Good, though it looked a bit like she was putting his number into her phone when I walked past."

"Who knows," said Ben. "Forget Blondie and King Dong, let's talk Ibiza. If you come along with us, I can guarantee there will be a hundred blondies all drunk, drugged and loved up, eager to introduce themselves to your micro weenie."

"Hilarious. I'll think about it."

"Don't think too long, we're off in five weeks. Maybe just enough time for you to get down to the local cosmetic surgeon for a pee narse enlargement."

"Presumably you've already been there. There's no bigger a pee narse than you."

"That's the spirit Marto, a bit of banter. Live a little. Join the Ibiza crew."

Wavering towards accepting the offer, but determined not to show it, Martin says, "I said I'll think about it, but Maureen has already booked one trip." He takes a sip of beer and as an afterthought adds, "I'm not sure if I want to use up all my leave in a space of a few weeks."

"Mate, a week in Ibiza with the lads and you'll need another quiet one with Maureen to get over it."

"We'll see," Martin empties his glass and stands up. "Right, I'm off. Drinking on two early weekday nights in a row, ain't good for me."

"Just think of it as pre-Ibiza training. I just going to hang around for a night cap. Got my eye on the barmaid."

Looking over to the bar, Martin smirks and says, "If it's the one with black hair, you've no chance. Punching well above your weight." With a parting shot, as he leaves, he points to an older grey-haired man serving customers further along the bar, "Best chance is with the other bartender."

4

IT'S JUST A SILLY PHASE
I'M GOING THROUGH.

"**A**re you feeling okay Martin? It's very hard work tonight. You've been sat opposite me looking like a wet weekend, not saying a word."

Opening his mouth to respond, he was beaten to the punch by the sound of an acoustic, guitar, violin and trumpet pumping out a tune he had heard a thousand times before. Friday night is date night and he is sitting opposite Maureen in their favourite local Mexican restaurant, Gringo and the Dashing Burrito. It was the third time the mini-Mariachi band had appeared, apparently from nowhere. The rotund manager of the restaurant plays the trumpet accompanied by the barman on guitar and a waitress on the violin. In front of them another waitress stands holding a small plate with a portion of chocolate cake topped with a sparkling candle. Three customers having a birthday on one night, it was beginning to wear thin.

Once the tune finishes and the applause from nearby tables subsides, the restaurant returns to normal with a background buzz of conversation and laughter. Finally, Martin can respond to Maureen's question. "Everything is fine, I'm just a little tired, it's been a busy week."

"Well perhaps if you didn't get drunk with your mate every evening after work, then you'd be less tired by the weekend. I've not seen you all week and I do think you could make more of an effort." Irritated, Maureen sits back, folding her arms and pouting.

"I don't normally drink during the week, do I? It's just there is a lot going on and I needed to de-brief with Ben," lies Martin.

Maureen stays silent, arms folded, re-doubling her pouting. Whenever she wore her sulky angry expression, Martin always thought she looked like she had swallowed a wasp. More disconcerting, Martin realises that she bears an uncanny resemblance to his mother. This was the same disapproving look that dear old Freda Hazel, God rest her soul, adopted when young Martin arrived back from school with scuffed new shoes, clutching a term report which recorded a clean sweep of C's. Martin is mentally transported back to his schooldays.

Deciding to offer up a further slice of humble pie, Martin leans forward to show his sincerity. "I'm sorry Maureen, I promise I'll do better." In the nick of time, he managed to correct himself from calling her Mum.

"Sometimes I think you don't love me," snaps Maureen, with a healthy dose of petulance.

"Of course I do," protests Martin, whilst wondering if he really does.

"Well, you don't show it. I've done all the work arranging our holiday and you've not shown one iota of interest. Sometimes I think you don't even want to go to Lanzarote."

"Of course I do," protests Martin once more, but this time he is now one hundred per cent certain that he doesn't.

"Well, what's the problem then, because I am damn sure I don't know what the hell is wrong with you?" Adjusting her pink Marks and Spencers cardigan, she resets herself and waits for Martins next move. After a short, but uncomfortable silence, Martin dips his toe in the water.

"Genuinely, I am tired and under pressure at the office as well as depressed at the sheer boredom of the work that Herring gives me. It's the sort of stuff he should be giving to junior staff. I don't know whether he's being patronising or just a dickhead."

"Well, that's hardly my fault. I've my own problems at work but I don't take them out on you."

"I'm sorry. I feel as though I just need a few days letting my hair down to take my mind of it. To reset and probably rethink my future."

"If that's the way you feel, just take a couple of days off. I'm sure you've got enough annual leave. We only go on holiday once a year."

Martin had not planned to have this conversation but a rare flash of inspiration hits him and he seizes the moment. "That's what Ben said. As a matter of fact, he invited me to join him and his mates for a few days on a sort of golfing trip."

"You don't play golf."

"No, but Ben and his mates do. I wasn't expecting to be invited but, knowing I am a bit down, Ben suggested I tag along. To be honest, it's just a boys drinking trip with a bit of golf thrown in. Sort of male bonding. I know it sounds crass, but I think it's what I need to shake me out of this mood."

Maureen's pout, tightened.

"What do you think? Should I go?" probes Martin, trying not to sound overly keen.

Now the onus of the decision has been placed on Maureen. Cleverly, Martin has engineered the situation so that an answer in the negative would come across as unreasonable, petulant and churlish. The hook has been baited and cast into the water. Narrowing her eyes, she tries to read Martin's thoughts. "So, are you now saying you want me to cancel Lanzarote?" A booby trap has been laid, but it wasn't buried deep enough to catch its prey.

"Oh! No, no, no. Ab-so-lutely NOT. I'm really looking forward to our trip. It will be lovely just to spend time together away from the trudge of commuting and work. If I had to choose only one, of course it would be Lanzarote but the boys' trip is a few weeks before ours. I think I could do with a break before we go away." It was time to ramp up the martyr and guilt index. "Anyway, don't worry, if that's how you feel I'll tell Ben it's a 'no.' The last thing I want to do is cause an argument over a short break with the boys. I'll tell Ben

I'm not able to go. I'll give him some excuse about lack of time or money."

Slackening her pout and unfolding her arms, Maureen leans forward. "I'm glad you feel that way about our trip because I'm really looking forward to it."

Game over then, no boys trip for me, thinks Ben.

She looks earnestly into his eyes. "No, really Ben, I wouldn't want you to miss out. There's no reason that you can't do both."

"Are you sure? Look I'm happy to tell Ben that I can't do it. I'll make an excuse about not having the cash for two holidays." Instantly, Martin regrets what he had said, has he pushed it too far and given her the opportunity to change her mind.

She reaches for his hand and smiles like a doting mother handing out a treat for good behaviour. Grasping it with both of hers, she looks into his eyes. "I wouldn't dream of it. Of course you should go. Just promise me you'll come back refreshed and that you'll leave Mister Grumpy in the Golf resort."

"Of course I will darling, it's a promise," replies Martin, with a forced chuckle.

"And one more thing, and I want the truth."

"Yes," replies Martin with trepidation. His mind races trying guess exactly what is 'the truth' she is looking for.

"Do you have a secret admirer?" she asks with a glint in her eye.

"What, sorry, I mean pardon."

Maureen points to a table in the corner behind Martin. He turns round to see who she is talking about. At that moment the mini-Mariachi band surrounds the table and plays the birthday song obscuring Martin's view of the lucky patrons who are the object of Maureen's attention. He turns to Maureen with his arms spread out to show that he cannot see who she was pointing to. She raises an index finger in response, telling him to wait a minute. The band clears and Martin can now see the couple at the table. His jaw drops, its Goatee beard man. Across the table sits a tall slender woman with her back to Martin. For a split second he thinks the woman is Unrequited love and follows up this thought wondering if he is becoming obsessed. Goatee's female companion throws her head back laughing and he gets a clearer view of her face. She is beautiful but she is not Unrequited love. Thank God.

"Don't keep staring Martin, he'll see."

"Who?"

"Your secret admirer, the cute man with black hair and one of those little beards. With those amazing grey eyes, he'd make a good hypnotist. I saw him looking over to you, though Gods knows why, especially when he has got that supermodel sitting opposite him. She is stunning."

"Oh! Him."

"Why do you say that? Do you know him?"

"No."

"Well, he was definitely giving you the once over like he knew you."

For the rest of their meal, Martin converses on auto pilot unable to stop thinking about Goatee and stealing the occasional furtive glance when Maureen is distracted or looking down to fork her food. When Goatee eventually rises from the table the Supermodel follows him. She goes to the reception desk to grab her coat from the row of wooden pegs next to the front door. Diverting his path for a visit to the toilets, Goatee looks back towards Martin and their eyes meet. Smirking, Goatee turns and enters the rest room. Excusing himself, Martin leaves the table.

Another customer on his way out passes Martin in the restroom doorway, and once inside Martin sees that it is empty except for Goatee who is at the urinal. Not wishing to repeat the last toilet encounter, Martin walks to the sinks and washes his hands, all the while looking into the mirror watching Goatee relieve himself. The sound reverberating on the metal urinal is loud and heavy. Finally, the stream comes to a halt, as if a hosepipe had been switched off. Still with his back to Martin, Goatee shuffles and calls over to Martin whilst zipping up his fly.

"We really have to stop meeting like this?"

Trying to compose a witty response, Martin hesitates and failing to think of one, replies tentatively.

"Guess you're right. I'm beginning to wonder if you're stalking me."

Goatee responds with a dismissive snigger. "Funny you should say that but to an objective outsider it would look very different."

"Whaddya mean?" asks Martin defensively.

"Well, I was in the restaurant at least a quarter of an hour before you came marching in. So, if there is any stalking being done, it's you, not me. You also followed me into the restroom."

"My girlfriend saw you staring at me," protests Martin desperately trying to regain the upper hand.

"I'm sure she did. Like I said, we arrived well before you and I saw you come in."

At an impasse, Martin struggles to work out his next move but his mind is a blank. Filling the awkward silence, Goatee takes the initiative. He walks towards the sinks and washes his hands in the bowl next to Martin, whilst Martin looks on haplessly. Goatee does not face Martin directly but looks at the image of them both in the wall mirror whilst he speaks.

"Well, I do hope you and your girlfriend have enjoyed your meal and please enjoy the rest of your evening Mister …?"

Goatee leaves the question hanging for Martin to respond. Martin hesitates then replies distractedly,

"It's Hazel" he mutters as Goatee exits the rest room. He doesn't know if Goatee heard his response nor did he take the opportunity to ask Goatee's name. By the time he comes out of the restroom, Goatee and the

Supermodel have left and, in an almost semi-hypnotic state, he wanders back to the table.

"Are you okay Martin?" asks Maureen, with a frown of concern.

"Oh! Yeah! Me? Yes, I'm okay, just a bit tired."

"You were ages. I thought you'd been flushed down the toilet. I've been a bit worried about you. You've not been yourself lately. You're no spring chicken now that you're in your thirties. Do you think you should get your prostate checked? Is it taking you much longer to pee?"

"Jeez Maureen, I'm thirty-two, I've a functioning bladder and no grey hairs … yet. I wasn't in the loo that long."

Re-setting her pout, she says, "And, as well as more frequent bathroom visits, you get tetchy a lot more easily nowadays. The sooner you have your golfing holiday the better. Let's hope it does some good," replies Maureen, huffily.

Discretion being the better part of valour, Martin mumbles an apology. Catching the waiter's eye, he mimes imaginary scribbles with his index finger on the palm of his other hand. They sit in silence until the waiter brings the bill and a handheld device which Martin swipes with his credit card.

"You didn't even check the bill," chides Maureen.

"The total looked about right," retorts Martin.

Back at his flat they make love because its Friday and Friday night is date night. Neither are overly enthusiastic and, as love making goes, it is unremarkable.

5
LITTLE DARLING, I FEEL THAT ICE IS SLOWLY MELTING.

Thursday. Alarm. Duvet exodus. Shivering. Warm shower. Instant coffee. Toast. Exits flat. Not raining but cloudy. Through barrier. The 7.05 is on time.

After an uneventful weekend, Martin returns to the grind and eventually reaches the point of the week where he feels the back of the drudgery has been broken and the next weekend can be seen on the horizon. Not that it necessary promises excitement and joy judging by the last two weekends, but at least he's not working. An added bonus is that he has, for the first time this week, secured his favourite seat. The previous day 'baldy man' had the impudence to take his self-allocated space. Uncharacteristically Martin had dawdled, too busy daydreaming about Unrequited love. What followed was a short trip into the world of non-verbal, commuter communication. With reserved English outrage, Martin gave baldy man a mildly indignant stare. Baldy man returned serve with an apologetic shrug which translated to 'sorry mate, but it was the only free seat.'

Still, no need to dwell on the past, today Martin is ensconced on his rightful throne, ear buds in but the novel resting in his coat pocket. He decides to give it a rest for a day or two before he makes the call to either persevere or abandon it. Instead, he sits back, closes his eyes and listens to his sixty's playlist. With the Beatles crooning into his ears, he almost doses off.

Gradually the train slows to a halt which precipitates an announcement by the driver. Hearing the muffled words through the intercom, Martin pauses the music and opens his eyes to hear the message.

"Apologies for the delay, we have had to stop just outside Archway until the train on our platform departs. There has been a small incident which has now been resolved, so we should not be too long."

Murmurs and groans pepper the carriage but are quickly silenced when the train moves again, this time slowly as it cautiously approaches the now vacant platform and then grinds to a halt. The doors open and the new passengers tentatively enter, edging past those already standing in the carriage. Disinterestedly, Martins sees the jockeying for position but his eyes widen at the vision of Unrequited love squeezing through the crowd to claim a gap in front of Martin's seat. She reaches for one of the hand straps to avoid stumbling when the train starts.

Martin looks up and is faced with the polite male commuter's dilemma. Does he offer his seat or does he look down pretending he hasn't noticed? Does he risk the embarrassment of a refusal being labelled a sexist or does he keep just looking down with dogged concentration. Will she think he's being patronising? Uncharacteristically, Martin decides that fortune favours the brave. He looks up, catches her eye, she smiles. God, she is beautiful.

"Can I offer you, my seat?"

A tense moment for Martin ensues, whilst she works out if he is talking to her. Tension replaces relief when her quizzical expression softens to another smile.

"That's very kind of you but I only have a couple of stops. But thank you all the same."

"No problem," says Martin, slightly embarrassed and self-conscious despite the positive response. He has put his neck above the parapet and publicly got a refusal. A slightly awkward four stops later, she alights.

For the rest of his journey, Martin bathes in the lukewarm water of partial success. True, she had not embraced his chivalry but also true that at some level he has broken the ice. If she has not noticed him before, she has now. She did smile even before he made the offer and it could well have been a smile of recognition. If he notices and recognises people he often sees on the train, why shouldn't she?

"So, you're saying you've laid the groundwork," says Ben as he tucks into a salami and cheese roll.

"That is not what I said," protests Martin, with his mouth full of minted lamb.

Both had decided to escape the office for a while and rather than take their sandwiches back to their desks, they sit on high stools resting against a narrow ledge next to the long window along the side of Mario's Sandwich Bar. It allows for a handful of customers to eat in, if they are willing to be frequently nudged, accidentally, by others queueing along the counter. The shop is long and narrow and it's a squeeze.

"Mate, it sounds as though you made contact, she smiled and thanked you."

"Yeah, but she didn't accept my offer, did she?"

"A man offering a seat to a woman means you are either locked in a televised dramatisation of a Jane Austen novel or you have the balls of a rampaging bull. Full respect to you. You took the risk and instead of being labelled a patronising, sexist pig by some radical lesbian, you came up trumps."

"I can see that investment that the company has made in inclusiveness training has paid dividends with you Ben." Munching on his roll, Martin pauses for thought. *Maybe, for once, Ben might have a valid point. She did smile and she didn't seem to be offended in any way. And ... their eyes met.*

With the bit between his teeth, Ben pursues his line of thinking.

"Next time you see her, you need to follow up. Did you check out any telltale red flags?"

"Such as?"

Ben sighs. "For God's sake, things like did she have a ring on her finger?"

"I'm not even sure people get engaged or married nowadays. But to answer your insightful question, no I didn't notice but I didn't really look. I was still mortified and couldn't keep eye contact."

"Mate, you'd give Casanova a run for his money. You're dynamite."

"If you are going to take the piss then I'm not going to share stuff like this with you anymore."

"Harden up Princess. On to more immediate matters, what's the story with the Ibiza trip? Did you give it any more thought?"

This time, Ben's question raises a smile because it gives Martin the perfect opportunity to re-instate some masculine credibility.

"Yeah, actually I have. Against my better judgement I will be joining the Muppet Show in the Balearics"

"Sorry?"

"Yes, I am joining you lot for the Ibiza trip, providing the offer is still open."

Raising his arms Ben gives muted cheer, so as not to draw too much attention in the crowded space. He then pats Martin on the shoulder. "Mate, I don't bloody believe it. Don't tell me you laid the law down with Maureen."

Maintaining his regained status of toxic masculinity, Martin winks. "Let's just say that I've had a discussion and I'm going, and leave it at that," replies Martin in a way that neither confirms nor denies Ben's premise. It is the perfect opportunity to gain further ground in the blokey respect stakes.

"Well bugger me, you've finally grown some balls."

"I believe the correct phrase in Ibiza would be cojones."

Ben laughs and pops the last bit of his sandwich into his mouth.

Squeezing past the queueing customers, they leave the shop and wander back to the office which takes longer than normal. Neither are in great hurry to return to their desk. Once settled in, Martin completes a leave request and emails it to Herring before returning to his half-completed spreadsheet. Some people find spreadsheets fascinating. Martin does not, but he is good at them.

Appearing by his side, Herring leans over to grab Martin's attention. Martin looks up. Mentally he sighs and silently prays that his sigh did not have an involuntary physical manifestation. He cannot be certain either way.

"Just letting you know that I've authorised your latest leave request."

Normally, the Human Resource application automatically sends the employee a message but clearly Herring is bored and fancies a chat.

"Yeah, thanks," replies Martin, hoping that this will end the interaction and Herring will bugger off. No such luck.

"Looks like you're really pushing the boat out. Where are you going this time. Or hasn't Maureen decided?" asks Herring, sarcastically.

"As a matter of fact, it's Ibiza." Nodding towards Ben's desk, he adds, "a boys trip organised by our resident entertainment manager."

"Aren't you a bit old for that sort of place?"

"Perhaps you are just old before your time Hezza," says Ben, who hearing the conversation has walked over to join them. Working in a different section to Martin, Ben is not as shackled in his dealings with Herring.

"It's Herring to you Watkins." Watching his boss walk away huffily and then firmly closing his office door, Martin considers it safe to talk.

"You're funny Ben and I appreciate your support, but he takes himself very seriously so I would dial back the banter."

"I don't give a shit. I'm not answerable to him thank God, and the bloke is a clown. Anyway, are you up for a drink tonight?"

"Better not, tomorrow is Friday night and I'm out with Maureen".

Giving his best 'are you serious' expression, Ben stays silent forcing Martin to justify himself."

"Oh! Go on then, just one."

Re-focussing, Martin turns back to his spreadsheet. The afternoon drags but the spreadsheet is completed. With palpable relief Martin tidies his desk, logs off, gives Ben the sign and they make their way to the Ship and Shovell.

Depositing himself in his favourite spot, Ben tells Martin that it's his round. Without complaint or protest, Martin goes to the bar to get the drinks, leaving Ben to scan the premises for 'talent'.

When he returns with two pints of beer, Martin says, "Here you go. I got served by that barmaid you fancy."

"Yeah, I saw. Tried to chat to her the other night after you buggered off. No luck. I was given the cold shoulder."

"Can't say I'm surprised. I told you that you were punching above your weight. Did you try the grandad?"

"My, my, my. We are getting to be the smartarse, aren't we? Obviously, Blondie has given you renewed confidence."

"Birds of a feather mate."

"You'll fit right in with the Ibiza crew."

They drink in silence until a memory pops into Ben's mind.

"Hey, I meant to tell you, I was in here the other day on my own. A swift half before heading home so to speak, and I got talking to your mate."

"What mate?"

"King Dong."

Momentarily confused, Martin tries to process the information but is unsuccessful. Ben assists.

"Y'know that bloke who tried to pick up blondie."

"Sorry?"

"King dong, the bloke with the monster dick. The one with the black hair and pissy little chin beard."

Realisation dawns. "You're fucking kidding me."

"Nope. He sat there," says Ben pointing to the table next to them. We were both drinking alone and he struck up a conversation. Quite a nice bloke, actually. Chatted about all sorts of things but get this."

"What?" asks Martin, still incredulous that one of his best mates is suddenly pals with his nemesis.

"You'll never fucking believe it. What a co-incidence."

"What?"

"We got chatting about what we do and ended up talking about holidays. Believe it or not when I told him about Ibiza, he laughed. It turns out that he's going to be in Ibiza the same time as us."

"For fucks sake Ben."

"Not only that but he is staying in the hotel next to our block of apartments. He arrives a day before us, so we agreed to meet in his hotel bar after we've checked in. The Ibiza crew grows from three to five."

"But you hardly know him," whines Martin.

"Mate, he's a clever, funny bloke and with his looks, and chat up skills, he'll be a real asset on the talent hunting. He got talking to your blondie in the wink of an eye."

"Yeah. Thanks for the reminder. Let's hope the twat doesn't wear Speedos around the pool. The local women will be choking on their cocktails."

"That's the spirit Martin. You're not only honing your smart-arse skills but you can also be funny. You're gonna fit right in. My round." Having drained his glass, Ben approaches the bar. He carefully avoids the section covered by the barmaid who rebuffed his suggestion of a romantic liaison. By the time he returns Martin has finished his first drink.

"Cheers mate, I said just one, so this is definitely my last before going home."

"Shame Marto, you were doing so well. Still, you've made progress. Gained a little independence from Mozza, grown some balls, acquired a sense of humour and turned into the banter king."

"This is my last one, definitely my last one then I am off and you are on your own," warns Martin.

6

OH, DEMON ALCOHOL, SAD MEMORIES I CAN'T RECALL.

If Martin had gained, or re-gained, the skills of independence, banter and humour, as Ben had claimed, then he had lost willpower in the process. Against his better judgement, he stayed until closing, during which he graduated from, just beer, to beer with a chaser, then onto downing double whiskies. Beyond that, he cannot remember a thing.

Having awoken with a severe hangover, he is in the midst of one of the worst working days of his life. It's hell on earth, frequently being hassled by Herring whilst all the time trying not to vomit over his keyboard. He clock-watches for two reasons. The main one is simply to see how long there is to go before he can reasonably excuse himself from damnation and return to the sanctuary of his flat to sleep it off. The subsidiary reason is to count down how long it is before he can safely take another double dose of aspirin to dull the throbbing pain in his head. A small demon is inside his skull, tapping it vigorously with a small, razor-sharp ice pick. He endures the torture until two o'clock and can bear it no more. Logging off after sending Herring an apologetic email explaining that he has a migraine, he leaves the office. For once, Martin is grateful for modern workplace regulations which allow an absence to go medically uncertified if less than three consecutive days. Of course, being a Friday, Herring assumes the worst after he reads the email. Clearly, it is an overt tactical move to extend the weekend, but what could a manager do? Short answer, nothing. Nevertheless, he makes a mental note to discuss it in the upcoming annual appraisal.

By three thirty Martin is home in bed asleep. A short beep on his phone letting him know of an unread text goes unheard, as does one that follows five minutes later. The first one is from Ben and has only one word. That word is 'Lightweight'. The second text from Maureen is slightly longer which reads 'See you at 7pm at On Cloud Wine.' It is their favourite wine bar. Rather, it is Maureen's favourite wine bar. Martin can take them or leave them. In his opinion they're the watering holes of wannabe sophisticates.

Magically, he's on the beach with the waves gently lapping, a sangria in one hand and a beautiful blond laid next to him. All the pain and feeling of nausea has gone and the blond leans into him caressing his stomach. Slowly her hand moves down to the top of his shorts and starts to creep under the elastic. The sound of lapping waves dissipates and is replaced by incessant piercing beeps from his phone, which rips him from his dream. He had set his alarm to give him enough time to shower for his date with Maureen. *He must remember to change the tone to something gentler.*

It's six thirty, leaving him just enough time to shower, change and get to the wine bar as arranged. Pleasantly surprised by his much-improved physical state, Martin jumps into the shower feeling rested and largely hangover free. Nausea and the headache have dissipated. Obviously the three aspirins he took before collapsing into his bed have done the trick, not to mention the extra three hours sleep. Refreshed and dressed, he is chipper and ready to go. He needs to be on his game this evening to keep Maureen on side and make sure he does not jeopardise the Ibiza trip.

Entering the wine bar with five minutes to spare, Martin sees a small table for two and sits down to claim it. So far so good, no sign of Maureen, she hates it when she arrives first. Not prone to Maureen's self-consciousness, Martin is happy to sit alone in any bar and so orders a bottle of their usual wine. The waitress brings the bottle and two glasses just as Maureen enters the bar. Perfect timing. He stands up as she approaches the table, gives her a peck on the cheek and they both sit down.

"You're turning into quite the gentleman," she says, as she settles herself and reaches for the wine he has just poured.

"How so?"

"Standing up when a lady approaches, pouring her wine, a respectful greeting. Need I say more?"

"All part of the silver service for the woman I love."

"Either you've been having coaching lessons from the local lothario or you want something. And I don't know of any local lotharios."

"Such cynicism from one so fair."

"Mmmm, I wonder," says Maureen as she takes a sip of wine. "Anyway, how's your day been?"

"Easy, a boring Friday. Just a normal day at work," lies Martin. "What about you?"

"Same I guess, anyway I want to take you through the arrangements I've finalised for our Lanzarote trip."

Making a concerted effort to convey interest, Martin keeps eye contact and gives occasional murmurs and nods to show he is taking in everything that she is telling him. She likes to take control, so although he absorbs only a fraction of what she had just told him, it will not make a difference. He'll just follow her through the airports, into the taxis and to and from the hotel, like a lapdog. Although fully zoned out by the end of her lecture, he feigns enthusiasm once she finally stops talking.

"Sounds great," he replies, with enough energy to avoid raising suspicion.

"And what about your plans?" she asks.

Initially thrown by the change of subject, it feels like they had been discussing Lanzarote for an hour, he is saved by Maureen's clarification. "I'm talking about the Ibiza trip."

"Oh! that, not much as far as I know. To be honest I'm more focussed on our trip. All I've done is book flights. I managed to get on the same flight as Ben. Basically, he's making all the arrangements and he'll meet me at the airport. Other than that, I haven't given it much thought."

It had the desired effect, Maureen smiles with satisfaction. He has said exactly the right thing, balancing apathy with ignorance to convince her of his ambivalence to the Ibiza trip compared to keen anticipation for Lanzarote. Munching through various small sharing plates the conversation is easy, if uninspiring.

During the meal, Martin had not looked around at other tables. Subconsciously he feared spoiling the good vibe by finding Goatee laughing and joking at a nearby table with yet another supermodel. He need not have worried, the restaurant is Goatee free and he wonders if, perhaps, he is getting a little obsessive. One never knew, he may get to know him better on the Ibiza trip and they could become good mates. Equally as probable, Unrequited Love may sit next to him on the train, grab him and give him a passionate kiss expressing her rampant desire for his body. Just as he develops that thought, an image of Goatee standing in Speedos inserts itself into his musings. Mercifully, the voice of Maureen snaps him out of it.

"Martin. Did you hear what I said?"

"Er, sorry. What"

"For goodness sake, I was asking you if we should order coffee. We could push the boat out and order Irish coffees."

"Oh! yeah, sorry. Sounds good."

Courtesy of half a bottle of wine and an Irish coffee, Maureen is tipsy and begins to give Martin that familiar leer which usually is a precursor of her desire for a spot of bedroom action. Unfortunately, the wine and food consumed this evening, after the previous night of unplanned debauchery, does not leave Martin quite as enthusiastic. *But a man's gotta do what a man's gotta do*, he thinks.

They arrive back at his flat and Martin offers a nightcap before they go to bed. The offer is left hanging. Maureen heads with intent and determination straight to the bedroom.

Mercifully, Maureen orgasms quickly and Martin rolls onto his back breathing heavily. Once he settles down, he looks to his side. Maureen's smile transforms into a slightly worried expression.

"Are you okay Martin?"

"Yeah, fine, why?"

"Well, you didn't, you know … finish."

"Sorry, I thought you came?"

"No silly. Obviously, I did. But I'm pretty sure you didn't".

"It was great Maureen. I'm just a bit tired and too drunk. Must be old age kicking in."

"You're in your thirties not sixties, you silly thing."

"Honestly it was good, let's not go on about it."

Satisfied both physically and with Martin's explanation, she cuddles up to him and quickly falls asleep. Martin, on the other hand is wide awake partly due to his unscheduled mid-afternoon nap but also due to an overactive mind. When insomnia kicks in, he tries to think of something pleasurable to distract him from work worries. This is often successful and usually sleep follows. One of the more frequent topics that pops randomly into his thoughts is Unrequited love, especially when travelling on the train where he was most likely to see her. But recently she had been relegated to second place with Goatee often invading the space. This is one of those moments.

Why the hell am I thinking about him, even when I'm lying in bed having made love to Maureen? What the hell is wrong with me?

To expunge Goatee from his brain, he focusses his thoughts onto Unrequited love. It works for a couple of minutes but then Goatee pops back into his consciousness, uninvited.

He kicks out Goatee by imagining Unrequited love dressed in exotic underwear, to keep other thought interlopers at bay. Smiling, he begins to doze with this welcome image. Finally, sleep takes hold.

In his dream, Goatee re-appears naked, except for a diamante laced leather jock strap that looks as though it is going to burst with the weight of its contents. With a mixture of disgust and fascination he is initially distracted by Goatee but realising that he has been lured into a trap, Martin expels the vision and Unrequited love re-appears. This time she is bent over his kitchen table, still in exotic lingerie. She looks back over her shoulder, wiggles her bottom and calls him over whilst pouting seductively. Unbuttoning his trousers, he walks slowly towards her only to find Goatee has suddenly materialised and is giving her pleasure. Staying silent, he looks on guiltily whilst he slips his hand under his shorts to grasp his own manhood. He knows he's dreaming, but somehow it starts to feel very real.

"Oooh! Martin, it looks like you have re-loaded," purrs Maureen, handling his erection. Not one to complain, he tells himself that there are worse ways to be pulled from a pleasant, if in this case slightly disturbing, dream. Smiling at him with cow eyes, Maureen is invigorated after her post orgasm slumber and is keen to go again. It is like re-living the first few weeks after they met. A time when physically they could not get enough of each other. Obliged to perform, he does so willingly and with more vigour than before. Post coital, he lays exhausted and analyses what just happened.

He knows what fuelled his libido but ponders on what might have triggered Maureen's. Who, or what, was she thinking about? His inner voice tells him that it may be best to let sleeping dogs lie.

Their unremarkable sex life became, possibly for one night only, slightly less unremarkable.

7
SEARCHING FOR
SOMETHING TO SAY.

Sunday evening and Maureen has left to prepare for work in the morning. Slight depression creeps in, as Martin considers what awaits him at work the following day. Mondays are the worst and what is in his calendar is the worst of the worst. To take his mind of it, he watches a wildlife documentary, he has seen the whole series and this is the last one. Ironically, considering the events of the weekend, it is about the varied world of animal re-production. Five minutes in, his viewing is interrupted. Seeing Ben's name appear on the screen, he answers the phone. In contrast to Martins mood, Ben is jovial and upbeat and enquires how the weekend went. Wanting to get it off his chest, Martin tells him about the events in the bedroom and instantly regrets doing so.

"Mate, are you kidding me? You're porking Maureen whilst thinking about Goatee wearing a diamond studded jock strap rogering Blondie doggie style?"

"Very tastefully put. You should write romantic novels. For the record it wasn't diamonds, it was diamante. And also, for the record, it sounds much more sordid when you put it like that. Furthermore, I wasn't thinking of them when making love to Maureen. It's just that this was what fired me up the second time."

"It doesn't matter how you dress it up mate, it's not a good look. You're obsessing and frankly I'm not sure with who."

"What do you mean?"

"I mean is it Maureen, Blondie or, dare I suggest, is it Goatee? You'll be telling me next that you're coming out of the closet. Either way it's not healthy. You need a good psychiatrist or else a good break to get away from it all to take your mind of it. Which, my friend, leads me nicely into the reason I called."

"Thank you, Sigmund Freud. So, what's the news?"

"Everything is booked for Ibiza; I'll email you the details of the apartment so you can check it out. I've ordered an Uber for the airport so all you need to do is get yourself over to my place on the morning we leave and then it's party time all the way. We'll meet the other lads in Ibiza because they are booked on an earlier flight. Twelve days to go and counting my friend."

"Sounds great, but I ,ight just make my own way to the airport," replies Martin, unenthusiastically.

"Mate, up your game. Give me more energy or you'll bring the whole group down."

"Maybe I could, if I didn't have to sit by the pool across from fucking Goatee. I can picture him now, lying on a lounger, cocktail in hand, packing a baby seal in his Speedos."

"You're obsessing again. I'm telling you mate; he's a good bloke. I had a real laugh with him and it ain't his fault that you fancy him."

"I don't fucking fancy him. If you're going to wind me up, then I'll bid you goodnight and see you at work tomorrow."

"See ya mate, or as they say in Ibiza, Adios. And sweet diamante dreams."

It had been a slow day in the office. Glancing up at the clock on the wall, Martin notes the time is twenty-six minutes to four. Almost another half hour of purgatory. He begins to feel as if the walls are closing in, being trapped in a glorified cupboard which serves as Herring's office. Far worse is being alone in it with Herring, enduring an annual appraisal. Their verbal exchanges throughout the meeting have mostly been strained and awkward.

Fighting an ever-increasing urge to punch his boss in the mouth, Martin's answers are becoming shorter and more strained. Annual review time for Martin is the worst time of the year in normal circumstances, but it's made more unpleasant by the debut of Herring as the appraiser.

"What do you consider to be your strengths?" asks Herring, reading from a pre-prepared set of standard questions developed by the Human Resources Department.

"My forte," replies Martin.

Scribbling down the answer, Herring is unsure of the meaning of forte but does not want to appear stupid. Blissfully unaware that the answer given is a synonym of his question, therefore meaningless, he pushes on.

"Anything else?" probes Herring, hoping for another response. One that is more comprehensible.

"Nothing that immediately springs to mind. What do you think is my forte, sorry I mean strength?" asks Martin.

"It's not for me to say, according to the HR guidelines. They tell me that the process must involve seeking answers to what you think, not what I think," bluffs Herring, finding the process increasingly uncomfortable. Conducting annual appraisals is not turning out to be as easy as he thought it might be. He decides to move on. "Okay, then, what about your weaknesses?"

"Not sure really. Perhaps it's a lack of confidence in the pool of competence around me."

"Right – e – o," replies Herring, as he makes a note of this response, mechanically writing all the responses down word for word. He takes comfort knowing he can make sense of the answers later when he is under less pressure. "And … any other weaknesses?"

"I think the open plan area could do with some extra natural light."

Unsure as to whether this constitutes a valid comment for an annual appraisal, Herring makes a note. He could check with HR later. Having lost his place on the form, Herring pauses, scratches his eyebrow and scans the list.

"Are we done Mister Herring?"

"I think so Martin. Er, let me process your answers and tidy up my notes and I'll get back to you." Martin perceives that Herring's use of his first name is a clear indicator that his confidence is low and he's struggling with this new and unfamiliar process.

No jocular use of 'Mister' now, thinks Martin, pleased with his efforts and the opportunity to cut the interview short by fifteen minutes. Leaving before Herring has a change of heart, Martin says "goodbye" and closes the office door behind him.

Seeing Martin back at his desk, Ben sidles across for a chat.

"How'd it go?"

"I have no fucking idea," replies Martin, looking back over to Herring's office, "and neither does he."

"What did you say?"

"Not a lot. It's not as though he's going to put me forward for promotion, is it? He's a dickhead who's out of his depth, so why waste my time trying to impress him?"

"Fair enough, fancy a quick drink?"

"Naw, I need an early night. Had quite a busy couple of days and knackered, as you know, with Maureen choosing to stay over all weekend. I'm just gonna watch TV and get an early night."

"Any more diamante dreams?"

"Fuck off."

With Ben's laughter echoing behind him, Martin packs up. Before he leaves, he looks over to Herring's office. Uncharacteristically, his boss is still behind his desk tapping away at the keyboard. Seems that the Annual Review process is taking its toll, having spent the whole day meeting back-to-back with every team member. Martin was lucky last, which he suspects will be where he is placed in the team ratings. It is hard to shine when assigned the more mundane jobs, but it is what it is.

Running down the subway tunnel, he jumps into the first carriage, just avoiding the closing doors. It's not his usual carriage but the electronic board showed a train was at the platform and destined for his branch line. The next one is not due for twelve minutes, hence the dash. Surveying the half empty carriage he grabs a seat. One of three in a row which are unoccupied. Popping in his ear buds, he plays a few of his seventy's favourites. Chicago is the first band up and he closes his eyes to focus on the music. At the next station he keeps his eyes closed listening to music but senses a presence next to him once the train leaves. When there is a pause between songs, he can hear the chatter of two female voices next to him. They are deep in conversation and he partially opens his eyes to steal a glance.

Requiring a double take, he cannot believe it. Unrequited love is in the next seat but with her back slightly turned away from him, so she can comfortably talk to her companion. Furtively, he pauses the music and strains to hear the conversation. Not able to hear full sentences, he can still piece together the general gist of the conversation. The relationship of her companion is under discussion and he gets the impression that it has, or is, coming to an end. Unrequited love is offering several standard platitudes such as, 'he's not worth it' and 'you're better off without him.' Frustratingly, the conversation is all about her companion. He is not learning anything about Unrequited love. With diminishing interest, he prepares to put his music back on, when she ends a sentence with 'I've never been happier since I ended it with Tim.' Or perhaps she said 'Jim', he is not sure, but it does not matter. It sounds as if she is currently single.

His heart beats a little faster, matching the rhythm of the train which accelerates up the Northern line. He strategizes. What should he do with this new piece of information? Nothing, as usual, or positive action. Take the bull by the horns? The balls in his court? What was the phrase used in the management training course he was put on last year? 'Bias for action', that was it. The strategic choice to act quickly, even when there are risks and uncertainty involved. But he is not normally a 'bias for action' sort of guy, although tonight turns out to be different.

When the train approaches Archway, Unrequited love and her friend both start to rise, then shuffle along the rocking carriage to the doors. They get off when the sliding doors open. After a moment of hesitation, Martin jumps up and just makes it through the doors before they close, almost bundling over a schoolboy walking past the carriage. Muttering an apology, he looks down the platform towards the exit signs and sees his targets walking side by side. Keeping a distance, he steps onto the moving escalator about ten steps down from Unrequited love and her friend. Three passengers riding above him provide cover. Not that he even thinks he needs cover. But better safe than sorry. She did see him the other day when he offered her his seat so she might recognise him. Seriously, who is he trying to kid.

Both women hesitate at the exit of the station and put out their hands to see if the rain has stopped. They smile at each other, step out onto the street and walk down Junction Road. He follows them down the road until they reach a majestic Victorian building which stands alone. Although he has heard about it from friends, he has never been to St John's Tavern, a celebrated Gastro pub. Now only twenty yards behind them, Martin stops when they turn and enter the pub. Starting to turn round, he decides to return to the tube station. He hesitates, re-thinks, does another about turn and strides back down the road then straight into the pub. Looking around, engulfed in an atmosphere of laughter and loud conversation, he takes in the surroundings of the famous pub. It's busy, being renowned for its food, and all the tables are either occupied or have a reserved sign. Unrequited love and friend are seated at a table for two in the corner. They had obviously made a reservation. Edging to the bar Martin catches the eye of a server who points to show that the stools at the bar are free. Martin sits.

"Did you make a reservation sir?" asks the server.

"Er no, I just popped in for a quick drink on my way home," says Martin.

"That's fine sir, we are fully booked tonight anyway, but you are welcome to just have a drink as long as you are happy sitting at the bar."

"Great, thanks," says Martin. Scrutinising the beer taps, he settles on ordering one of the boutique lagers.

He taps the handheld device offered by the barman and the beer is placed in front of him. Taking a sip, he turns toward the main area filled with customers and tries to act as naturally as a man sat alone at a bar can. Unrequited love and friend examine the menus and a server approaches them to take the order.

Martin manages to stretch his hour long stay to just two beers, the price of them is eye watering, before there is movement at the table. The two women get up to leave and Martin, with no idea what the hell he is doing, follows them. They make their way back to the tube station with their unknown stalker following a few yards behind. He has a lapse of concentration as he looks down at his phone attempting to be unobtrusive and almost walks into them when they come to an abrupt halt at the station entrance. He swerves just in time to avoid the friend, who reaches to kiss Unrequited love on the cheek. Physically committed, he must continue into the station without looking back to avoid suspicion. Tapping his card, he squeezes through the ticket barrier and rides down the escalator. On his platform he lets a train pass, in the hope that they will follow him down to catch a train. Momentarily his hopes rise when the friend appears, but she is alone. She catches him staring at her and responds with a tentative smile. Embarrassed, he smiles back before looking down, pretending to examine his phone.

One stop along she disembarks.

Two further stops later he does the same.

What the hell was I thinking? he wonders, as he walks to his flat.

8
TALKING BOUT MONROE AND WALKING ON SNOW WHITE.

"What the hell were you thinking, mate?" asks Ben, as he rises to get another round.

By the time Martin has given a full account of how he had followed Unrequited love to St. John's Tavern, they have finished their first beer. He asked Ben not to comment before he finished the whole story and Ben, who had agreed to this condition, is true to his word. However, Ben's initial observation, as he rose to go to the bar, left Martin uncertain as to what pearls of wisdom would be forthcoming. He would just have to wait until his friend returned. To fill time, Martin studies the landscape within the Ship and Shovell, to see if the subject of his story is present, but there is no serendipity to be had.

"Here you go mate, drink up, it sounds as if you need it?"

"Well?" asks Martin.

"Well, what?"

"Don't be bloody obtuse, you know what. What's your take on it?"

"Better to be obtuse than a bleeding stalker is my opening thought. I repeat, what were you thinking? Were you intending to talk to her? What do you think her reaction would be if some creepy bloke who had been following in the shadows, suddenly jumped out and asked for a date?"

"I don't know. It was a spur of the moment thing. You're always saying I'm Mister Conservative, now you're criticising me for doing something."

"Well, you're a different sort of conservative now, more like one of those Conservative Members of Parliament, preying on young women. The Right Honourable Martin Hazel, Minister for Pervy Affairs."

"I knew I shouldn't have asked."

"Now, now. Don't get your diamante knickers in a twist. It's just a bit hard to get my head round it. You're with Maureen and have been for quite a while. You seem to be going okay. Holidays together, cosy dates and, judging by the other night, engaging in rampant sex. Even if the latter was being fuelled by Blondie and the meat master."

"For God's sake."

Raising his hands to placate Martin, Ben says, "No, no, let me go on. You asked for my thoughts, so I am going to give you the benefit of my wisdom and experience. I think there are three basic questions to address. The first, and don't get angry but hear me out, is the question of sexuality. Are you in the closet?"

"For fucks sake."

"Look mate, even a stud muffin like me can appreciate that Goatee is a very good-looking bloke. Not to mention his obvious endowments. For me, that's where it starts and finishes. I'm not the one who's dreaming about him in a diamond jock strap." Ben holds up his hand to prevent further interruption. "Discounting the possibility that you have propensity for a bit of cock, let's move on to Maureen. The question here is, do you still love her?" Ben pauses and nods, prompting Martin for an answer.

"I think so."

"Or is it that you have affection for her but not the deep meaningful, soul mate kind of love that exists in the movies, if not in real life. Are you still with her out of habit, rather than love?"

Frowning Martin, does not answer the question.

"Okay Marto, park that for a while. This then moves me on to my final comment. What about Blondie? You seem very, for want of a better word, captivated by her. Do you have feelings for her or do you just want to give her a good seeing to."

"Good seeing to?"

"I was trying to think of a less vulgar expression than 'shag,' respecting the gravitas of our conversation. But never mind the semantics, let me summarise. You need to sort out and find resolution to these three questions.

"Which are? asks Martin, now wishing that he had never raised the subject.

"Are you gay? Do you still love Maureen? Do you want to shag Blondie?"

Ben leans into the back of his stool and takes a long pull of his beer. Satisfied he has delivered a telling evaluation of the situation, he raises his left eyebrow and takes another drink. Leaving Martin to ponder without further interruption, Ben scans the pub for 'talent'. When he finishes scouting the room, finding no prospects in sight, he turns back to Martin who is ready to respond.

"My answers are, in the order of which you posed them, 'no', 'not sure' and 'yes'. But I don't want to hurt Maureen, and my feelings are very confused."

"You see mate, that's your dilemma. You've got good old Maureen. She's a safe bet. She loves you, I assume, and you've been together for a fair old while. The proverbial bird in the hand. She's nice, non-threatening, a sort of fairytale little goody two shoes princess. Maybe not as beautiful as a fairytale princess, but nice looking. No offence, but you know what I mean."

"And?" asks Martin irritably, having taken offence.

"And then you've got the blond bombshell waiting in the wings. Except, at this point, she isn't waiting in the wings but is about twenty yards ahead of you. The reality is that currently she's totally unaware of your existence whilst you are stalking behind in the shadows like a bitch on heat. If she was, aware of you that is, you'd probably be arrested by now."

"Sometimes I think you're in the wrong career. You should be a bloody diplomat. And for the record, I can't be a bitch on heat because that would be a female dog," mutters Martin, sulkily.

"A diplomat? I thought for a minute you were going to say a psychiatrist or a relationship counsellor. But I'll take that."

"I'm being sarcastic."

"I know mate, so am I. But you asked me and I've been honest. Just to throw a bit more coal into the fire there may be, as the song goes, trouble ahead."

"What are you talking about? What song?"

"It an old one, you'll have heard of it. It goes something like this. There may be trouble ahead … blah blah blah, can't remember the words, but it ends with, let's face the music and dance."

"I don't know what drugs you've been taking, but I have no idea what you are talking about."

"Let's face the music and dance. Maureen, mate. You're no longer at the boyfriend stroke girlfriend stage. The ground is giving way under you and you're slipping into the sinkhole of a serious long-term relationship. Her clock is ticking, she's done the hard yards, she invested in you, she's in her thirties."

"So?"

"Mate, she is going to want more. She is going to want to move on to the next stage. Co-living, joint mortgages maybe even the patter of shitty nappies."

This, of course, is no new revelation for Martin, but hearing it spoken aloud makes him slightly nauseous with nerves. "I suppose you have, for once, made a valid point," he admits.

"I certainly have. It's your move and if you make the wrong one it's checkmate."

"Well, I'm off to the toilet, I'll get another round on the way back."

"Spoken like a man versed at ignoring problems, in the hope that they will go away. Yes, my friend, it is your round," says Ben draining his glass, "On your way back make sure you get the beers in."

Walking though the main area, Martin looks across the room to check that his nemesis, Goatee, is not in the house. A flash back in his mind creates the vision of Goatee chatting to Unrequited love, so he looks over to the table they were sitting at. Tonight, it is occupied by two grey haired, suited men, enjoying an after-work beverage. Nearby, another customer feeds money into the jukebox. The manager recently installed it to give the pub a retro feel and create a bit of an atmosphere. A David Bowie classic pumps through the speakers.

Not convinced he is free from a surprise Goatee appearance, Martin tentatively opens the restroom doors, peers in and sees two occupants washing their hands. More suits, neither is Goatee. Emptying his bladder into the urinal, he covertly monitors his surroundings. No-one else enters and, once he has zipped up and washed his hands, he leaves quickly, not wishing to push his luck. Diverting his path from their table, towards the bar, he grabs the attention of the barmaid. She's the one that rejected Ben 's advances. Handing over the drinks, she smiles warmly. Pleased with himself, he has ammunition to give Ben a bit of his own medicine. No harm in reminding his mate that even the self-titled chick magnet, does not always come up smelling of roses when dealing with the opposite sex.

Laden with the drinks, Martin eases his way to the table to avoid spillage. His eyes lift from the beers, which have taken up his full concentration during the short journey, to Ben. About to give Ben grief about the barmaid, Martin stops a metre short of the table and screws up his eyes in confusion at Ben's odd behaviour. Winking and nodding his head sideways with slight, but rapid movements, Ben looks as though he has developed a particularly severe nervous tick. Martin shrugs to show he does not understand. Frustrated, Ben tries a new approach. He widens his eyes as if surprised and startled, then shifts them to his left urging Martin to look in the same direction. To Ben's relief, Martin finally looks where Ben is indicating and sees two women on the next table. Nearly dropping both pint glasses in surprise, he spots Unrequited love with her friend from Archway. Both are engrossed in a deep conversation oblivious of their surroundings. Martin shuffles into a position at the table which places Ben between himself and the eyeline of the two women. To further reduce the likelihood of being seen, he hunches in his seat.

"What are you doing mate. You look like you're playing hide and fucking seek?"

Whispering, Martin replies, "Keep your voice down mate."

"Why?" whispers Ben, in a sarcastic tone.

"I don't want them to see me in case they spotted me at Archway the other night."

"Are you bloody serious?"

"Yes mate, for once just do as I ask."

"Okay, if that's what you want. You do realise we are not back in schoolyard. Next, you'll be asking me to go over and say, 'my friend fancies you'."

"Just shut the fuck up and change the subject."

Ben is not letting it drop that easily.. Adopting the tone and voice of a pre-pubescent schoolkid, he says, "Excuse me, but would you and your friend like to go to the pictures with me and my friend, cos he wants to be your friend's boyfriend. He's got his pocket money today and he'll pay for the tickets."

"Can you stop it, you dickhead. They might hear," pleads Martin.

"I will mate, but you're thirty not thirteen. Just go and talk to her."

"Leave it. Can't you see they're deep in conversation? The last thing they'll want is a couple of likely lads trying to chat them up. Anyway, I'm with Maureen, aren't I?"

Ben changes the subject as requested, and they move on to the usual current topics of work, football and the Ibiza trip. Struggling to concentrate, Martin sneaks the occasional glance at the two women when he is sure that Ben isn't looking. Last orders are about to be called, so Martin goes to the bar. Bringing back the drinks, he sees that their table is now empty. Noticing his friend look over, Ben says, "They've gone mate, you've missed your chance."

Setting down the fresh drinks, Martin does not answer. His mind is occupied with what Ben has said about Maureen and the next stages of their relationship. Ben, on the other hand, is on a dating app, swiping right on his mobile phone.

9
I DON'T HEAR A WORD THEY'RE SAYING.

"To conclude. It's all about being future ready, gaining competitive advantage and consolidating on your unique offerings in the market. Thank you and good luck."

A smattering of applause follows the summary of the speaker. Joining in, Martin tries to show enthusiasm, which after four hours is now proving to be a challenge. Herring has appointed a consultant to assist the process of strategic planning. Being locked in the training room with Herring, the other seven team members and no natural light, was only the beginning of the torture. It has been PowerPoint hell, interspersed with awkwardness where most of the team failed offer any contributions of value. Five of the seven, as well as Martin, are nursing a hangover acquired from a leaving function the previous night. Herring's management style has already seen off one capable staff member, who jumped ship to join a competitor.

Two of the team are hangover free and both had dominated the discussions led by the consultant. They are Herring's proteges, both desperate to impress whilst their boss smiles and dotes over them like a benign uncle. It's not only the effect of the drinking session last night that makes Martin nauseous. If he hears anybody utter words such as mission statement, risk profiles and value propositions, he may decide to end his life.

"Any questions before Justin leaves us?" asks Herring. Both Herring and the consultant, Justin Beauchamp, had attended the same private school.

The slightly high-pitched voice of Simon Jennings, Protégé one, cuts through the stale air of the meeting room. "I think that we ought to do a deep dive into our value propositions as a next step."

For fucks sake, thinks Martin, hoping he did not accidentally mutter this thought aloud.

"Good idea Simon," says Herring.

"That's certainly one of the things you could look at," says Beauchamp, diplomatically. It's obvious to Martin that Beauchamp does not think that the suggestion made has any merit but the consultant can see Herring supports the idea. He adds "Yes, you could do that once the priority tasks we have identified in the session are addressed."

"Yes, good thinking Justin," agrees Herring. "We can circle back and pick off the low hanging fruit."

Martin has heard enough and speaks up. "I thought we have agreed in the first break out session that the value propositions were all good. With all the deep diving and circling back, I don't know whether I've got the bends or motion sickness."

Muted chuckles around the room cause Herring's mouth to twist in annoyance.

Beauchamp tries to mediate. "Actually, Martin has a point, but I'd say that nothing at this stage is baked in but rather has been put on the backburner."

"All this talk about fruit and cooking is making me hungry," says Martin.

More chuckles around the room prompts a strained laugh from Herring, who wants to be one of the boys and not appear humourless. "Very good Martin, very funny. Which brings us neatly to lunch time." He waits for chuckles at his own joke, but the room stays silent. "Okay then, forty minutes and we'll re-convene. Thank you again Justin. We can take it from here and work on our agreed actions in readiness for our session next week."

Sitting in Marios Sandwich Bar with Ben, Martin sighs and takes a first bite of his minted lamb roll.

"How was your strategy session?" asks Ben. With his mouth full, Martin gives a non-verbal reply, by raising his eyes skyward.

Ben chuckles. "That good eh Marto! Our team is starting next week, so that'll be something to look forward to. What's Herring been like?"

Swallowing, Martin replies. "An absolute tosser accompanied by some inbred cliché-ridden idiot who he went to school with."

"The old boys' network eh!"

"Looks that way. To be fair the bloke is no worse than any of the other consultants we've had in the past and I get the impression that he thinks Herring is a bit of a fool. Obviously, Herring is paying his bill, so he plays the game."

"How's the thinking going?"

"We've got another session after lunch, then we have to agree a workplan."

"I'm not talking about the departmental strategy; I'm talking about your love life strategy. Our discussion the other night. Maureen, nappies, mortgage, shackles and the rest, or the blond bombshell."

"No closer, but to be honest all I have, as you so nicely summarised it, is the bird in the hand. The blond bombshell is not even an option at this stage. To quote Herring's consultant mate, I'll put it on the back burner until after Ibiza."

"Well, to continue the corporate theme, you've got to be wary of having too many balls in the air. You may not have the bandwidth to cope."

"Very good Ben. Ever thought of going into management consultancy?"

Protégé two, Nicholas Humberstone, takes the floor, worried that his rival, Jennings, had gained too much ground in the morning session.

"I feel that that we are in danger of mission creep and may be spreading ourselves too thin. We've got to make sure we don't limit ourselves by drinking the Kool-Aid of senior management. I wonder if it's worth a brain dump to see what we come up with."

Challenging senior management did not seem a good idea to Herring, who, new to the role, did not want to rock the boat. As much as he liked Humberstone, he begins to wonder if one of his protégés is getting a bit too big for his boots. Giving a slight cough to ensure he gains the floor, Herring decides it is time to nip this in the bud.

"Before we all get ahead of ourselves, let's make sure we get all our ducks in a row prior to considering any potential game changers. I admire your enthusiasm Nick, but let's park it for now. If we want to suggest radical new ideas, we are going to have to run them up the flagpole to ensure that the Directors have buy in and skin in the game."

"Totally agree, Mister Herring, we won't' get traction otherwise," responds Jennings, seeing the opportunity to score further points against his competitor.

Humberstone scowls knowing he has lost further ground. "On reflection Mister Herring, I can see the wisdom of your strategy."

Jennings smirks.

Martin yawns and looks up at the clock, preparing himself for the longest hour of his life. Most of the remaining sixty minutes are spent daydreaming and thinking about Unrequited love.

"Okay team let's wrap this up. You've all been assigned tasks so let's re-convene next Monday with, hopefully, everything completed so we can move onto the next stage."

Chatter fills the room, and they laugh and joke with the relief of finishing a long day in the stifling atmosphere of the meeting room. Rustling of papers and scraping of chairs precede the evacuation of the room, leaving Herring and Martin alone. In the coffee break, Herring had asked Martin to hang back once the session finishes. Both stay seated and Herring only speaks after the last team member has left, closing the door behind him.

"How did you think today went Martin?"

"Okay, I suppose. I think we've made some progress and everyone has plenty to do before the next session."

"I ask, because I feel that you were dis-engaged for a substantial portion of the day."

"Really?"

"Yes Martin. Other than your witty little interventions, I didn't feel you contributed much."

"Sorry you feel that way. I thought I did okay."

"Maybe try to bring a bit more energy to the next session. What do you say?"

"I'll certainly reflect on it and do my best. Is that all?"

"No, there was one more thing."

"Yes."

Seeing Herring shuffle uncomfortably and look down before answering, Martin braces himself for bad news.

"I have some bad news. I'm afraid I am not putting you forward for promotion this year."

Inwardly, Martin sighs with relief. It is not bad news; it's expected news. He isn't even sure he has the energy for more responsibility in his current mental state. Next year he might think differently. The lofty role of Assistant Manager entails more pressure for precious little extra money. Martin thinks that Herring is threatened by his skills and experience and never intended to promote him. Struggling in his new role, Herring needs Martin's experience and cannot afford to lose him.

"Oh right! Can I ask why?"

Martin barely listens to the vague reasons being doled out by his rambling boss. He asked the question more out of mischief than seeking clarification, just to make the meeting as uncomfortable for Herring as possible. When Herring eventually runs out of steam, Martin asks another question. "So, who did you put up for promotion?"

"Actually nobody, I don't think anyone in the team is quite ready to be an Assistant Manager."

I can think of two, thinks Martin. Looking Herring directly in the eyes, he says, "Oh really? I'm surprised, but I guess it's your decision."

"Yes, it is and I am a hundred percent confident in my decision," replies Herring curtly, sensing he is being challenged.

"What an absolute wanker," says Ben before taking a large pull of his beer.

The pause allows Martin to think of a suitable witty response but he can't find one. It's been a long day and he's exhausted. "Mate, I am only staying for one, I am absolutely knackered."

"Never mind that mate, aren't you angry?"

"Not in the least. Frankly I can't be arsed managing everyone else's problems and the rest of the bollocks that goes with it. It's not as though it comes with much more money."

"Okay, well as long as you're alright with it. I guess there's next year."

"I'm not even sure whether I'll be here next year. It's time for a change."

"I've told you before, you can't go and leave me here alone with the likes of Herring."

"Every man for himself mate." Martin downs his half pint and makes to leave. "Sorry, I'm buggered and off home. See yer tomorrow."

On his way to Embankment station, his mobile rings. It's Maureen.

"Hi love, what's up?"

"Another lovely greeting. You need to work on your telephone manner. I am ringing to check in and see if you've heard anything about your promotion."

"As a matter of fact, I have. There is to be no promotion, at least not this year."

"Oh! I'm so sorry Martin. You must be devastated."

"I'm fine Maureen, honestly, I'm fine. I've been thinking about the future and after days like today, I feel more inclined to leave."

"What, because of the promotion news?"

"Not really, it's been a shitty day. In fact, it's been a shitty few weeks."

"You never said so,"

"I sort of did. Just didn't want to go on and on about it. You've got your own issues," replies Martiin.

"Don't be silly. I'm your life partner; we should be sharing the ups and the downs."

Life partner, thinks Martin, trying to process the implications.

"Are you still there, Martin, you've gone quiet?"

"Yeah sorry, just exhausted."

"Okay then, I'll let you go. Where are you?"

"On my way to the tube station."

"Okay, chin up and get some sleep. We can catch up tomorrow."

On autopilot, Martin makes his way to the station and boards the first train. It is late and mid-week. The carriage is almost empty. Two young students sit further up chatting and sharing pictures on their phones. They are his only co-passengers and after two stops they jump up and run out of the carriage when the doors open. Now alone he closes his eyes. Fatigue takes over.

Minutes later, the train jolts and he opens his eyes. Immediately he panics thinking he has fallen asleep and missed his stop. Peering through the window he sees that he did doze off and miss a few stops, but he is still only at Tufnell Park. Thinking he is alone in the carriage he closes his eyes again but opens them a few seconds later when he imagines that he hears a voice. Sitting two seats to his right he sees the outline of a man from the corner of his eye. He was so focussed on looking ahead to see the sign of the station when the train stopped, that he hadn't noticed there was a fellow passenger. He does not want to look directly at the man. It is late at night and better not to engage with strangers, especially when alone. He closes his eyes only to re-open them seconds later.

"I said, we meet again," says the passenger, repeating himself.

Turning, Martin is surprised to see Goatee. Trying to appear nonchalant, he says, "Oh! it's you, the stalker."

"Now let's not go down that route again," suggests Goatee. "You're the one followed me into that restaurant if you recall. Not to mention the toilets."

Feeling a little contrite, Martin reluctantly offers a semi-apology. "Yeah! Maybe. Take no notice of me, I've just had a long day."

"I fully understand," replies Goatee with a grin. "Actually, this chance meeting could be described as fortuitous."

"Fortuitous? How so?" asks Martin, with a furrowed brow.

"I'm sure that our mutual friend Ben has mentioned that he invited me to join your little get together in Ibiza. I'm staying in the hotel next the block of apartments where you are going to be."

"Yep, he did tell me. How long have you known him?"

"Barely two weeks. We got chatting in your local hostelry after work."

"The Ship and Shovell."

"Yes. It came up in conversation that we're both going to Ibiza and, imagine our surprise when it not only turned out we are going at the same time but we are also staying next to each other. Isn't that incredible."

"Yeah, incredible," replies Martin with a hint of sarcasm, which Goatee ignores.

"So, my friend, that's why I think this meeting is fortuitous. I don't want to step on anyone's toes and hang around where I'm not welcome. I feel we've got off to a poor start and I thought that we could possibly meet for a drink and not so much bury the hatchet but break the ice. What do you say?"

Martin felt hi-jacked and struggled to respond. Goatee rescued him.

"I'm only proposing a quick drink. A quick get to know you drink, that's all."

The man has handed out the olive branch and what he proposes makes good sense. He did not want any awkwardness either. The trip is only for a few days and too short to act like quarrelling schoolboys. Goatee holds out his hand. Thinking it is a clumsy attempt at a handshake, Martin reaches across the seats but realises that a handshake isn't on offer. In Goatee's hand is an embossed business card with silver lettering.

"Take this Martin. If it suits, I'll see you tomorrow at around six at the Ship and Shovell. I believe you finish work around that time."

"How do you know that?"

"Not sure really, I think Ben may have mentioned that you often go there around that time to debrief after a day's work."

"Oh! I see," said Martin, doubtfully.

"If we don't end up strangling each other, I may have an added incentive for you to join me tomorrow. Something to make it worth sparing me some of your time."

Creases appear at the corner of Martin's eyes as he looks at Goatee with a mixture of suspicion and curiosity. Goatee elucidates.

"No need to look so worried Martin. I had a good chat with Ben and he mentioned what you both do for a living. He also hinted that you may have had enough of your current employer and may be looking for a way out in the near future. Keeping an eye out for opportunities, so to speak."

"He seems to have said a lot in a short time to a relative stranger."

"Perhaps, but he means well."

"Okay, tell me, what's this proposal you have."

The train begins to slow as it approaches the next station.

"No time now Martin. This is my stop and to be frank you look exhausted and my proposal has its complexities. It requires time to explain and equally as much time for you to consider the implications. I can guarantee that if you are interested, then it will take a couple of meetings to iron out the details."

"Really?"

The train comes to a halt. Goatee rises and moves towards the doors. As they open, he shouts back to Martin. "All I can tell you for now is that if you accept my offer and are successful then it will be highly profitable for you. Life changing, in fact."

Goatee steps through the doors, walks at a brisk pace towards the exit tunnel and disappears out of sight.

Momentarily in a daze, he begins to question whether he has dreamt the whole thing but in his hand is a very real business card. It is white, with a grapevine embossed around the edges. He reads the silver lettering.

Sebastian Balfour

Director

Life Solutions

The card offers no contact details. No address, no email and no mobile number.

10
AND CATCH YOUR TRAIN
IN THE MORNING RAIN.

Thursday. Alarm. Duvet exodus. Shivering. Warm shower. Instant coffee. Toast. Exits flat. Raining. Hunched shoulders. Through barrier. Exit tube station. Enter workplace. Log on.

"Morning Mister Hazel."

Martin looks up from his screen and greets Herring with as much enthusiasm as he can muster. Which is very little. Instead of following his urge to say, 'fuck off', Martin responds with 'Good morning.' His body language sends the clear signal that he is not interested in a friendly morning chat. Martin's attention returns to the screen. He cannot bring himself to go through the motions of the pathetic office joke. So, there is no 'Mister' Herring today. Feeling a little awkward after the brevity of Martin's response, Herring wrestles for something to say and settles on asking if he is prepared for the next strategy session in a few days. Martin's eyes are still fixed on his spreadsheet as he types, but gives a single word response, 'Yes'. Herring scuttles back to his office. Still with eyes glued to his screen. Martin allows himself a brief smile.

Lunchtime comes after a productive morning. Sitting in Marios Sandwich Bar, Ben says, "How was your morning, mate?"

"Good actually, I've got a lot done without Herring hassling me. He came over first thing but I didn't engage in all the 'Mister' nonsense. He buggered off and I haven't seen him all morning."

"Sent him away with a flea in his ear, eh!"

"Yep. Anyway, I've something to tell you," Handing over Goatee's card, Martin takes a bite of his prawn sandwich whilst his friend exams it.

"Well bugger me. It's your mate Goatee. He told me he was called Seb when I bumped into him in the pub. Card looks like he's got money and he's important. What the fuck is 'Life Solutions.' Sounds like a life coach or a counsellor. He doesn't look like a counsellor."

"I have no idea what he is, but whatever it is that he does, he's interested in me doing it as well, I think."

"What?"

"He says he has a proposal for me, so I assume it is something to do with his work."

"You're kidding me. I wonder what it is. Didn't he tell you?"

"No. I saw him on the train last night after our session. I was a bit pissed, dozed off and the next thing I knew, he was sitting near me. We got chatting, he said he wanted to break the ice as we'd be seeing each other in Ibiza. Then he said he knew what I did for a living. Apparently, you told him, and he had a proposal for me. Then his stop came and he got off. Before he left, he handed me his card and we agreed to meet in the Ship and Shovell."

"When?"

"Tonight. Do you want to come along. Afterall you are big mates and arrange holidays together."

"No need to be sarky. No can do tonight. I've been swiping," says Ben, with a smirk.

"What. You've been using that online dating site again."

"Yep. She looks hot and she accepted my invite."

"She could be hot, providing the woman that you're meeting is the same one that's in the picture. And, if it turns out to be the same woman, that the photo isn't twenty years old."

"Never mind all that. Back to Seb. He must have said something about the proposal."

"I guess I'll have to call him Sebastian now. I can't call him Goatee."

"Yes mate, but what about the proposal. He must have said something?" asks Ben, frustrated at having to repeat himself.

"No, there was no time and he said it was complicated and may require a couple of meetings to work it through."

"Sounds serious."

He did say it would be worth my while. In fact, he claimed it would be life changing."

"Fuck me. You're gonna have to tell me all about it tomorrow. Anyway, check out my date." Ben hands over his phone and Martin examines the picture.

"Well, she looks very attractive and must be in her late twenties. Let's see if you end up having a drink with a woman in her late fifties, and five minutes later you're desperately finding an exit route to cut the date short. So, ditto. You're also gonna have to tell me about it tomorrow."

Time moves at the snail's pace. Martin spends the afternoon in a daze in front of his laptop. On the positive side, Herring continues to avoid him and he remains unmolested other than the occasional enquiry by junior team members struggling with the strategy workplans.

Each time he looks at the clock in the bottom corner of his screen, he is disheartened. At the same time, his anticipation is followed by a reality check. Why is he getting so worked up? Probably, the bloke is a monumental bullshitter. Ben, the master bullshitter, likes him for God's sake, if that's not a red flag, what is? Best not to raise your hopes, only for them to be dashed. There again, he dresses well, expensive suits, meticulously groomed, and his business card doesn't look like it is the product of a discount deal at Prontoprint.

This thought prompts him to take Sebastian's card out of the wallet. He muses. *Silver lettering. It looks expensive. There's such a thing as gold leaf, is there such a thing as silver leaf?* Stroking the card with his index finger, he feels the embossed pattern. *The letters look like they are real silver. Not sure about the diamante jock strap though. To be fair that bit was a dream, not reality.*

"Wakey, wakey mate. It's time to go." Ben taps him on the shoulder. "If you don't get a shift on you may jeopardise your bright future.

"Oh! okay, yeah sure." Martin returns slowly to reality and looks at the time stamp on his laptop. It reads 17.26. He looks up, but Ben, with his own fish to fry, has made a quick exit.

With thirty minutes to pass before his life changing meeting, he continues writing the concluding section of his report. Increasingly distracted as his meeting with Goatee draws closer, it has taken far longer than expected. He considers leaving the rest of it until tomorrow but decides to write another couple of paragraphs. The pub is barely five minutes' walk away and he doesn't want to arrive early and appear desperate. Ironically, he is now the one that is deferring the moment. Running his draft through the spell and grammar check, he finds it much more error prone than normal.

Finally, the time has come. Martin clicks save, checks the time stamp on his screen, 17.54, and logs off. It is time to discover what his future holds or, more likely, endure yet another of life's disappointments. The man is probably a bullshitter and a charlatan.

11
PLEASE ALLOW ME TO INTRODUCE MYSELF.

The Ship and Shovell is uncharacteristically quiet. Normally, there would be the buzz of chatter and laughter from bored white-collar workers energised by alcohol after being set free for the day. All wanting to let off steam after long hours in the quiet sedate environment of their offices. Not today.

Echoing around the empty bar, the Rolling Stones are playing on the jukebox to an audience whose number barely breaks single figures. Martin undertakes a visual inventory of the handful of customers scattered around, but there is no sign of Goatee. He makes a mental note to refer to him as Sebastian going forward. Checking his mobile phone, he sees it is just after six o'clock and when he looks up to search for Sebastian once more, he almost falls off his stool. Smiling, Sebastian is standing in front of him, holding a pint of beer in one hand and a whisky in the other. Handing the beer to Martin, he pulls out a nearby stool and sits down.

"I believe this is your tipple."

"Er, actually yes, it is, how did you know?"

"Lucky guess," replies Sebastian, taking a sip of his whisky before setting it down.

They make small talk, all the while Martin desperate to hear what Sebastian has to say but rapidly reaching the conclusion no such proposal exists. For all his good looks, immaculate grooming and smooth taking, the man is probably just a timewaster. At the point where Martin has resolved raise the topic of the proposal, Sebastian fiddles with his Rolex watch before looking Martin straight in the eye.

"You probably have forgotten, but I did promise you that I have a proposition that may be of interest. If, of course, you still wish to hear it."

Martin's heartbeat quickens, but he tries to appear nonchalant.

"Yeah, I'm always willing to listen to any idea, but can't guarantee I'll agree to it. At least not until after I've heard it and thought it through. I'm sure you understand."

"Of course, Martin. I would not expect anything else. But I also have a caveat."

"Fair enough, what is it?"

"I have made this proposal to people I've selected many times. More times than you could imagine. I can tell you with absolute certainty that the process will take at least three meetings, and sometimes more, before both parties can come to an agreement."

"And, after all of that, do both parties always agree?"

"Not all, but most do."

Intrigued, Martin asks, "Why does the process take so long? Why do some refuse?"

"Ah! Two questions already, even before I've explained the proposal. To answer your first question, it takes a while because it is complex and people must understand and accept the situation before going ahead. I will not answer the second question in detail because you will gain an understanding as you learn more about my offer. It will become clear why most accept but some refuse."

"Okay, shall we get down to it then?"

"Certainly, but before we do, can I have your agreement that we take this slowly and that you are willing to have as many meetings as it takes, before you can make an informed decision."

"You can't expect me to agree to that until I know what it is I am agreeing to."

"I am not asking you to agree to the proposal, but I am asking you to pursue the process to the end and keep an open mind. In my experience, as I mentioned before, we are talking a minimum of three meetings of about an hour."

"Okay, then where do we start?"

"Let's make a start. Firstly, I have a few introductory questions to run by you."

"Okay, fire away."

"If I offered you a sum of money, enough to live your life free from financial worries, how much would you ask for? Make it an amount within reason of course."

Stunned, Martin tries to process the question.

"Take your time on this one," recommends Sebastian.

Trying to focus on a suitable answer a bundle of supplementary questions pop into Martin's mind, distracting him. Who is this man? How wealthy must he be? How has he acquired this wealth? What on earth will he want in return? How much should I pitch? What's his limit?

Losing track of time, these thoughts swirl around his mind like dead leaves on a windy day. Three minutes pass.

Glancing at his Rolex, Sebastian speaks. "I don't want to rush you Martin, but we have a lot to get through. There are far more challenging issues you are going to have to grasp, so I'll need an answer."

Martin blurts out, "Five million." He is surprised to see there is no obvious change in the expression on Sebastian's face. Certainly not an expression of surprise or shock at the amount requested.

"Good, we have a figure. I will offer you five million pounds and as a gesture of good will, a ten percent deposit will be set aside upon signing the agreement."

Stunned, once more, Martin nods but stays silent. He cannot believe this man is serious. Should he have asked for more?

"Now Martin, I realise that you will, doubtless, be keen to find out what you must do to earn your five million. Unfortunately, this cannot be addressed until the second or possibly even the third meeting."

"Why can't we just get straight to it?"

"Because you need to accept a few things which most find hard to accept, at least in the first instance. What we now must concentrate on, is a discussion about me. I agree that this makes me sound a little narcissistic but, believe me, it is central to the agreement. Do you know who I am?"

"Well groomed, expensive suit, high end accessories like the Rolex. I also notice tonight you have a diamond stud in your left ear. Some sort of businessman, maybe a stockbroker?"

Reaching inside his wallet, Sebastian pulls out a black credit card.

"I am showing you this to convince you that you need not worry about my ability to pay your price. As I am sure you know it's an American Express Centurion credit card."

"Yeah, I know," replies Martin, who has no idea what a Centurion card is.

"Good. Now I am going to give you a clue about my name. On my way to the toilet, you will hear a song on the jukebox. When I come back, we can discuss it."

Martin tracks Sebastian's progress to the toilet, but notices that he walks straight past the jukebox and neither puts any money in it nor selects a tune. *Thought so, he's full of shit*, thinks Martin. To fill in time, he googles 'American Express Centurion' on his mobile phone. *Bugger me,* he thinks reading from his phone. *It says it's the highest tier of an American Express card. Jesus, it's made from fucking Titanium and issued only on invitation.*

Whilst his concentration is focussed on the phone, the Rolling Stones start to play on the jukebox. He misses the iconic instrumental beginning of the tune with Jagger shouting "yeow" accompanied by the jungle beat of congas and maracas. But once he turns his attention to the song, he picks up the middle of the first verse and recognises it. Jagger's vocals are more story telling than singing.

"I've been around for a long, long year,

stole many a man's soul and faith …"

Seriously, thinks Martin. *He must think I'm a right dickhead if he thinks I'm going to swallow this.*

The song finishes and is followed by Yazz, beating out 'The only way is up.'

Sebastian rejoins Martin with another beer and a whisky.

"You're joking, right?" asks Martin.

"So, you heard the song then?"

"If you are referring to the Stones, yes. You want me to believe you're the devil," snorts Martin.

"Is that so hard to believe?"

"Frankly yes."

"Why?"

"Because the devil doesn't exist and if he does, you, my friend, don't have horns and a pointy fucking tail."

With a patronising chuckle, Sebastian says, "You can see why I said that this would take a few meetings. We are in the first stage of the process, which is establishing belief."

"Mate, we aren't gonna get beyond the start line if you expect me to believe that you're the devil. It isn't gonna happen."

Sebastian leans back into his stool and offers no immediate response. His demeanour and piercing grey eyes unsettle Martin. The silence between them begins to make Martin feel slightly uncomfortable. In contrast, Sebastian smiles knowingly with the expression of a father who is has discovered his six-year-old child has been naughty and stolen an extra piece of cake at a birthday party.

"Yeah, it isn't gonna happen," repeats Martin, sulkily, feeling the need to fill the silence.

Appraising him for a few more seconds, Sebastian sits up straight and leans forward to show that he is being earnest.

"Don't worry Martin, I've had this conversation a thousand times, more in fact. One of the more tried and tested paths that follows this revelation, is the demand for proof."

"Yeah, good idea, prove it. Show me your horns and pointy tail."

"Oh, deary me. Can I ask you something? Tell me, do you believe in God, the bible and all that stuff?"

"Not really." Martin thinks this is a clever response which cuts off the argument that if you believe there is good and a God, it follows that you must believe there is evil and a devil.

"Well, that's a good start Martin, not least because the Bible was written by a bunch of misogynistic racists."

Their discussion was not following the direction he expected. "Pardon?"

"The old horns and pointed tail chestnut comes from various sources including the Book of Revelation and the Old Testament which demonises ancient pagan Gods like Pan and vilifies goats and other symbolic animals in Jewish tradition."

"What about the pointy tail?"

"The same my friend, the book of Revelation talks about a dragon with seven heads, ten horns and a massive tail. It's all basically a work of fiction created by a load of old men to subjugate the common people and particularly control women.

"Control women? You said the church is run by misogynists."

"Look at the Catholic Church, they still won't ordain women because their official teachings say they have no authority to alter the male-only priesthood established by Christ."

Martin is struggling to pick holes in Sebastian's arguments and finds another intellectual ledge to cling to. "Hang on, you also said they were racist. You're surely not claiming that racism is built into religion."

"Absolutely I do. All the do-gooders rattle on about racism but, to use one of their phrases, 'let them without sin cast the first stone'. Let me give you a history lesson. In the north of England, a place called Hartlepool, they captured a monkey which had been washed ashore from a ship during the Napoleonic Wars. Subsequently, they hung it as a French spy."

"So?" asks Martin petulantly.

"So, they believed anybody from France looks like a monkey. I've no doubt those who gave the order were devout Christians. In other words, it's no different from the Christians who believe that anybody who does not accept their work of fiction has horns and a pointy tail. It's bloody racist, if you'll pardon my French."

Attributing his confusion partly to the beer he has consumed, Martin feels like he is sitting on a cognitive merry go round. The discussion with Sebastian was moving along but it was not going anywhere. Sebastian seemed to have all the answers but it was stagnating. Martin is desperate to get to the crux of the matter and learn what he needs to do to earn his money.

"While you are mulling all that over Martin, think on this. The poor old church women are only fit for cleaning the church, making the sandwiches and fund raising for one of the world's most wealthy institutions. Go figure. And let's not get into the dodgy stuff the randy clerics get up to, abusing their power and all that. If the women, and my good self for that matter, nipped off to the Equality and Human Rights Commission, we would have cast iron cases for sex and racial discrimination. And if can you believe it, I'm supposed to be the evil one.

"I'm confused," says Martin.

"I'm simply saying that there are no pointy tails, it's a myth. I cannot show you my horns or pointy tail because I don't have any."

Mulling this over for a few seconds, another mental lightbulb clicks on and Martin decides on a different tack. "Right then. If you are the devil, do something to prove it."

"Here we go, another old chestnut." chuckles Sebastian, "I assume you mean something like a miracle. I tend to leave the thunderbolt, parting of seas and turning water into wine tricks, to the other side. That sort of stuff is their bag. Let me ask you this. Have you ever approached a Vicar and asked them to perform a miracle to prove there is a God?"

"Well, no."

"So why subject me to this rigour. And before you answer, who said the devil is all powerful like your God.

I never made this claim. I can't make you float off the ground or make the clock at Big Ben spin backwards or with the waves of my hand issue forth a plague of locusts. Even if I could, that sort of tawdry ostentatious behaviour it's not my style."

"Surely you must have some powers. More so than we mere mortals?" says Martin sarcastically.

"I'll ignore the fact that you assume I'm not human and answer you directly. I do have some powers but generally I prefer to rely on persuasion, temptation and hypnotic suggestion with a bit of good old bribery thrown in."

Seeing that Martin looks deflated and tired, as well a slightly drunk, Sebastian offers a couple of titbits to keep his interest.

"Okay then. I told you, before I went to the toilet, that the song you would hear whilst I was in the urinals would give you a clue as to my identity. You managed, at least, to work that one out. But let me ask you this. Did you see me approach the jukebox and put in money to select the song?"

"No, you went straight to the toilet," admits Martin.

"There you go, explain that."

"Co-incidence. Someone else happened to put it on. It's a popular old song."

"Come on Martin, that's a bit weak. Alright, let me try another tack. What do you think of my diamante jock strap?

Unable to avoid opening his mouth in surprise, Martin stutters but cannot dredge up an immediate answer. Sebastian adds, "How can you explain that I appear in your dreams. More importantly, how do I even know that I appear in your dreams?"

Feeling a bit woozy, Martin slouches in his stool. It has been a long day and he is drinking too much lately. Stretching his normal intake from two nights a week at the most, he now finds himself drinking four or five with his regular liaisons with Ben and Maureen. Let alone adding Sebastian onto the drinking session list. Now also bored, he is rapidly getting to the point where he has had enough of the circular religious philosophical debate.

"Okay then Sebastian, I have one more question."

"Call me Seb, it's easier."

"Okay Seb. If you are the devil, shouldn't you have some clever name which reveals that you are what you are saying you are. If you get my meaning?"

"Oh! another chestnut. I think I know where this is going. You mean like DeNiro in that movie Angel Heart. The one where he plays a character called Louis Cyphre. I mean really, Louis Cyphre. Lucifer! Give me a break. All a bit crass don't you think?"

"Maybe."

"If I came to you in the form of a woman calling myself something like Belle Zeebub, would you have been more convinced?"

"Probably not."

"How about if I dressed as Father Christmas, Santa being an anagram of Satan and all that nonsense."

"Okay Seb, point taken. Now I'm knackered, a bit pissed and need my bed. How about we cut to the chase and you tell me what I must do to get my hands on the five million?"

"We are not at that stage in the proceedings, I'm afraid. First you must believe I am who I say I am or there is no value in getting you to fulfill your part of the contract. When you have had time to process our discussion tonight, call me and we'll set up another meeting. And one final thing for now."

"Yes," says Martin, warily.

I do not want you discussing any of our business with a third party. It will invalidate the agreement if you do."

Disappointed at the failure of their first meeting to reveal what fulfilling his part of the deal would entail, Martin agrees. He's too fatigued to argue and does not want to jeopardise the five million pounds that's been put on the table. Evidently, judging by the credit card, Seb is loaded and the five million is still in play. "We have an agreement Seb. When do you want to meet next?"

"Like I said, give me a call. Take heed of my warning, if you discuss the nature of our arrangement then the deal is off." Leaving the pub, Sebastian waves goodbye, before walking out into the night.

"I don't even know what the sodding deal is at the moment," mutters Martin, to himself.

Steeling himself for the tube journey home, Martin stands up, a little shaky but holds onto the table to steady himself. Concentrating on walking in a straight line, he makes his way out of the pub and to the tube station.

On the train home he plays through the events of the evening and the bizarre conversation. Maybe Seb is a lonely rich eccentric with more money than he knows what to do with. A game player, and strange games at that, to keep himself amused. If he plays along with Seb, Martin thinks he may acquire a far healthier bank balance. Equally, it could all end up just a waste of time humouring some madman. He visualises the figure of five million appearing on his bank statement. Replaying their discussion repeatedly in his mind, he dwells on the parting instruction to call when he is ready for a second meeting. This prompts a minor panic. Butterflies burst in his stomach when he realises that he does not have Seb's number. Certain that it was not on the business card, he pulls his wallet out and extracts the card to re-examine it. The front of the card is exactly as he remembers it when Seb handed it to him. There is no number, just Seb's name, job title and his company, Life Solutions. He flips the card over, although he knows he checked it when he got the card originally and it was blank.

At first glance it still looks blank but his eyes widen in surprise. A mobile number appears in silver lettering once the card is held at an angle that catches the light. Relieved, he reads the number.

7734999

12
TO HAVE A GIRL LIKE HER IS TRULY A DREAM COME TRUE.

In Mario's Sandwich Bar, Martin and Ben discuss the events of the previous evening. Ben starts his story, whilst Martin tucks into a minted lamb roll.

"Anyway, I turned up five minutes early and looked around for this bird."

"You can't say 'bird' nowadays, it's disrespectful and misogynistic," replies Martin, reflecting on the religious misogyny conversation with Sebastian last night.

"Do you want to hear this story or not. We can have a discussion on political correctness later for fucks sake."

"Go on," mumbles Martin, with his mouth full.

"Cheers mate. So, I'm looking around for this bird that I've arranged to meet and straight away I see her. I say straight away, because normally it takes a lot longer."

"Why?"

"Because usually they look nothing like their photos when you see them in the flesh. Not the case last night,

I can tell you. She's the spitting image of her photo. She is, mate, stunning. I wandered over trying to be all cool, introduced myself and apologised for being late, even though I was actually a bit early. She assured me I wasn't late and asked what I was drinking. Being the gentleman, I declined her offer, ordered a beer and got the barman to replenish her drink."

"Very smooth," replies Martin, sarcastically.

"Anyway, the evening went well and the conversation was light and easy. I was floating on cloud nine."

"Why do I feel a 'but' coming?"

"Because mate, there is a big 'but'. It is the 'but' to end all 'buts'. It is devastating."

"Go on," urged Martin, whose interest has been piqued.

"As I say, we were getting on like a house on fire. The evening draws to a close and she asks if I want to go to hers for a nightcap. It's getting better and better my friend. Apparently, she lives around the corner from the wine bar we were in. Trying to play it mega cool, I said it would be nice to extend the evening for a little bit longer."

"Sounds like you hit paydirt."

"I hit a brick wall. She then says, putting her hand on my arm before we go, that she wants to clarify something. My first thought was that she was going to say it's just a coffee and nothing more. She doesn't do anything on her first date. I look her in the eyes and she says if I am not comfortable with what she has to say, then that's okay."

"Was she on her period or something?"

"Oh no mate. If only she had periods. She's transitioning but calmly explains that it will be a while before she completes her gender affirming surgery. Obviously, I didn't immediately understand what she meant, but she explained it all to me in excruciating detail. For some of the bits I had to cross my legs in subconscious sympathy."

"So, you're saying she still had a cock."

"It's not exactly how she expressed it, but in a nutshell, yes."

Straining to keep a straight face, Martin says, "But you told me she's stunning."

"She is mate. Her father is English and her mother is Malaysian. Before she dropped the bombshell, I complimented her on her beauty. She told me her mother was a model."

"Come on then. You can't leave it there. What did you do?"

"Well, she explained that there are some things she can do. Y'know, oral, hands and stuff."

"And stuff?" asks Martin. He knew exactly what Ben meant but wants to hear him say it out loud.

"Y'know. Other stuff."

"What other stuff?"

"Stuff … like anal."

It's too much. Unable to contain himself, Martin lets out a loud guffaw, which prompts an expression of rebuke from Mario who leans over the counter and shushes him. Overcome by the humour of the moment, Martin can't speak, so waves an apology, with his chest shaking in mirth. Once he composes himself, he asks, "So did you go to her place then?"

"No, I fucking didn't."

Martin bursts out laughing again and waves a further apology at Mario who is now scowling at him. "Sorry Mario, I'll pipe down," he calls over.

Annoyed, Ben says, "Well, I'm glad I provided you with the entertainment. I was hoping for a bit more understanding."

Covering his mouth with his hand, Martin's shoulders shake with supressed laughter whilst Ben watches on. Annoyed, Ben opts to change the subject.

"Moving on from my unfortunate evening, what's your story? Did you get a job offer?"

This has the desired effect of supressing Martin's giggles.

"Well mate, in contrast to your night it was all very sedate. We talked a bit, had a drink and got to know each other. Which was useful I suppose, as you've kindly arranged for us to holiday together. I doubt we are going to end up besties."

"Never mind all that mate. What about the proposal? What's on offer."

"Not as good as your proposal mate. It is all a bit vague to be honest. Just the possibility of working for him if I choose to leave my current job."

"Doing what?" asks Ben.

"Oh! it sounds like something not dissimilar to what I'm doing now. As I said, it was all a bit vague. A bit of a disappointment really," lies Martin. Inside his head, Sebastian's voice echoes, *'Well done Martin, mum's the word.'*

"Is that it! That all sounds underwhelming. I hope he's going to be more fun in Ibiza."

'I am sure he will be,' thinks Martin, as they both climb off their stools.

Back in the office, very little work is done in the afternoon. They have a constant exchange of emails. Most of the those that Martin sends are about transitioning and gender re-assignment, all attached with images. Most of Ben's responses are emojis giving Martin the finger.

Although it's Friday, there is no date night. Maureen has called it off because she has a sniffle and does not want to spread it around and infect Martin. Relieved, Martin looks forward to a quiet night in the flat watching a movie and having a break from alcohol consumption. Learning of Martin's availability, Ben urges him to have an after-work beverage but he resists all the pleading and cajoling. Having drunk more than he intended at his meeting with Sebastian, he resolves to have a weekend off the booze and on the wagon.

On the train he mentally pats himself on the back for keeping his resolve and not giving in to Ben's peer pressure. He further resolves to take it a step further and have an alcohol-free weekend with healthy eating and exercise. He might even go for a run on Saturday. He doesn't know what Sebastian has in mind, but if it involves something physical, he'll need to get back into shape. When he grabs a spare seat, he buries his head in his book, oblivious of his surroundings. Two stops later, he raises his head from the book. Immediately opposite, sits Unrequited love. His heart misses a beat. She must have boarded at the previous station, when his attention was focussed on the increasingly interesting plot of his novel.

Their eyes meet and he is sure her pout widens slightly into a half smile. Once he decides to return a smile of his own, she's is already looking back down at her mobile phone.

Sebastian's voice enters his head.

'Five million dollars. Quite the aphrodisiac.'

Unsure what is happening, or how, Martin responds in thought.

'Is this my imagination or is that you Sebastian?'

There is no response. Martin offers another thought.

'If that is you, are you doing the devil temptation thing? I'm with Maureen so it doesn't matter how much money I get from you. It ain't gonna happen.'

A few moments silence then Sebastian's voice re-enters his mind.

'To quote one of my favourite authors, Irvine Welsh, a standing prick hath no conscience. I do love that man's work. It's the subject matter, so raw. The man is a degenerate. My type of novelist.'

'Never read his stuff, but I've seen the film, Trainspotting.'

'There you go Martin. Now don't let me distract you. The woman of your dreams sits opposite.'

Martin looks across, she is still there, eyes glued to her mobile. He sinks back into his thoughts *'Literally, that man has got into my head. I'm now having imaginary conversations with him. I need to get a grip.'*

'Are you sure it's just your imagination?' replies Sebastian, his voice echoing through Martin's mind.

To evict Sebastian from his mind, Martin turns on his music. It works. He looks across. She is still there, eyes glued to her mobile.

Three stops later she gets off. This time Martin doesn't follow.

Saturday morning, hangover free, feeling chipper, Martin makes himself an instant coffee. He must try sobriety more often. Settling down on his couch to read the paper, the tone of his mobile breaks the peaceful serenity. Tutting, he answers it.

"Yes mate."

It's Ben. "Just ringing to see if you've heard anything from Seb. I don't have his number and want to finalise a few holiday arrangements. I'm going to book a few things for us to do and want to know if he's interested in joining us."

They discuss their respective Friday nights. Martin remembers he has Sebastian's number, takes out the card, turns it over and takes a photo.

"I've just emailed you Sebastian's number. It's on the back of the card he gave me. I've sent you a photo of it."

There is a pause in the conversation whilst Ben opens the attachment on Martin's text.

"Got it mate. Weird font. Old fashioned, a bit like how numbers looked on those old calculators. Hang on, it's not proper number, it says, Six, six, six, hell. No wait, the picture is upside down. Got it, seven, seven, three, four, nine, nine, nine." Cheers mate.

"What do you mean six, six, six hell?" asks Martin.

"God, this takes me back. Do you remember when you used to have competitions at school with your mates, trying to make words by turning the calculator upside down. An upside down four looks like an 'h' and a three turns into an 'E'. The longest word I ever got was 'hoses. The five turns into an 's' as well."

"And the seven looks like an 'L'. Yes, now you say that I do remember," replies Martin. He dwells on what Sebastian's number reveals when read upside down.

"Anyway mate. Maybe he's not as cashed up as we think. Errors on business cards are not a good look. That isn't a valid number, it's missing a couple of digits. You were telling me you saw Blondie but still didn't make a move."

"Nope."

"Are you seeing Maureen this weekend?"

"Nope."

"Do you want to meet up for a drink then?"

"Nope, I am drying out for a couple of days. I'm toying with the idea of returning to the gym."

"If we're going to talk about exercise, I'll love you and leave you. See you mate and if Sebastian calls tell him I want to speak to him. He's got my number but I don't have his."

Just after finishing the sports section, he receives another call. It's not showing a caller ID, but he answers anyway.

"Hello. This is Martin Hazel."

A familiar, educated voice with a smooth timbre, responds. "Good morning, Martin, it's Sebastian."

"Morning Seb, you must have read my mind."

"Are you surprised, given who I am?" jokes Sebastian.

"I was going to call you but the number on your business card isn't valid, as I'm sure you know."

"Yes. I don't like to give out my private number, for reasons which I am sure you can imagine. It was just my little joke between our good selves."

"Well, I unwittingly gave it to Ben. He wants to speak to you but he realised it is not complete."

"Noted. I'll touch base with him. But let's discuss you."

"Very clever."

"Clever?"

"Your number thing. Not Louis Cyphre or Belle Zebub, but three sixes, the number of the biblical beast, followed by the word 'hell'. A very nice touch and it shames me to say that it took Ben to notice it."

"I must admit, I was pleased with myself. But I do hope you haven't shared our business with him. That would be a shame considering my warning."

"No, I haven't said a word. I accidentally took the photo upside down and sent it to him, He read it then realised that it was the wrong way up. I assure you that I'm keen to pursue the matter."

"Jolly good. As you now realise, you have no way of contacting me, so I decided to give you a call. I propose we reconvene next Tuesday evening, same time at the same location. Thoughts?"

"Sounds good. I'll see you there. One question before you go. Were you getting into my head the other day? It felt like we were having a conversation on the tube."

"Possibly Martin or possibly my proposal is occupying your mind, along with Blondie of course. Goodbye."

How the hell did he know Blondie was on the train? The Devil? Surely, not,' thinks Martin, placing his mobile on the table.

Sunday morning and the sunshine is out, prompting Martin to risk a short jog around the local park. Avoiding a hamstring strain, he returns to the flat and takes a shower. When he finishes dressing, the doorbell rings. He presses the button on his intercom and enquires as to who is at the front door. A voice with a strong mid-west American accent asks if he is willing to spare a few minutes of his time to discuss God on this holy day. The Mormons have timed their visit to perfection. Normally, Martin would have responded brusquely in the negative, but he sees this as a homework opportunity in preparation for his second meeting with Sebastian.

He opens the door to find two, thin, twenty somethings, in poorly tailored black suits. Smiling through his pale complexion, the taller one speaks.

"Hello. I'm Elder Miller and this is my companion, Elder Berry, we would like to share with you today, a brief message of hope. If you have time, we would also be delighted to discuss the Gospel of Jesus Christ."

Elder Berry, nods, does not say a word, but is slightly put out by Martin's chuckle.

"Look, it's nice to meet you and I am happy to talk, but please excuse me for laughing. It's not at you; it's just the name. Ignore my childish behaviour. Let's start afresh, my name is Martin."

"That's quite alright sir; we are used to people laughing at Elder Berry's name. We fully understand the unfortunate similarity to the fruit. We have considered changing our introduction but it is a requirement of our church that we introduce ourselves in this manner."

"Okay. Once more, apologies. What's this message of hope you bring?" asks Martin, narrowing his eyes to convey that he is taking them seriously.

Elder Miller spends five uninterrupted minutes explaining that the message of hope is based on faith in Jesus Christ, the saviour, and his atonement. Martin is not exactly sure what this means, so remains silent. Elder Miller explains that having faith in Jesus Christ means that believers can confidently expect fulfillment of eternal promises.

"Eternal promises? What exactly are these?" asks Martin.

"Resurrection and eternal life," answers Elder Berry, who has now decided to speak up. As the senior team member, Elder Miller has the sole responsibility to speak and teach. With a sideways glance of annoyance at his colleague, he then turns to Martin and asks if he has any further questions. Martin says that he has a few, and Elder Miller gives him a nod of encouragement to go ahead.

"Do you believe in the Devil?"

The pair exchange glances, slightly concerned at the direction that the discussion could potentially follow. Their research had not revealed the existence of devil worshippers or covens in the Finchley area.

"We do sir. We certainly do. We call him Satan, Lucifer or sometimes simply the adversary," answers Elder Miller, re-asserting his position as spokesperson and teacher.

"Does he have special powers like God?"

"God is all powerful, he is omnipotent. He cast Satan down to earth as an evil spirit. Satan or Lucifer as some call him, is here to tempt, deceive and create misery. But, to answer your question, he lacks the power to force people to do evil."

Martin struggles to recall what Sebastian said when he asked him if he had special powers. Dredging his memory, scraps of information creep to the forefront of his mind. He recalls that Sebastian did not claim to have superpowers and opted to use persuasion and temptation. It appears representatives from both sides of the religious fence, heaven and hell, seem to be aligning. *Interesting, there is some consistency,* thinks Martin.

Seeing Martin fall silent for a minute, Elder Miller elucidates. "God's gift to man is Agency."

"Agency?" asks Martin, wondering what agency he is talking about.

"Yes Agency. It's a privilege that God gives us to choose and act for ourselves. Without it, we would be unable to make the right choices."

"Mmmm, but isn't the flipside of that, the ability to make wrong choices?" asks Martin.

"Indeed, that is the point of giving us Agency. If we choose to commit sin, we lose the opportunity to be with the Heavenly Father again. This is why the Heavenly Father provides a Saviour, in the form of Jesus Christ. He who suffered for our sins and enables redemption, if we repent."

"Mmm," says Martin.

Feeling the need to explain further, Elder Miller offers more information. "Four principles must be in force if there is to be Agency. The laws of God that can be obeyed or disobeyed must exist. Secondly, there must be good and evil. Thirdly, those who are to enjoy Agency must know the difference between good and evil so they are making their choice with full knowledge and not through ignorance. Finally, there must be an unfettered power to choose."

"Mmm," repeats Martin. He is beginning to struggle to understand the logic of Elder Miller's arguments. "I'm not sure I'm following you. It all seems convoluted and a rather odd way of dealing with things."

"How so?" asks Elder Miller

"Well, you say the saviour is Jesus, the son of God. It doesn't make sense to send down his son to save us, only to end up nailed to a cross. That's gotta hurt. Why would God even put Jesus into the mix. Give man free will and if he chooses evil then downstairs he goes. If he chooses good, it's a one-way ticket to paradise. It doesn't make sense for God to say that those who choose evil get a second chance to repent, just because he allowed his son was nailed to the cross by the Romans."

The Elders look at each other, unsure how to respond. Seeing them struggle to craft a response, Martin pursues his thinking.

"Look don't worry about answering that. Getting back to the Devil, you're sure he exists?"

"Lucifer? Yes."

"You talk a lot about Agency, and having a freedom to choose evil or good, but isn't he a bit redundant?"

Now Elder Miller was confused. "I'm sorry, who are you saying is redundant?"

"Lucifer. Isn't he redundant in the scheme of things? Regardless of this Agency, of the ability to choose, it looks like the outcome is inevitable no matter what Lucifer does. If we choose good then we go to Heaven and even if we follow Lucifer's path, we will still end up there because Jesus has been sent down to suffer on our behalf and redeem us?"

All three of them are losing energy and secretly want to end the discussion. Martin is beginning to find the conversation confusing, and the Mormons still have a lot of streets to cover before they can call it a day.

Elder Miller makes the first move. "Well thank you for your time, Martin. I hope we have brought you a little enlightenment. If you have no other questions, we will leave you in peace and may God be with you."

"Enlightenment? Yes, I think you may well have," confirms Martin, as he waves them goodbye. Thanks to the Mormons, Martin has drawn comfort that Lucifer has significant limitations. If Sebastian is some sort of beast, it's a cash cow rather than a horned, cloven hooved monster. Game on. He goes back into the flat with the bit between his teeth and the intention to do a bit more research on the matter. If only lessons on religious studies were this interesting when he was in school.

13

HE WAS IN A BIND AND WILLING TO MAKE A DEAL.

Bringing a whisky over to the table, Martin sits down and joins his companion for the evening. He has arrived early and bought himself a beer which has barely been touched by the time Sebastian arrives. Tonight, he intends to keep a clear head and having researched several religious academic papers dealing with the existence of the Devil, he is prepared for battle.

"How have you been Martin?"

"Busy Seb, very busy. I've been conducting research."

"Really, how very conscientious of you. About what?"

"Whether or not you exist."

"Well, here I am. You can see me with your own eyes."

"I certainly can, but how do I know you're not just some prankster with more money than sense."

"Fair point. Okay then, fire away. It's an excellent topic to address in our second session. Let's discuss whether the Devil exists, or not. Where do you want to start."

Martin pulls out a piece of paper. "I've got some prompts. I'm not going to fall into your last trap and get tied up in knots again. I take it you don't mind me using them?"

"Be my guest."

"Firstly, I think you mentioned God last time and presume if you do exist then God must."

"Yes, go on."

"I'm assuming you have a single adversary, God. There's not several of them, like say the Hindus have?"

"You mean like Brahma, Vishnu, Ganesha and all the rest? Goodness me, no. I've not seen any with an Elephant head that's for sure, nor the rest for that matter. Frankly, if there were as many as the Hindus think, I'd be hopelessly outnumbered."

"Does that mean we are looking at Christianity. Just the one God."

"Let's just say 'yes' for the time being."

"Ah ha! In that case you've fallen at the first hurdle."

"It makes a change from grace."

"Pardon?"

"Usually, the narrative runs that I have fallen from grace."

Worried that already he is being given the run around, Martin re-groups.

"Christianity is a …" Martin pauses to check his notes, "… is a Monotheistic religion. Is it not? In other words, there is only one God. Therefore, in a Monotheistic religion, the devil cannot exist."

"Pray tell me why?"

Turning the paper to read his notes on the back, Martin says, triumphantly, "Because such a belief system cannot accommodate two eternal forces responsible for the events in the world." He pauses then adds, "If the monotheistic God is all powerful and dominant, then there is no room for the devil and therefore the devil cannot exist."

"Not sure I either follow you or accept your logic."

Undeterred, Martin has the bit between his teeth. "The Devil is purely a fictional character created by men who cannot accept responsibility for their actions. Take Hansie Cronje."

"Who is Hansie Cronje?" asks Sebastian.

"A cricketer, he's South African."

"I hate cricket, too boring," says Sebastian.

"I'm not saying you have to like cricket."

"Oh! right."

With slight irritation, Martin snaps, "The point I am trying to make is that Hansie Cronje was caught match fixing".

"Nothing to do with me for the record, in case this is where your story is going."

"Can you please stop interrupting and let me finish my point?"

"Sorry."

"When he was caught cheating, Hansie Cronje's defence was that the Devil made him do it."

"There you go. I knew I was right. I told you so. I knew this was where your argument was going. I can categorically confirm that I played no part in this match fixing. I hate cricket."

"Actually, this is exactly my point. You admit that you played no part in it. The Devil is just a fictional creation by men, in this example Hansie Cronje, who are unable to take responsibility for their bad deeds."

"An interesting, and to some degree valid, point. Certainly, the Devil is often slandered and blamed for the behaviour of others. But let me ask you this in return. If the devil is fictional, what do you have to lose, other than five million pounds if you don't accept my proposal?"

"That's exactly the reason I'm trying to find out who or what you are, and then work out what you want?"

"So, what if I am the Devil? How does it help you decide whether or not to proceed?"

"Well, if you are the Devil, then I presume you'll want something from me and it may not be good."

"And what do you think that might be?"

"Something like selling you my soul, which leaves me in eternal damnation."

Bursting into a raucous laugh, Sebastian almost falls off his stool and steadies himself by holding onto the table. Perplexed and irritated at the same time, Martin watches on, patiently waiting for the attack of mirth to subside. A tear escapes the corner of Sebastians eye, which he wipes with his hand as he struggles to control himself. Calming himself down, Sebastian sinks the rest of the whisky in his glass.

"I'm so sorry Martin, but you caught me off guard there. I must tell you that this has made my day. Let me get you another drink." Without waiting for a response, Sebastian hops off his stool. As he heads off to the bar, he calls back, "Listen to the next song whilst I'm getting the drinks in."

Previously oblivious to the background music, Martin listens whilst the current song finishes and waits for the next one. He immediately recognises it from the energetic introductory fiddle playing.

"The Devil went down to Georgia,

He was looking for a soul to steal,

He was in a bind because he was way behind

And was willing to make a deal."

Rejoining Martin, Sebastian sets down the fresh drinks. "I think you deserve something stronger so I bought you a whisky. I'm sure one more drink won't dull your thinking too much. Right, where were we?"

"The song. It's about doing a deal with the Devil. Selling souls."

Controlling himself after a final chuckle escapes involuntarily, Sebastian says, "I am so sorry, but really Martin, you shouldn't believe everything you read or hear. There's a lot of false news bandied about. Ask Donald Trump."

"Really, is that so?" replies Martin sulkily, having been made to feel foolish and naïve.

"I'm afraid so. Look I can assure you that souls aren't something you can sell. You've either booked your spot in Heaven or not. You're either going up or down and that's determined by what you do with your life. It can't be decided by some sort of transaction with the Devil who, incidentally, doesn't exist according to your research."

Peeved, Martin snaps back. "So, what's your take on it then?"

"Not so much a take, but a fact. Actions decide the nature and direction of your journey. Hitler and Mother Theresa went very different ways once their mortal coils were snipped due to what they did while they were here. Currently, we've got the likes of Trump, Putin and Maradona who've all already booked their spot in you know where."

"I get Trump and Putin, but Maradona?"

"Well, the fat little Argentinian did cheat and exacerbated that sinful act with his comment that his handball was the hand of God. Very blasphemous. How does the second commandment go? Let me think. Ah! Yes. You shall not take the name of the Lord your God in vain."

"Really, are you seriously telling me he's going to hell because of that?"

"No Martin, of course he's not. That was my little joke. I may not like cricket but I do love football. All that diving and cheating, it's my sort of game. Also, I thought that you, being English, would appreciate the humour."

"I'm not sure I'm in the mood for jokes. I think my fucking head is going to explode."

"The thing is, Martin, on my side of the fence I don't require faith. Those who follow God, demand it. Faith is a weakness. One of my favourite thinkers, Bertrand Russell, summed it up perfectly. I must say, I did like him whilst he was around. I'd often attend his lectures."

Sebastian pauses and looks up in the air wistfully before he continues.

"Anyway, I digress. Old Berty said all faiths cause harm, and I have to say that in Hell we don't consider that this is necessarily a negative thing. His analysis is that we only speak of faith when we wish use emotion instead of evidence. Different groups substitute different emotions, and that leads to problems. Conflicts, wars, torture, subjugation and so on. Again, from our perspective not a negative thing."

"Okay so you say that being the Devil, you don't require me to have faith?"

"Correct. As Bertie said, it's a weakness. Despite that, I have provided you with evidence, devoid of any emotion, but that's still not enough for you. How did that song appear on the jukebox just now. I didn't go near it, did I? Now consider another excellent thinker, dear old Albert."

"Einstein," replies Martin, now confident he is following the conversation.

"No, Camus. Albert Camus, a Frenchman. He wrote about 'the Absurd'. This being the collision between man's desperate search for meaning in an unintelligent universe which, in response, stays doggedly silent. He talks about the conflict between the human tendency to find inherent value and meaning in life and the inability of the universe, that they live in, to provide them with evidence and the answers. Therefore, having got no answers, humans invent something which is unprovable and therefore requires faith.

"I don't know what I think, so I certainly can't get my head around the ramblings of a bloody maths teacher and a French bloke."

"My point is, Martin, I don't need you to. Nor do I require you to have faith and therefore believe in God or the Devil. To progress to the next stage, I really need you to, at the very least, be convinced that I have the money and wherewithal to keep my part of the bargain. This will ensure that you will be fully committed to trying to fulfil your part of the deal. It is vitally important for my proposal."

"I'm still not sure I fully understand."

"My proposal is essentially a test. It is evaluating a proposition. The proposition cannot be rigorously assessed unless you believe that, if you pass the test, you will profit. In this case to the tune of five million. If you doubt that passing the test will result in the promised outcome, then I cannot be sure you have put in one hundred percent of effort. Believing I am the Devil would achieve this because you know that I have the capability to fulfill the bargain. However, unlike the other side, I don't necessarily need your faith. If you choose to think I am a few sticks short of a bundle and won't keep my promise, then it will not work. So as a backup, if you won't accept that I am the Devil, you can at least accept that if you co-operate then you'll get the money."

"You've got to admit that if you were in my shoes you'd consider the possibility that someone claiming to be the Devil isn't playing with a full deck?"

"Of course, I can see your point entirely. But I have given you a few demonstrations of my power in an attempt to convince you that I'm the Devil. So where do you stand now?"

"I don't know."

"Okay Martin, let's take a break. We've made considerable progress and this is sufficient to move forward at our next meeting. Time to get some rest, you look as though you need it."

Not sharing Sebastian's optimism on the amount of progress they've made, Martin agrees that it is time to call it a night. They finish their drinks and make their way home, going in opposite directions after they step outside the doors of the pub. The fresh night air clears his head during his walk to the tube station. With two meetings completed, his first thought is that he is no nearer to deciding whether Sebastian is from the burning halls of Hell or the Lambeth Psychiatric Hospital just down the road. He certainly walked off in that direction, when they parted ways outside the pub.

Moments before they made their way into the night, Sebastian encouraged Martin not to rely on faith but consider the evidence. Were the timing of the songs co-incidence or were they put on the jukebox by the Devil using preternatural powers. What about the dreams and the voices that had materialised in Martin's mind. More co-incidence? Hypnotic suggestion? Martin had not a clue. Before they parted, he had offered Martin a final bit of proof. "Just keep your eyes peeled on your journey home, I'll give you a glimpse of something to warm the cockles of your heart," he said. Martin assumed it could only be Unrequited Love.

It's late and the train is half empty. Taking the first available seat, he scours the length and breadth of his carriage. No sign of Unrequited love. Disappointment. Rising from his seat, he walks to the door between the carriages and looks through the window. Still no sign of Blondie. Defeated, he sits down on a nearby seat. His expectancy increases as the journey progresses. Two more stops pass and he stares in anticipation when the carriage doors open at the third stop. Two men enter with a blond woman following closely behind them. He strains to look around the men, to get a clear view of her face. When they sit down, the woman comes clearly into view. She is Blond but she is not Blondie. She looks at least ten years older. Chastising himself for believing Sebastian, he takes out his book and starts to read.

Archway arrives; the train doors slide open. Struggling to concentrate on his book, he glances outside onto the platform. Within the small group walking up to the exit he spots the back of a woman's head, her hair is blond and the style is similar but she is too far away to be certain it is her. The doors close and she is no longer in sight. The rest of the journey is uneventful but his frustration simmers within his thoughts. *Why did I allow myself to be drawn in? Am I that sad and desperate for God's sake? I'm not even sure that was her on the platform. The man is just a bullshitter. What am I thinking? What am I doing even entertaining this nutbag?*

Hauling himself up from his seat, he lets out a big sigh as the train pulls into Finchley Central. With no enthusiasm, he thinks ahead to tomorrow and another day on the treadmill with Herring watching from the sidelines. If he needs an incentive to accept Sebastian's offer, all he needs to do is visualise what tomorrow brings. Then, after visualising tomorrow, visualise the day that follows and then the day after that. According to Sebastian, souls cannot be sold. Providing the contract does not involve him acting illegally, or putting his life in danger, what's to lose?

Settled in the flat, with a hot chocolate before bedtime, Sebastian's proposal runs through his mind. He revisits the snippets of evidence that Sebastian claimed to engineer. He works through the logic and arguments that Sebastian put forward. He considers Sebastian's claim that he is the Devil, though thinking about it, had he ever categorically said those words? In fact, Sebastian had insisted that it didn't matter whether Martin believed this or not. In the end all he needs from Martin is a firm belief that Sebastian can meet the financial side of the bargain. This is the one thing that Martin has no doubt about. Martin has seen clear indications of Sebastian's wealth. The clothes, the accessories and most pertinently, the American Express Centurion card. Not to mention that Sebastian oozes the confidence of a man with money and power, used to getting what he wants. In the final analysis whether Sebastian is the Devil or not, Martin can be sure that a significant amount of cash could come his way. Ten percent was promised up front. Half a million pounds in his bank account is a hefty insurance that he would not come out of the deal empty handed. It all boils down to the nature of the deal. Should he stop pandering to this man's potential fantasy or follow it through. Should he see this to the end or stop wasting his time with a delusional prankster.

Sebastian has made it clear that he does not require Martin to believe he is the devil, but Martin is convinced that Sebastian clearly believes he is.

What to do? Draining his mug of the last drop of hot chocolate, Martin goes to bed.

His mind is made up.

14
YOU MAKE ME FORGET MYSELF.

Either the alcohol, the hot chocolate, the decision to go ahead, or all three, results in a good night's rest. No dreams of diamante jockstraps nor of his semi-naked blond haired Unrequited love pouting alluringly. Just pure, restful, unadulterated, uninterrupted sleep. Coming to a decision removes a weight from his mind and, unusually for a Wednesday, he walks to Finchley Central with a spring in his step.

Invigorated from the restful night and the anticipation of his next meeting with Sebastian, the prospect of work, once he logs on at his desk, borders enthusiasm. An email from Herring informing Martin that he would be out of the office, taking a wellness day, further enhances his mood. Martin hunkers down to the tasks of the day.

A gentle tap on the shoulder wrests him away from the screen. Tapping his watch, Ben smiles then mimics eating a sandwich. Martin checks the time and can barely believe it is half past one already. Like a man possessed he has cleared all his emails and completed his latest report, which Herring is not expecting for two days. On their way to Mario's Sandwich bar, Martin decides that if today is a new dawn then he will celebrate with a new sandwich.

"I'll have a salami and Swiss cheese on multigrain today."

Raising his bushy black left eyebrow, Mario grins, "Is this a special day?"

"Just a good one Mario and I'm in the mood to broaden my horizons. In fact, I'll try one of your coffee Frappuccino's as well, whilst I'm at it."

They find two spare stools by the window and place their food and drinks on the ledge. "What's got in to you today, Marto. A bit of mid-week nookie last night?" asks Ben.

Working through his first bite, Martin wonders why he had not tried this before, the sandwich is delicious.

"Well?" prompts Ben.

"Well, what?"

"Why the good mood, did Maureen come over to yours gasping for your body?"

"Nope. Just had a good night's sleep and the day was made better when I found out Herring is not coming in today."

"A managers' meeting?"

"No, he's having a wellness day. Must be his fourth since he's been promoted."

"But you're only allowed two per year, aren't you. Or is it different for senior management?" replies Ben, sarcastically.

"No, it isn't, but I think he finds his new role much harder than he thought it would be."

"You could be right. He's brown nosed his way up and probably finds he's not up to it."

"Could be. But I've had a good day. Got plenty done and finished my latest project ahead of schedule."

Widening his eyes expectantly, Ben says, "Does this mean that you're going to stay then?"

"I wouldn't say that. I've been thinking about the meeting with Sebastian and I think I'm going to press him to see what he has got to offer or, at least, to see if he is just full of shit as I suspect. I'm in the mood for change."

"I could see that when you ordered the sandwich. Mario almost fainted."

"Very funny."

Back in the office Martin continues where he left off and starts a new project ahead of schedule. Smiling to himself, Martin visualises Herring basking in the reflected glory of his team's productivity when progress reports are delivered up the line. The only break he takes in the afternoon is to grab a coffee and text Sebastian.

Hi. Given everything a bit of thought and decided I'm keen to proceed to the next stage.

In seconds Martin's phone pings, notifying him of a message received.

Hello Martin. Excellent. Same time, same place tomorrow?

After sending a 'thumbs up' emoji, Martin tidies his desk and, on his way out, looks over to Ben who responds with a beer drinking mimic. Martin waves away the offer and strides out of the office to avoid dealing with any attempt to persuade him to re-consider. Having left earlier than usual, Martin finds the tube station less busy and experiences the rare pleasure of seeing a seat available when he boards the train. Three stops later, two students sitting opposite leave the train and engrossed in his book he does not notice the new passenger who occupies one of the vacated seats. Once he looks up to stretch his neck and rest his eyes for a moment, he is presented with a vision of beauty. Unrequited love sits opposite and when he accidentally catches her eye, she rewards him with a tentative smile before looking back down at her phone screen. With a slightly increased heart rate Martin steals glimpses whilst pretending to read his book, until she leaves at Archway station. He cannot be sure, but he thinks that she gives him a backward glance just before she exits through the train door.

Back at his flat, Martin heats up a meal for one that he bought from the supermarket he passes on the way home. Settling down in front of the television, he watches the news whilst unenthusiastically working his way through the fisherman's pie which the food factory processing plant has rendered devoid of flavour. When the news transforms into the weather forecast, he goes to the kitchen, tips the half-eaten pie into the bin and puts his fork into the dishwasher.

His mobile rings and seeing Maureen's name on the screen, he answers it.

"Hi Maureen, how's your day been?"

"I've had a bit of a mare …"

She proceeds to regale him of all the minor dramas that befell her life that day. He murmurs and makes sufficient sympathetic noises to show he is listening intently. His mind wanders away from Maureen towards Unrequited love, recalling his brief encounter on the train.

"So, is that okay with you then?" she asks.

"Eh! sorry. Is what okay?"

"Haven't you been listening?"

"Yeah. Sorry, of course. I was distracted for a moment; there's footage of some explosion on the telly. I've got the news on," he lies.

"Really, what happened?"

"I don't know. I turned the sound down when you rang."

"Well, never mind that. I was saying that that I won't' come round tomorrow because I have an after-work thing. Sonya is leaving and I'm doing her leaving speech. But maybe we could go to a film on Friday, there's a new one with Jude Law that I want to see."

"Yeah, sure that's okay."

When Maureen finished the call, he sat down realising he has just had a close shave. He forgot that he had arranged to see Maureen tomorrow when he accepted Sebastians invitation. Luckily, Maureen has just cancelled leaving him blameless. It is one of those rare days where everything just works out perfectly, apart from the fisherman's pie.

His phone pings with a message notification. It's Sebastian.

Lucky that Martin. A close call. See you tomorrow.

Martin replies.

What's a close call?

He gets an immediate response.

You know my friend.

Peeved, Martin texts.

Have you bugged my flat or something?

Another immediate response.

No Martin, scout's honour. Just giving you a bit more 'evidence'. Have a good night. Sweet dreams.

Sleep that night is less restful than the previous one. The dream starts mundane. Martin is riding on the train home from work, reading his book. Then it turns strange. He looks up and sees Unrequited love sitting opposite, she smiles at him dressed in erotic underwear.

Next to her is Sebastian, grinning lasciviously. He whispers something into her ear. She stands up and walks towards him and …

15
WHAT'S PUZZLING YOU IS THE NATURE OF MY GAME.

The alarm sounds…

Another workday begins. Duvet exodus. Shivering. Warm shower. Instant coffee. Toast. Exits flat. Raining. Hunched shoulders. Through barrier. On the platform standing in his usual spot.

Everything is back to normal, yesterday a distant memory. Feeling as though he has not slept, Martin's energy and motivation levels are reset to low. Any possibility of them rising again dissolves with the appearance of Herring at his desk. Mechanically, Martin responds to Herring's cheery greeting. The small talk is one sided. Herring describes his day off and Martin nods, his mind wandering elsewhere. Sensing, from the change of tone in his boss's voice, that Herring's small talk is coming to an end, he tunes back in.

"Oh! well Martin, that was my day. Just popped by to touch base and give you a little nudge that the report on Henley and Son is due tomorrow."

Martin grunts an acknowledgement, not bothering to tell Herring that the report was completed yesterday. He's in no mood for work. An unofficial day off, spent at his desk surfing the internet, is the order of the day. Once he sees Herring is safely back in his office, Martin starts to google. His first search is for Sebastian Balfour. Forty minutes trawling social media draws a complete blank. He tries Linked In. Nothing. Whoever or whatever Sebastian is, he is digitally invisible. He scours the internet broadening his search. Pulling out Sebastian's card from his wallet, Martin re-reads it. He googles the name of Sebastian's company. There are plenty of hits for 'Life Solutions,' none of which have a director called Sebastian Balfour. The search widens.

Ben taps him on the shoulder. Martin has lost track of time.

"C'mon mate. It's one o'clock, let's go and grab a sarnie".

The culinary experiment is over. Sitting beside Ben in Mario's Sandwich Bar, Martin unenthusiastically works his way through a minted lamb roll, washed down with a normal coffee. No Frappuccino today.

"You seem a bit down mate. You were on top form yesterday, today you're a bit miserable. What's changed. What's up?"

"Didn't get much sleep. Just knackered."

"Cheer up mate. Won't be long before we are partying in Ibiza."

"Yeah sure, with your new best mate."

"Sebastian? He'll be fine. I reckon he's gonna be a bit of a laugh."

Tutting dismissively, Martin says, "Him? A laugh? The international man of mystery."

"What are you talking about?"

"Old Seb. The invisible man. I've been checking him out this morning. Or at least trying to. He can't be found anywhere. Facebook, Tik Tok, Instagram, Linked In. Nothing about him anywhere."

"Mate, have you been stalking again? First Blondie, now Seb. I'm getting worried about you," laughs Ben.

"I'm serious mate. It's not stalking. He says he's got a proposal. It's perfectly reasonable to check him out and what he does. Isn't it?"

"Yeah, fair comment mate. Keep your hair on, I was only joking. So, you found nothing?"

"Not a fucking thing. You'd think that I would have found something about his company. Who runs a company that isn't on the internet nowadays? Ask yourself that."

"Once again, fair point mate. Maybe he runs one of those exclusive, word of mouth, type of businesses. Y'know, it's so exclusive that he selects his clients, they don't select him. Maybe he's one of those lifestyle consultants and provides a specialist high end service. He looks to me like he's loaded, so maybe he serves the rich and famous. Discretion is paramount. Services by word of mouth. Exclusive, high end. All that sort of thing."

Pondering Ben's comments, Martin finishes his roll and drains his cup of coffee. He has not thought of that angle. Ben waits patiently for a response.

"You may have a point Ben, but you've got to admit it's pretty strange. Aside from that, if he's some sort of mentor to the rich and famous, why the hell would he want to talk to me? It's not as though I'm exactly high-profile."

Laughing, Ben says, "Once again mate, fair comment. You're not exactly Mister Personality either."

"Fuck off."

Checking his watch, Martin tuts. A pint of beer and a whiskey sit untouched on his table. It is ten past six o'clock and Sebastian is late. Looking around, he sees only two other customers. Both sat alone nursing their drinks. *I'm not the only sad sack*, he thinks. Rapidly concluding that the whole thing has been some sort of pathetic hoax, Martin picks up his beer intending to drink it quickly and then leave. Before he takes a drink, the jukebox fires into life. The introduction of the song is familiar. Jagger's voice fills the pub. Hearing another voice behind him, Martin swings round.

"Evening Martin, please accept my apologies for the tardiness in my time keeping."

"No worries," replies Martin, pointing to the glass of whiskey. "Sympathy for the Devil, a nice touch to accompany your entry."

"Thank you, Martin, I'm glad you noticed."

"Another piece of evidence?" asks Martin, wanting to appear relaxed and unfazed by Sebastian's late arrival.

"If you wish," replies Sebastian.

"I've been researching you."

"Oh! really. Well, I must admit there has been a lot written about me over the centuries," replies Sebastian, proudly.

"Well, certainly a lot more than has been written about Sebastian Balfour. You are literally invisible."

"But here I am, in the flesh," replies Sebastian, obtusely.

"I mean digitally. There is nothing about you anywhere. If you have a company called Life Solutions, you clearly don't look to advertise it. You also don't bother with social media."

"I suppose it's more of a job description than a business name," replies Sebastian, smirking whilst taking a sip of whiskey. Martin shakes his head. Sebastian asks, "Having done all this research, what's your conclusion?"

"My conclusion is that I don't know who or what you are. Certainly, you're enigmatic. Also, I've thought about what you said."

"Which bit?"

"You told me that I don't have to believe you're the devil, only that you have the capability to pay me so that

I will give it my full commitment. And I need to be fully committed to validate your test. If I'm not all in, then the test would be invalid. Is all that, correct?"

"Spot on Martin. Well done."

"So having resolved that, all that remains is to move on to the details of the proposition. Or put simply, what is it I've got to do to earn my five million and, equally important, what happens if I fail."

"Hence our previous soul selling discussion." says Sebastian.

"Indeed," confirms Martin.

Stepping off his high stool, Sebastian suggests that he replenishes the drinks before they get to the crux of the matter. Martin agrees and whilst Sebastian is at the bar, he goes to the toilet. Standing at the urinal, he gets the feeling of butterflies in his midriff as blood flows from his stomach in anticipation. Zipping up, he thinks, *finally, one way or another, I'm going to know what this is all about.*

"Before we start, I want to run a couple of things by you."

"Certainly," says Sebastian.

"I had a chat with a couple of Mormons and they talked about Agency."

"Mormons. Now there's a belief system with a whole raft of contradictions. An interesting bunch."

"Yeah right. Anyway, they talked about committing sin but man having Agency, being a gift from God."

"Well, I suppose an Escort Agency is a hotbed of lust. That's a sin. An Estate Agency is full of charlatans charging extortionate fees. That's greed, more sinning there. Staff in a PR Agency often think they are, pardon my blasphemy, God's gift. That's pride, another sin."

"NO. NO. Let me explain," says Martin, raising his voice in frustration. "By Agency, they meant that we have a choice. A choice to do the right thing or do the wrong thing. And if we do the wrong thing, we can get out of it by repenting because Jesus redeemed us. So even if I did something wrong because of your proposition I'm not guaranteed a trip to your place anyway. Even if I signed a contract, I could get out of it by repenting."

"Excellent Martin. You've cracked it. No one goes to hell by selling their soul for money. It's all about what you do."

"In that case let's get to it."

"That's the spirit. I take it you have heard of the seven deadly sins I was just alluding to."

"Yes, but a reminder wouldn't go amiss."

"Look you don't have to commit today. But I suggest you do a bit of revision back at the flat. Because it is important that you know exactly what they are. You will need to know them in detail, if you commit to my proposal. They are, for the record, Pride, Greed, Wrath, Envy, Lust, Gluttony and Sloth."

"What has this got to do with me?

"In the eternal fight between good and evil, there are a lot of cases where it is black and white. Trump, Putin, Hitler, Jack the Ripper and all the rest are hell bound. They are the easy ones to deal with. The no-brainers. On the other side, the likes of Abraham Lincoln, Mother Theresa and Oprah Winfrey are going to the other place."

"Like the Pope," interrupts Martin.

"Not all of them, but certainly most of the modern ones."

"Oh! okay!"

"But most of the people who live on this little rock in the far reaches of the universe, are somewhere in the middle. They are a bit, how can I put this politely without causing offence, boring. It is this lot which really tests who has the most influence and power."

"Basically, you're saying I am boring."

"Let's not dwell on that for a moment, Martin. Not everything is about you."

"Sorry."

"Not a problem. So, the mid-range group, of which you are a member, is the real test. Can Mister Average, that's you for the record but no offence intended, be persuaded to do the bidding of our side or the other? Strictly speaking we believe that the other lot have a massive advantage. People don't commit any serious sins because most of them are conservative and conformists by nature. Not to mention they fear the consequences of the laws that man has created. It's not an even playing field and to be fair to the other lot, they recognise this."

"I'm with you so far but I'm not sure where we are going with this."

"It's simple really. Every year I have a little competition with one of my opposite numbers."

"Opposite number? You mean God."

"Not exactly."

"Hang on mate. If you're the devil then your opposite number must be God."

"You've assumed that's what I am. You haven't heard me say as much. In the eternal struggle of good versus evil, there is no 'i' in team. You've been doing a fair bit of research apparently, so I will refer you to the Gospel of Mark. A man possessed by many demons is asked his name. The response is, 'My name is Legion for we are many.' So, you see, it's not all about the two head honchos. It's a team game."

"Okay, I get there's a lot on both sides, but what are you, a demon?"

"That's not important at this stage. What are names, but labels. The seven sins I mentioned earlier, pride, greed and so on are the test ground. According to Western religions, Lucifer is associated with pride and Beelzebub with gluttony, and Mammon with greed."

"Sloth?"

"Yes, we have specialists in all areas. Belphegor has sloth covered. But let's move on. I want to focus on your part of the bargain."

"Good idea let's get to it. Basically, I think I understand. There's an annual competition between you and a hitherto unnamed opponent, to test who can persuade Mister Average to be good or in your case, bad."

"Nice summary Martin. Once you have signed up, the competition will run over the following seven weeks and in that time, you will either embrace or repel the temptation to commit each of the seven deadly sins."

"So how do you win or lose this competition?"

"There are seven, conveniently an odd number. First to four, wins."

"If, say, I commit four sins and you win, what does that mean for me?"

"If you are asking me whether you are destined for eternal damnation, the short answer is no. In the cosmic scheme of things, the sins committed by participants are normally relatively minor. We aren't talking genocide here. There are no consequences for you in the eternity arena. As for your duration on this rock, I can't say. That depends upon what you do when, or if, you commit one of the sins."

"Not sure I get your drift."

"If, in an act of greed, you rob a bank and get caught by the Police, then a consequence of committing that sin is that you might go to jail. Of course, you may get away with it. I have no influence either way. The only outcome for me is a point on the board."

"What if I commit mass murder?"

"Martin, my dear Martin, haven't you been listening. Those we select are in the herd. The mainstream, Mister and Missus Average. With all due respect, you are no Ted Bundy, Jeffrey Dahmer or Fred West. I mean if you were, it wouldn't be a competition, would it now? I'd win hands down."

Martin sits in silence, pontificating, whilst Sebastian looks on patiently, sipping his whiskey. Seeing that Martin is struggling to formulate his next response, Sebastian goes to the bar and brings back another beer and whiskey. When he places the beer on the table, Martin looks up.

"Forgive me, but if you are the devil, or one of his team as you call it, how can I trust you?"

"Fair point. To ensure everything is above board there is a contract prepared and signed by both sides, remember my opponent is trustworthy. It only requires your signature to execute the agreement."

"There are no consequences for me?"

"None other than I mentioned earlier. If you rob a bank, get caught and jailed, that's on you. That's in your control, not mine. It's that Agency thing you were talking about with the Mormons. Your choice, under your control."

Narrowing his eyes, Martin asks, "So, what do I have to do to get the five million?"

"Sign the contract. Wait until the seven-week period is up. Collect your money."

"As simple as that."

"Essentially yes. I will of course be setting several tests to encourage your participation in the seven sins of course."

"Just you?"

"In the main yes. I may of course seek the assistance of one or two of my colleagues who specialise in certain areas."

With a frown, Martin asks, "Are you allowed to cause me harm?"

"No, of course not Martin. That is not allowed in the rules. There would be an immediate forfeit and the other side would go into guardian angel mode to ensure your safety. That said, if you come to harm because of a choice you've made, then that's a different matter. What's more, you can't rely on a guardian angel bailing you out."

"Why not?"

"We are back to the Mormons again. Agency, choice and control. If, for example, you choose to sleep with Ben's girlfriend and he finds out … well … the consequences are on you. Let's just say we won't be footing the hospital bill."

"Shouldn't be a risk there. There isn't any woman in their right mind that would give him the time of day. Right, for now I'm done. Where's the contract?"

"I'll email it to you tomorrow so you can have a good read at work and we can meet back here to cover any queries or final questions."

"Email it? I thought it would be written on parchment and I'd have to sign it with a quill pen."

"I think you've been watching too many films. It's not Hollywood and we're in the twenty first century, not the eighteenth. After our meeting tomorrow, you can sign it when you get back into the office the following day. Let me give you a reminder about confidentiality. You can't let anybody else read it."

"Don't you want me to print it off and sign it. If it's all kosher, I can bring it with me tomorrow?"

"Martin, we're in the twenty first century, the contract will be set up with DocuSign. If you are happy with it, just flick it back when we are done. However, I recommend that you wait until after tomorrow night's meeting. You may have questions and amendments to put to me. In fact, after further consideration, I insist that you wait. I can assure you that the other party is very keen to ensure you haven't been pressured into a rushed decision. That would also be a forfeit and I don't want to lose this year. Not good for the old ego."

"Understood, fancy another drink?"

"Not for me, I've another appointment with a local vicar. The poor chap is having a bit of a crisis of faith.

Until tomorrow then." Sebastian rises from his stool and walks towards the exit. Another thought enters Martins mind, which is already swirling with conflict and emotions. He calls over to Sebastian who is at the pub door.

"Hey, Seb, wait. You don't have my email address."

Looking over his shoulder, Sebastian gives a knowing smile and walks out into the night.

16
ALL I NEED IS JUST A LITTLE PATIENCE.

The alarm sounds. Instant coffee. Toast. Exits flat. On the platform standing in his usual spot. Arrives at Embankment, disembarks. Greets colleagues as walks through open plan. Logs on.

With a rare feeling of anticipation, Martin clicks on to Outlook to check his emails. There are only four unread messages. Two are spam, which he forwards to the IT Department to investigate and block future attempts from that email address. One is from Ben which has a meme about Donald Trump. The fourth is from Herring which he deletes. Disappointed by the lack of any email from Sebastian, he sighs and clicks on to Word, to open his draft report. He intends to give it one final edit before submitting it to Herring before the deadline. Once the file is opened, he pauses for thought. There were two spam messages this morning. Normally, the security measures on the server were sufficient to block unknown or suspicious sources and processes were tightened following a bad virus that breached the systems several months ago. What if Sebastian's message is blocked? It's from an unknown source and will have a document attached which increases the likelihood of it being picked up by the anti-virus software. He sends a message to the IT Department requesting that they scan the Junk Emails to see if a message from a person with the surname Balfour, has been received.

The morning drags but at least he has finalised his report and sent it to Herring. Constant checking of his emails, only to find nothing from Sebastian nor from the IT Department, does not help the slow passing of time. Lunchtime arrives and he feels the need to get some fresh air. Ben is on a one-day external course, so with the prospect of dining alone, he gets a take-away sandwich, today is a prawn day, and goes for a walk along the South Bank. He finds a bench and looks across the muddy Thames at the Houses of Parliament. The familiarity of the scene drags him from the surreal events of the last month back to reality. Nibbling on his sandwich, he mulls it over.

What was he thinking? A contract with the devil. Ridiculous. The man is a fraud, a hoaxer. But, what about the dreams and the predictions. What predictions? Not exactly earth shattering. Lucky guesses with a bit of mind play and mental suggestion. As for the erotic dreams, he has been obsessing a bit about Unrequited love. Thirty somethings can have wet dreams; it is not the sole privilege of pre-pubescent teenagers.

Returning to the office with a mixture of expectancy and hope, Martin logs back on. No unread emails. He gathers up some papers for his meeting with Herring to go through the report he had sent in the morning. Their meeting is relatively short because either Herring has not read it or he doesn't understand it. Or both.

Whatever the reason, Martin is grateful for the brevity of their get together and sits back down at his desk to contemplate whether he has the emotional or mental energy to start on the next job at two thirty in the afternoon. He taps the keyboard which causes the screen to light up from snooze mode. His heart rate quickens when his eye catches the bold font showing there is an unread message. It's from Life Solutions with a paperclip symbol showing that the message has an attachment. After looking around the office to ensure no-one is near, he clicks on the message.

Dear Martin,

As promised, I attach a draft contract. It is relatively short, so please review and we can discuss this evening. Once we have your signature it will be sent to the other two parties who will sign within twenty-four hours and then you will be provided with a final signed copy. Upon receipt of the final copy, the agreement commences for a period of seven weeks.

Regards,
Sebastian Balfour

Moving the cursor to the attachment and double clicking, the file opens. He scans the PDF document and finds it is only three pages long. At the bottom of the third page there is a Docusign symbol for Martin to click on to sign electronically. Heeding Sebastian's advice, he does not sign but scans back to the beginning of the document. His first reading takes barely five minutes. The terms are clear, devoid of legalistic language and the conditions are exactly as Sebastian described. He reads and re-reads the sections on confidentiality, limitation of liability and termination. It is made clear that discussing the existence of the agreement, or even the activities described in the scope, with a third party immediately renders it void. The consideration is exactly as described by Sebastian, five million pounds with ten percent up front. The termination clause indicates that the terms of the agreement have been met seven weeks after all parties have signed. When he reaches the end, having read and re-read each clause along the way, he examines the signatories in addition to his own. Two other names are printed, with a space for their signature.

Signatories to the agreement.
Asmodeus (Head of Malevolence)
Zadkiel (Head of Benevolence)

Having satisfied himself that the agreement is in line with Sebastian's promises, Martin decides to do a little more research. There is an hour and a half to kill before his meeting. He googles Zadkiel and immediately gets a hit. There is not a great deal of information offered and the different hits recycle the same information. Zadkiel, an archangel known for mercy. He repeats the process for the other signatory, Asmodeus. This character has a few more entries. There are several versions and stories associated with him but the most common one describes him as an archdemon whose specialty is lust. Another entry gives him the lofty title of King of the demons. Martin ponders what he has learnt and feels fully prepared for his meeting.

When he enters the Ship and Shovell it is precisely six o'clock. The place is full, awash with the buzz of conversation and laughter. Looking around the bar, he spots Sebastian, who waves and gestures to the stool next to him. When he approaches, Martin sees there is a glass of beer waiting for him.

"Welcome Martin, busy day?"

"Yes, actually it was," replies Martin.

"Not too busy I trust. I hope you've had enough time to read the draft contract."

Emptying a third of his glass, Martin puts down his beer. "I have."

"Excellent. Now tell me do you have any concerns or queries."

"Just a couple. The main one is that I notice that if I do not complete the seven weeks, I lose the deposit and must pay interest on it for the period at a rate of fifteen percent per annum."

"That is correct. We're not running a charity here Martin and you are being paid handsomely. In your case, over one hundred thousand pounds per day for the seven-week period. I think if you pull out of the agreement in that time, it's a perfectly reasonable requirement. You would end up having to pay around ten thousand pounds interest on the deposit. We feel it gives you a little financial skin in the game and provides us a bit more assurance that you will think twice before pulling out."

"Once the half million deposit is transferred, what's to stop me keeping the money and bidding you goodbye?"

"Whilst we have a very strong legal department - look what we did with Cardinal Pell - we rarely resort to lawyers. It takes too long and it's far too messy. We do have more direct and efficacious methods, but they have been rarely used and frankly are quite crude. Demonic possession, that sort of thing. The overwhelming number of clients tend to play by the rules knowing who they are dealing with."

Reflecting on the answer, Martin drains his glass whilst keeping eye contact to gauge any further reaction. He makes a mental note to google the Cardinal Pell case. Returning Martin's stare, the corner of Sebastian's eyes wrinkle, accompanied by the slightest of smiles.

"I'll get you another drink whilst you are thinking about it," says Sebastian. He goes towards the crowded bar and, as he approaches, effortlessly catches the eye of the busy barmaid. She serves him at once to the annoyance of others already stood at the bar, hustling for attention. He returns with a beer in one hand and a whiskey in the other.

"Cheers. Do you know her?" asks Martin.

"Know who?"

"The barmaid, she served you before a crowd of punters who were already waiting."

"Not really, just put it down to my animal magnetism."

"Talking of animals, are you the demon, Asmodeus?" Hoping to catch him of guard, Martin looks for a reaction, but Sebastian stays expressionless.

"Good to see you have read the contract fully. I can confirm that Asmodeus is indeed the, how shall I put it, assigned contract manager for this little venture."

"That doesn't answer my question."

"Does it make a difference who I am. If I said I am Asmodeus, does that change anything. Would you believe it if I said yes, any more than you believe I am the devil. I'll tell you one thing that is certain. I cannot be both, but I can be neither."

"You seem to be evading the question."

"Not really Martin. As I have said previously, I don't need you to believe I am the devil, nor Asmodeus, nor some inpatient from Lambeth Psychiatric Hospital. I just need you to be convinced that I can meet my side of the financial bargain. I am certain of one thing. If I told you I am Asmodeus, you wouldn't believe it anyway. At the very best, you'd be highly sceptical."

"Fair enough. But there is one thing I am certain of."

"What's that, Martin?"

"You aren't Zadkiel."

Bursting into raucous laughter, Sebastian pats Martin on the shoulder. "Bravo Martin, a bit of humour at last. That's the spirit."

"I'm ready to sign."

"Excellent. When you have, send it back and I'll get the other two to put their monikers on it. Then I'll email the fully signed copy back."

"Sounds good. When does the contract begin?"

"From the time and date stamp of the email which has the fully signed copy. Precisely seven weeks, or forty-nine days, or one thousand one hundred and seventy-six hours later, the contract will be ended. What is more, at that point in time you will be five million pounds wealthier providing, of course, you have fully complied with the terms of the contract."

"So, we are done then. It's all systems go. Can I get you another whiskey to celebrate?"

Raising his hand to decline the offer, Sebastian says, "No thankyou Martin. I've got people to meet, places to go."

"Anyone I know?"

Chuckling, Sebastian replies, "Naughty, naughty Martin. You know very well that these things remain confidential between the parties involved. Do you know something Martin, I'm beginning to warm to you. Yes, indeed. I think I'm going to like collaborating with Mister Martin Hazel. Look I can't disclose details but I've still got this vicar on the go. He's proving to be quite needy, so I'm afraid I'll have to tootle off to church but I'll message you tomorrow."

"Won't you set on fire or something if you walk into a place of God."

"Tut, tut Martin. We covered off on the horns and pointy tail stuff ages ago. We are not in Hollywood. No, I won't spontaneously combust."

"I suppose where you live, you're used to the heat anyway."

"Very good Martin, very good. Keep up the humour, it makes these things much more fun. Must dash. Will be in touch tomorrow."

17
DESTINY IS CALLING ME, OPEN UP MY EAGER EYES.

In the office almost an hour early, Martin is tapping his keyboard energetically. After his meeting with Sebastian, he went home and decided to get an early night. Sleeping the sleep of the righteous, his mind is surprisingly clear of anxiety for a man who is about to sign a deal with the devil. Or Asmodeus. Or Sebastian. Or whoever.

He has grabbed the bull, of his next project, by the horns and is already confident that meeting his next deadline will be a walk in the park. He checked his emails as his priority when he arrived, but there was no signed contract waiting in the inbox. It doesn't worry him. Surrounded by a cushion of the tranquillity of an empty office, he works on a new spreadsheet.

Herring arrives thirty minutes later, having also decided to come into the office early. Expecting an empty open plan area, he is taken aback by the vision of Martin tapping vigorously, with his eyes glued to the screen. Slightly peeved that he cannot piously lay claim to being first in the office, Herring gives Martin a cursory greeting as he passes by and secretes himself in his office. Focussed on his spreadsheet, Martin barely notices his boss's arrival.

The office gradually fills but Martin is still oblivious to those around him and by mid-morning he completes his task, presses save and leaves his desk to make his first coffee of the day. Bleary eyed, Ben follows Martin into the kitchen.

"Jeez, what were you on last night. I've been watching you and you're like a man possessed. Mister bloody Brightside."

Returning Ben's comment with a wide grin, Martin retorts. "Unlike your good self. You look like death warmed up. On the piss last night, were you?"

"Yeah mate. Was with the boys finalising our Ibiza plans. Only twelve days to go. Are you all sorted?"

Martin has not given the trip any thought, his mind totally occupied by Sebastian and his proposal. Nothing is 'sorted', but he doubts whether there is much to sort anyway. His passport is still valid for another six years and all he needs to do is pack a few clothes for the short trip. "Yeah mate, all good," replies Martin.

"Do you have any paracetamol?"

"Sorry mate, I don't."

"Bugger," exclaims Ben, who immediately regrets raising his voice which amplifies the thumping in his head.

"Try HR, they will dole them out, providing you're not addicted to prescription drugs."

Martin shakes his head as he watches Ben trudge off down to the HR Department, then returns to his desk.

Immediately after keying in his password to unlock the screen, he sees a new unread message with an attachment. There is a short message from Sebastian.

Dear Martin,

Please find attached the contract signed by all parties. The term of the contract runs for seven weeks and will end in precisely one thousand, one hundred and seventy-six hours from the date stamp of this email. It is customary that we meet with new clients at our earliest convenience to complete the induction process. With tomorrow being Saturday, I do not expect you to make the trip to meet at our usual venue. Instead, I am happy to meet you near your flat and suggest midday at the Black Cat Café in Finchley Central. Please confirm that this is suitable.

Regards
Sebastian Balfour

Realising Friday night is date night, Martin works through the logistics. They had booked a table at Gringos and the Dashing Burrito, so Maureen would be staying at his flat. Her Saturday Pilates Class is at eleven near her place, so midday at the Black Cat Café works well. He presses the 'reply to' icon and types, 'Great, see you there.'

With a look of surprise and a wry smile, Maureen watches Martin cheering and clapping. The mini-Mariachi band finishes playing after the waitress places a portion of chocolate cake, topped with a sparkling candle, in front of a slightly embarrassed young woman. With a self-conscious look around the restaurant, she blows out the candle which re-ignites the applause, led by Martin. Maureen smiles benignly at the young couple sat on the next table, then raises her eyebrow at Martin who has, unusually, embraced the contrived jolliness of the event.

"Well, somebody is in a good mood tonight. You've been a real live wire. Have you won the lottery or something?"

"Every night with you Maureen, is like winning the lottery."

"I don't know whether to giggle like a schoolgirl or vomit. You're not yourself. Something has happened. You're up to something. C'mon share the gossip.".

"No nothing," protests Martin, "I've just come to accept things and move on. Herring got the undeserved promotion above me and I need to live with it, apply myself, and make sure that next time it's me. I've been mega efficient these last few weeks, and if I keep it up senior management will have no choice but to give it to me next time."

"Good on you Martin. A very mature approach. I'm impressed."

"Cheers. I've been working hard and need a break. I intend to let my hair down in Ibiza then re-group for the final push when I return. I've decided to take control of my destiny. I'm hoping to get the nod by the time we fly off to Lanzarote." In the nick of time Martin realises that it is diplomatic to reference their planned trip as well. It did the trick, Maureen smiles and extends her arms so they can hold hands across the table.

Their conversation throughout the evening flows easily, occasionally borderline flirting like they used to in the early months of their relationship. The mini-Mariachi band plays twice more in front of self-conscious customers, both times Martin cheers and claps along with others on nearby tables. When the bill arrives, Martin swipes his credit card on the handheld device. After the waitress leaves them, Martin smiles at Maureen.

"What?" she asks.

"Nothing, I just feel invigorated. I feel like a new man."

"So do I," replies Maureen, suggestively.

Back in the flat, there are no night caps offered or asked for, they both head straight to the bedroom. Forty minutes later, after a session of uncharacteristically lustful, physical and, at times, experimental sex, they roll onto their backs, exhausted. Sleep overcomes them.

Waking from a deep slumber, Martin is barely conscious enough to register the sound of Maureen's voice calling "goodbye" in the hallway, followed by the jarring noise of the front door being slammed. Groggily, he checks his phone and the time is quarter to eleven. He dozes off until he is re-awoken by the sound of the phone's alarm. This time the screen reads eleven thirty, with the calendar notification reminding him of a twelve o'clock appointment with Sebastian.

It takes a further five minutes to steel himself to crawl into the shower and by the time he is dressed and fully groomed, it is ten minutes to twelve. The Black Café is barely five minutes' walk.

When he enters the café, Martin sees Sebastian already ensconced in the corner with a cup of coffee in front of him and a second cup placed opposite on the small table. Gesturing for his guest to take a seat, Sebastian greets Martin.

"Bang on time Martin. How was your night out?"

"Good thanks, I was with Maureen at our favourite Mexican restaurant."

"Yes, I know."

Ignoring the remark, not wanting to pursue how Sebastian could possibly know, Martin asks, "So this is an induction, apparently, where do we start?"

"In a sense we have already started. The seven weeks were triggered from the date of the email. So, you are almost at the end of day one. We feel it is only fair to outline some basic rules to ensure there is no misunderstanding and, to some extent, put your mind at rest."

"Sounds good, so what are the rules."

"Firstly, the adjudication of whether you have committed one of the deadly sins, is determined independently."

"Okay. I guess in a sense it doesn't matter to me anyway. I just need to complete the seven weeks, right?"

Sebastian smiles. "The second thing to know is that if you have committed a sin, as determined independently, you will be told."

"Okay, again I presume that for the purposes of earning the five million it does not matter. Just out of interest, who is the independent adjudicator. Is it God?" asks Martin.

Laughing dismissively, Sebastian says, "Oh! now come on Martin. If it was God that would hardly be independent, would it?"

"If not God, who?" Martin cannot quite believe the surreal conversation he is having with a rich guy who probably is totally divorced from reality, but he wants to humour him.

"You may have heard of Saint Michael, the Angel of Purgatory. Perhaps you came across him in your extensive research."

"Nope, but I know that Purgatory is the place between heaven and hell. Is that right? Is that why this Angel of Purgatory is independent."

"Sort of Martin."

"Okay Sebastian. What else do I need to know?"

"By the time you get back to your flat, the deposit will appear in your bank account. It will be what is termed a 'Scheduled Deposit' which will be activated precisely seven weeks from the date of your email."

"That's not fair, it's not what was agreed. You told me a deposit would be made up front. What's to stop you cancelling it?"

"If you doubt our honestly, call your bank and they will confirm they hold the funds and that they are legally obliged to credit your account at the agreed date."

Raising his voice slightly in frustration, Martin says, "Doubt your honesty! Forgive me if I am being disrespectful, but your lot don't have the best track record and reputation for playing with a straight bat. You bet your bloody life I'll be calling the bank."

"Of course, Martin, but you must also appreciate that our dealings with human morals and behaviour over the centuries have left us as somewhat sceptical about your propensity as a race to always do the right thing. This sort of behaviour is what has kept us in business, so to speak."

"Fair comment, but I'll be ringing the bank and if I'm unhappy with the answer, the deal's off."

"That's perfectly fine Martin. Please do so and let me know if you are dissatisfied with what you are told."

"Don't worry, I will. What else do I need to know?"

"As you can appreciate Martin, the other side have expressed concern that this annual exercise can result in significant acts of evil of which they will be partly responsible for causing. They feel that by taking part in this process they are potentially complicit in encouraging bad behaviour. Therefore, I am duty bound, by the terms of our agreement, to encourage you not to take part in anything heinous."

"Assuming I do fall off the moral perch a couple of times, who determines heinous?"

"Both parties have had enough experience in this exercise to make that judgement. And, believe me, it's a judgment. It must be a sin but it need not be a serious misdemeanour. Take your date last night and how you finished it."

"Jesus, were you in the fucking bedroom?"

"No, no Martin, but we have our ways. Putting it delicately, you were both very enthusiastic, were you not?"

"Bloody hell. Where are you going with this? Are you saying that it is classed as sinful. Lust is a sin, isn't it?"

"Well done, Martin, Lust certainly is a deadly sin. That is another rule incidentally. You must be clear and have in your mind, all the deadly sins. So, if you commit one, you are doing so knowingly. But returning to your point about your little night session, this does not count as a sin for the purposes of our project, because it was an act undertaken with a committed partner in a loving relationship by two willing parties. Now were it with another person, male or female, naming no names, then it would qualify as sinful and lustful."

"Presumably you mean Blondie. In other words, if through lust I was unfaithful this would qualify as a sin in your game."

"Precisely."

"Anything else. Any other rules?"

Furrowing his brow, Sebastian gives it some thought, whilst Martin finishes his coffee.

"Nothing I can think of Martin. There is one other thing. We need to meet this week for a question-and-answer session. Perhaps you could come to my office this Wednesday."

"Questioning and answering what exactly?"

"Just the final part of the induction process. After that we can go full steam ahead."

"But we're already in the seven weeks?" asks Martin, suspicious that there may be some delaying tactic when his money is due.

"Oh yes, don't worry about that. The clock is ticking. Still seven weeks from the date of the email."

Checking the calendar on his phone Martin agrees to the meeting, deciding to take a wellness day to save his annual leave.

18
ALL THE THINGS I COULD DO IF I HAD A LITTLE MONEY.

On Tuesday, the work hours had crept sluggishly. At the end of the day Martin packs up his desk thinking about his meeting with Sebastian, as he has done for the last three hours. He does not notice Herring passing by on his way out.

"Enjoy your day off and see you Thursday Mister Hazel."

Looking around Martin sees Herring about to walk through the door and quickly responds by shouting 'thankyou', which Herring acknowledges with a wave as he exits. Across the open plan area, Ben catches his eye and mimes drinking a beer. Martin shakes his head. He wants to get home and make sure he has a clear head for Sebastian's question and answer session. The vagueness of the response, when he asked Sebastian for more detail about what the session entailed, aroused his suspicion.

After an uneventful journey home, Martin pops his head into the fridge. Sitting alone on the middle shelf, is a meal for one. Unenthusiastically, he watches it slowly spin round in the microwave. He takes the meal into the living room, places it on the small side table next to his armchair, presses the remote and settles in to watch television.

The seven o'clock news offers little in the way of positive stories around the world. Slightly depressed, he sets his half-eaten meal aside and picks up his phone. There are no messages, not even from Maureen. Mindlessly, he flicks through the channels, unable to settle on any one program for more than a couple of minutes until a worrisome thought enters his mind, which brings a halt to the channel surfing. There is a slight problem. When Sebastian invited him to his office, he didn't tell Martin where it's located.

When he opens his phone to write Sebastian a text, he is surprised to find a message from him. which he is sure was not there when he checked his phone a few minutes earlier. He finds that there is no greeting, just simply an address.

4 Hays Mews, Mayfair.

A late alarm, purposely set, gives Martin a gentle start to the day. He has the luxury of lying in bed for a few minutes to slowly rouse himself before taking a shower and treating himself to a late cooked breakfast at the Black Cat Café.

With only one other customer in the café, Martin is served quickly and he is soon tucking into his breakfast. Once he has finished, he orders a second coffee and sits at his table to google the address that Sebastian had sent him. Having planned his tube journey, he searches for information about the address, Hays Mews. As he suspected, Wikipedia informs him that the address is a very exclusive. It originally served as a service street for stables and coach houses behind the grandiose 'town' abodes of the wealthy. More evidence, if he needed any, of Sebastian's financial credentials.

His tube journey takes him to Green Park, a station he generally passes through rather than disembarks as he is doing today. He walks up Berkeley Street and turns into Berkeley Square. Weaving his way through the Mayfair, Sebastian finds himself at the corner of Hays Mews, next to a pub called the Coach and Horses. A sign near the door lays claim to it being the oldest public house in Mayfair, dating back to the 1740's.

Number four is a three-storey sand coloured brick building with a gleaming white door. There is no sign to indicate that it is a place of business, so he tentatively rings the doorbell. A young man in a stylish mid grey suit answers the door. His accent is dripping private school.

"Good morning, you must be Mister Hazel. My name is Harry; I am Mister Balfour's personal assistant. He's expecting you."

Not waiting for Martin's confirm that he is, indeed, Mister hazel, Harry gestures for him to enter and closes the door behind them. Squeezing past Martin, Harry invites him to follow and they walk to a room at the back of the house. Harry knocks and then opens the door without waiting for a response. He gestures Martin through and closes the door behind him. Sebastian rises from behind his desk, greets Martin and invites him to take a seat opposite. The room is tastefully decorated, predominately in Alabaster white paint. Behind Sebastian is a cream Georgian limestone fireplace and to his right are French windows which lead to a small, pristine garden.

"Hope you found the place easily. It's a bit of a hidden gem away from the bustle of Piccadilly. I use this place as a pied de terre, usually to conduct any business I have in London."

"Very nice," replies Martin, not quite sure what else to say.

"Good. Let's get straight to it. Tell me, are you clear as to what the seven deadly sins are, so if you committed one you would do so knowingly?"

"Yes."

"Would you be so kind as to list them, to remove any doubt."

Bugger thinks Martin, trawling his memory.

"Er, Lust, Greed, Gluttony, Envy, Sloth," replies Martin, then hesitates to think. "Oh yes, Pride."

"Very good Martin, that's six, there's one more."

Struggling to remember the seventh one, Martin beings to panic which turns to anger and frustration. There is five million pounds at stake and he cannot even retain seven names. A flash of inspiration in his anger jogs his memory and he blurts out the missing sin, "Wrath!"

"Excellent Martin. Now let's move on. Have you discussed this venture with anybody?"

"No."

"Are you clear on the terms of the contract?"

"Yes."

"Do you wish to pull out? Like all good contracts, there is a cooling off period. It would not be valid if you were coerced. Those on the other side wouldn't allow it, being the sanctimonious lot that they are. Holier than thou, if you get my drift."

"I do," replies Martin, smiling at Sebastian's irony, he is beginning to like him. "That is, I do get your drift, but I don't want to pull out."

"Now there is no right or wrong answer to the next question, it's more of a point of interest for both parties involved. Faith and all that sort of thing. Who or what do you believe I am?"

Martin pauses and looks up to his side to process his thoughts. His eyebrows arch slightly whilst he rests his index finger on his chin. Sebastian waits patiently for an answer.

"My overriding thought is, genuinely, that I don't know what I think. I'm struggling with the idea that you are the Devil or a Demon because frankly I don't believe in Heaven and Hell and all that stuff."

"If I am neither of those things, what other options have you considered? And don't worry, I won't get offended."

"Okay then. I did wonder if you were some nu …" Martin stops himself to find a more diplomatic expression. "I did wonder if you were some sort of rich eccentric with a penchant for game playing."

"And what would be the purpose of my game playing, were I to be a rich nutter?"

Martin let's out an involuntary guffaw at Sebastian's perception. "Sorry, I didn't mean to be offensive but you did ask. To be honest I've no idea. Maybe you've so much money that you don't know what to do with it and you have an interest in human psychology and motivation. Or maybe you like just disrupting the lives of ordinary guinea pigs like me. Or even that there is another nu … eccentric in the mix and you've both had a bet."

"Interesting thoughts Martin."

"To be honest they don't make any more sense or seem any more credible than the assertion that you are the Devil. And to be fair, you've sort of hinted along those lines."

"I can see your dilemma. But thank you for sharing. I have to say that it is refreshing to work with someone more sceptical. It's very boring when we have participants who just swallow everything that we tell them without question. Usually, they're Christians and therefore the concept of the Devil is already ingrained into them. Let's face it, they do self-identify as sheep in the bible and follow the flock."

"Thanks," replies Martin.

"No worries."

"If you are the Devil, isn't the choice of Christians giving your opponents an unfair advantage. Aren't they less likely to commit a sin?"

"Not at all Martin, in some ways they're the worst or should I say from our perspective, the best. There's a lot of hypocrisy as you can imagine."

"Really?"

"Oh! yes. Your average Christian does good because they believe that is what God wants. Those that don't believe in God, do good because they fundamentally believe it is the right thing to do. The Christian faith is based on fear. The flock do good with the belief that there will be consequences if they don't. Hell, fire and brimstone. Eternal damnation, that sort of thing. Non-believers act out of pure good will, not through fear of the consequences if they don't do good. In one sense, their actions have much greater purity."

"Interesting, I can see your point," says Martin.

"Not only that, the same applies to an act of evil. Our most valued clientele doesn't believe in Heaven and Hell either. Do you think they would act the way they do if they truly believed that, after they depart here, they will spend eternity suffering. Hitler and the rest would think twice, wouldn't they. None of them are exactly brave."

"Another good point," says Martin.

"It's a particularly delicious irony that some of those that are deeply evil such as the clergy paedophiles, wear their cassocks, spruiking the will of God, when, they clearly don't believe in God or Hell. If they did, they wouldn't do it, would they?"

"Interesting," says Martin.

"Anyway Martin, I didn't call you over here to discuss religious and spiritual foibles. I don't want to cloud your thinking. Free will, and all that."

Sebastian's phone rings, He examines the screen, raises his index finger to signal to Martin that he must take the call. Seeing Martin begin to rise, he holds up his free hand, indicating that he should remain seated. The conversation is short and one sided. Sebastian's only contribution is to say "Understood," before disconnecting the call.

"That Martin, was the go-ahead. All parties are satisfied and there is no turning back."

"Excellent, is that everything then. If so, I'll make my way back home."

"All the admin is done. But I'd appreciate a couple more minutes of your time, if that's okay by you?"

"Sure."

"So, you've signed up to a life changing project. For my own interest, tell me what made you do it?"

"I'm not sure I understand?"

"What convinced you to participate in what could possibly be the delusional game of a rich madman, so to speak?"

"It's obvious, isn't it? The five million pounds."

"But aren't you concerned about committing the sins at all? As you know, we will be doing our utmost to tempt you and you are only human."

"Not really."

"So, committing a sin doesn't' worry you?"

"You said the sins are not heinous. So no, not when there are five million pounds on offer."

"So, the only driving motivation is the money?"

"Yes, I guess so."

Once again, Sebastian's phone rings and he answers it. Martin realises he is expected to wait as he did during the earlier call. This time there is a little more conversation.

"Yes absolutely," says Sebastian to the unknown caller. "I don't think you can deny that this is one up to our team."

Martin listens with interest, whilst Sebastian continues his conversation.

"He was given ample opportunity I think you'll agree. So that is agreed then?" After a pause listening to the final words of his caller, Sebastian ends the call and places his phone back on the desk. He looks up to Martin and says, "Well thank you Martin, you're free to go."

"Hang on, what was all that about? It sounded as though you were talking about me."

Grinning, Sebastian replies. "Yes, we were Martin. We were agreeing that I had scored the first point."

"Come again," says Martin.

"You've committed your first sin, three more and it's a win for the bad guys."

"What?"

"Greed, Martin. Greed. Defined as an inordinate desire to acquire more than one needs, especially with respect to material wealth."

"Who wouldn't have chosen what I did?"

"Many Martin. But more pertinently, your desire for wealth is to the exclusion of everything else. I asked you if you weren't concerned about committing sins, especially when we will do our utmost to tempt you. Your response was, and I quote, 'not when there are five million pounds on offer'. Sounds a pretty good example of greed to me."

"That's not fair."

"Well, you could have said something about using the money, or at least some portion of it, for good. Or if not that altruistic, even perhaps just to say it would be good to set up a comfortable life for yourself and Maureen. But no, you admitted that your driving motivation was simply to get the money. There wasn't even any concern about others or the impact of committing sins on those around you."

"That's not fair either."

"Isn't it? How would Maureen feel about it if you fell prey to Lust, for example? She's not as cavalier as you about committing sins, I suspect. She would, be very, very upset to find you in flagrante delicto with Blondie. Of that I'm certain. Anyway Martin, as we've discussed and as per the contract, the decision doesn't affect you nor your greedy desire for money. Whatever mitigating factors you wish to plead, they're now irrelevant. Both sides have come to an agreement that you've committed a sin. Irrespective of what you think, it is one point for me and we all need to move on. Now, if you'll be so good as to excuse me, I've a very busy day ahead of me." He winks mischievously, "Sins don't just commit themselves, y'know."

"But …"

"No 'buts' Martin. If you feel hoodwinked then, what did you expect from the Devil, or a demon or some rich, slightly mad, eccentric person?"

The door to the office opens and Harry appears in the doorway and says, "If you would be so kind Mister

Hazel, could you please follow me and I'll show you out."

Once Martin reaches the doorway Sebastian calls over without looking up from his papers, "We'll be in touch Martin."

"Can't wait,' replies Martin, petulantly.

Harry leads Martin to the front door and wishes him 'good day.' Still angry, Martin gives no response as he exits. Making his way back to Green Park tube station, he reflects on the events of the morning and calms down. He reminds himself that it's a game, and given the characters involved, it is no more than he should expect. Taking the Victoria line, he changes at Warren Street and at once catches a train on the Northern line bound for High Barnet, which takes him directly home.

That evening Maureen calls in with a Chinese takeaway on her way home from work. They make small talk in between chomping on noodles, sweet and sour pork and beef with black bean sauce. She asks him what he got up to on his wellness day. Not much, he tells her. She perceives he is not in the mood for conversation, so she regales him with the woes of her own workday. He barely listens, still slightly irked at the outcome with Sebastian. His angst is not directed at whether he was tricked, he accepts that greed is a fair call. It's the ease with which he was bested that annoys him. With barely half a week into the contract, he has succumbed to a sin. Is he that much of a pushover? Is he that predictable? Sebastian only needs three more 'sins' to win his game. That gives him over two weeks per sin to break Martin down. At this rate he will end up committing all seven. On the other hand, why does he care, if he gets the five million?

"That's the spirit," echoes Sebastian's voice in Martin's mind.

"So, what do you think? asks Maureen.

"About what?"

"For God's sake Martin, haven't you heard a word I've said. You're clearly too tired or too occupied with your own thoughts to give me any attention. I'd best get off."

"Oh! aren't you staying tonight?"

"No Martin. As I've just told you, I've got an early start and a long day tomorrow. Good night."

After delivering a cursory peck on his cheek, she leaves. Although the door is not slammed shut, it is closed with enough vigour to be heard by the neighbours across the hall.

19
LAZIN ON A SUNNY AFTERNOON.

A week has passed and there is no sign of Sebastian nor, as far as Martin could tell, any further incident testing him on the seven deadly sins. It had been a particularly boring and uneventful week. Maureen kept her distance because she had COVID. Ben had been away on a course, so Martin had been abstemious to the point where he would not feel out of place at the local temperance society. Even Blondie hadn't popped up in one of his journeys to work, to break the monotony. Nor in his dreams for that matter. Since the start of the seven-week testing period, he decided to refer to her as Blondie rather than Unrequited love, as it seems less sinful in the circumstances, especially as Maureen is ill. He didn't want to risk falling foul of more Sebastian trickery and have this claimed as infidelity and therefore one of the sins, such as Lust or Pride. He hasn't entirely gotten over the determination of Greed, following Sebastian's interrogation, but he is trying to move on.

On his trip into work, he has two conflicting emotions about the day ahead. Ben is due back and this will liven up his life a little bit, added to which, they were assigned to work together for the next two days. Ben's participation has put his imaginary ledger in credit. On the debit side they were assigned a task everyone does their best to avoid - the annual clear-out of the archive store.

The third team member is a junior called Ronald. Martin had no idea what Ronald's parents were thinking when they named him, but it seemed to suit his somewhat feeble character. Ronald is the sort of person who was bullied at school because he naturally presents as a vulnerable target. The sort of person who would be categorised, in adulthood, as nice and unthreatening. There's nothing offensive about Ronald, but when he speaks in a group situation, people unwittingly talk over him. For all intents and purposes, he is invisible. The only negative thought about Ronald that Martin can muster is that he is Herring's lapdog. Herring being Herring, embraces the situation, enjoying the unique experience of someone who genuinely respects him on a professional level.

Martin logs on. Keen to clear all his emails before heading to the archive room. Half an hour passes and just as he finishes the last of the unread emails, Ben joins him and sits on the corner of the desk.

"How are you doing, mate?"

"Good Ben, and good to have you back in the fold. It's been quiet around here."

"Wish I could share your enthusiasm mate, but coming back to the bloody archive audit isn't exactly the most exciting prospect."

"Mate, it's the luck of the draw. Once we've got through it, that's us done for a few years."

"You talk as if you're here for life."

Martin logs off and rises. "C'mon, let's go and get Mister Personality."

They had agreed to meet in the kitchen at nine thirty. Ben and Martin walk in together to find Ronald sitting at the table with a cup of coffee, waiting for them with the eager expression of a dog expecting a treat.

Ben greets him. "Hi there Ronster, how's it hanging?"

"Good thanks Ben. Hi Martin."

"Hi Ronald. C'mon let's get this show on the road. The sooner we start, the sooner we finish," says Martin with forced enthusiasm.

They walk together to the elevator and take it down to the basement. At the end of a very narrow corridor, they reach the archive room. Ronald, who was charged with getting the key from HR, unlocks the door and all three stare into the pitch black. Devoid of any natural light the darkness of the room is expunged when Ben reaches round the door jamb and flicks on a switch. Dust particles float in the yellow light and they enter the uninviting space which will be their home for the next two days.

Three years ago, a new manager, who had transferred from a regional office, inadvertently asked a question about record keeping. It was her first managers meeting and she was learning the ropes. Murmuring, head scratching and blank stares around the room, as each manager sought inspiration from colleagues, yielded no sensible answers. Certain documents had to be kept for a period of seven years and then could be destroyed. It then became apparent that the Company had never cleared out the old records in the thirty-two years it had occupied the building. In theory, two thirds of the storeroom was probably housing unneeded rubbish. Having come from a regional office, she pointed out the extortionate cost per foot of real estate office space in central London and recommended a course of action.

Since that fateful meeting, it was agreed that there would be an annual two-day clear-out of the records which would continue until everyone is satisfied that only files within the seven-year time frame remained. Although this sort of work is far outside the job descriptions of the professional staff, one bright spark on the management team suggested it would be good for morale and team building for everyone to muck in and 'get their hands dirty.' That's everyone except for management.

The morning passes quickly. Ben has a couple of stories to tell about the happenings on his residential course. Rumours of a liaison between Agnes in Marketing and Dennis from Accounts on the third day, or rather, the third night, sparked things up a bit. The course itself turned out to be far more interesting than Ben expected and he tells Martin that whilst nothing happened in his personal pursuits, he may have laid some useful groundwork with Sarah, the new PA of the Managing Director. Having seen Sarah, who is stunning, Martin is less confident about Ben's chances but holds his own counsel. Ronald does not offer much in terms of banter, gossip or jokes but at least he's very diligent making their output look respectable.

Following the initial spark and enthusiasm at the novelty of the activity, the afternoon is like wading through deep mud carrying a sack of potatoes. The task is laborious. They dig out unlabelled files, read them to find the date they were prepared, and then either replace them or put the older ones into a confidential waste bin. Sometimes the date of the file is obvious from the first page, on other occasions a far longer examination is needed. By the time the day comes to an end, Ben and Martin want to resign. In contrast, Ronald gives them a cheery 'goodbye' and a 'see you tomorrow'.

Once they step out into the street outside the offices, they take a deep breath of air. It feels fresh even though it is infected by the exhaust from the capital's traffic. Then they soak in the natural light.

"Oh! well, one more day mate, then we're done," says Martin, before they part ways.

"Not sure I can do that again," replies Ben.

"You'd better not take a sickie and leave me to do it with Ronald."

"No mate, I have a plan. See you tomorrow."

Covered in dust and boredom, Ben outlines his plan. After looking at his watch, he throws another file into the confidential waste bin and then turns to Martin.

"It's five to twelve mate. Time to start operation Bunkoff."

"And what exactly is that?" asks Martin.

"We go to the Ship and Shovell for lunch and return around four o'clock to free Ronald from his incarceration. I told him that we have an unscheduled client meeting over lunch so we would be late back."

"And he swallowed that, did he?

"Hook, line and sinker mate."

In no mood to argue, whilst quietly pleased he's being let off the hook, Martin agrees to the plan. He feels morally exonerated because it's not his idea. *A bit like the Nazis in World War Two who claimed they were just following orders*, he thinks.

"See yer Ronster," calls Ben over a pile of files. "We'll get back as soon as we can. Are you gonna be okay?"

"Yes, no problem." Ronald gives the thumb's up, eager to please.

In the Ship and Shovell, Ben gets the first round. They are sitting in Ben's favourite observation spot. There are a few office workers in, for a pub lunch.

Scanning the bar, Ben's eyes settle on a table near the jukebox. Tapping Martin on the shoulder, he points and says, "Check that out mate."

Three young women are chatting and laughing.

"They are barely old enough to be out of school. You're turning into a sad old thirty something pervert."

"What's a decade between friends?"

"A jail sentence," replies Martin.

By the time Martin brings the second round to their table he is beginning to have second thoughts about Ben's plan. Glancing at the clock behind the bar, he sees that they've been gone for forty minutes. Although he normally only takes a half hour for lunch, they are entitled to an hour.

"Mate, I'm not sure about spending the afternoon here, leaving Ronald to do all the work."

"Are you serious? Are you worried about getting the sack or something?"

"Not at all," protests Martin. "I'm not happy about dumping all that on him just because it's Ronald. You wouldn't pull this stunt with anyone else."

"Seriously mate. It's a nice day, we could go and sit in the pub garden, catch a few rays and just chill."

"Sorry mate. It's how I feel. I'm not comfortable with just lazing around whilst the office victim does all the work."

"For fuck's sake, Martin."

"Sorry mate. I'm off." Martin leaves his pint half full and leaves. Sinking his own drink, Ben catches him up halfway back to their office. All efforts to get Martin to reconsider fall on deaf ears.

"You're back early," says Ronald, happy to see he has company he was not expecting.

"Yeah mate," replies Ben, looking petulantly at Martin, who, in turn, studiously ignores him. "It turned out to be a much quicker catch up than we planned."

Time slows almost to a halt in the afternoon. Enduring repeated glances from Ben, which serve to reproach him for abandoning their plan, Martin does not feel any regret for his decision. Ronald goes about his business making the occasional cheery aside, unaware of the tension between the two friends. By the end of the day, they have filled several bins.

Back in his flat, Martin settles in front of the television with a meal for one on his lap. This evening, he has gone Italian with Tuscan Chicken. He half watches the News whilst occasionally glancing at his phone. He messages Maureen to check in, not wanting to call her in case she is sleeping. She texts back at once so he calls for a chat. Drained from the effect of the virus, she keeps the conversation relatively short by her standards. Once the call ends, he notices he has received a text message. It's from Ben. When he opens it, an emoji of a cat pops onto the screen with the word 'pussy' typed next to it.

Still sulking, thinks Martin.

He watches a program about people watching television programs and wonders to himself what the world is coming to. This thought is amplified when he switches over and discovers a dating show where a female contestant has five potential suitors who are stood naked behind a screen. Different parts of their bodies are revealed, including genitals, before the contestant selects a partner, at which point she sees their faces. None of the contestants would win a Mister Universe contest. Horrified at the whole concept of the program, Martin switches over to something more palatable.

His mobile rings. Picking it up he sees it's Sebastian and it's almost ten o'clock.

"Hello Sebastian, long time no hear."

"Hello Martin, how are you?"

"I'm fine thanks. To what do I owe the pleasure at this late hour. I was beginning to think you'd abandoned me."

"I'm actually calling to discuss your latest challenge."

"Okay, when is it?"

"It has been and gone Martin."

"I've no idea what you're talking about Sebastian. I've not done any challenge. I've not even heard from you since the last one, which incidentally you tricked me into failing."

"My dear Martin, if bearing grudges and sulking were sins, you'd have failed both of those as well. Believe me you have been tested. Tests can happen at any time without warning, otherwise your reaction may be more contrived than natural."

"I suppose you're ringing me to gloat about another victory but I have honestly no idea what you're talking about."

"It's Sloth, Martin."

"Three toed," jokes Martin.

"Sloth Martin. Defined as a disinclination to exertion or work. A mind state that gives rise to boredom, apathy and a passive or sluggish mentation. The sin finds expression in laziness, idleness and indolence."

"Not sure I understand half of what you just said. I certainly don't understand what test you gave me to accuse me of Sloth."

"Actually Martin, and unfortunately for me, you passed the test. I refer you to today's events. You were tempted, this time by a supposed friend, to avoid work and your duties. You were encouraged to leave an unfortunate colleague to carry out all the work whilst you rested in the sun with your friend, drinking alcohol."

"Are you telling me Ben is in on this?"

"Not at all Martin. We have our methods and just used your friend as an unwitting tool."

"He's a tool alright."

"Now, now Martin. I can assure you he had no idea about his role in this. We just saw an opportunity and took it. Sloth is a funny old sin to test, and this was a perfect opportunity. Yes, Sloth is quite a tricky one. The other sins are more about proactively committing immoral acts, whilst this one is a sin of avoiding responsibilities. A sin of doing nothing, so to speak."

"If you say so."

"Listen Martin. If anyone should be angry it's me. You passed the test. Instead of doing the easy thing and sitting in a pub garden, soaking in the sunshine whilst quaffing beer, your conscience made you return to work, no matter how unpalatable the prospect. You chose to toil away at the most mind numbing, laborious of tasks and not leave that poor little colleague of yours to carry the can."

"Ronald?"

"Is that his name? Nothing worse than an ineffectual do-gooder. I'm surprised you even gave him a moment's thought. I'd have been sipping whiskey with you, without a single care in the world for him. Now that friend of yours, Ben, he'd be far more entertaining but I doubt he would pass muster as an acceptable candidate. He'd get black balled by the other side, I suspect. Just as our side would black ball dear little goody two shoes Ronald."

"So where does this leave us?"

"For you it makes little difference. For me it leaves the score at one all, with five to play. Currently the other lot are high fiving and drinking to your good health."

"Do they drink?"

"No Martin, it's just an expression. They may occasionally partake in something non-alcoholic."

"Where you're concerned, I never know what to believe, what to take seriously and what to write off as a joke."

"Devilish, isn't it. Well Martin, up here it's all to play for."

"When are we due to meet up again?"

"Definitely in a few days when we go to Ibiza, or maybe before. It depends on what opportunities arise. Until then be good … or preferably, be bad."

Lost in thought, Martin continues to hold the mobile phone to his ear even when the line is disconnected. One all, with a point to the good guys. Strangely, he feels quite pleased with himself, but he cannot put his finger on why this is the case. Maybe it's simply because he did the right thing. Maybe he is one of the good guys.

Sebastian's voice enters his mind.

Or maybe Martin it's a case of schadenfreude. Maybe you're deriving pleasure at my misfortune. Or maybe it's Pride, which incidentally is a mortal sin. I predict it will be two one to the bad guys within the week. Sleep well my friend, sweet dreams.

Martin did have a dream that night. More salacious than sweet. He's in the nude, prone over a table, face down. Wiggling his wrists and ankles, he discovers he is restrained by leather straps connected to the legs of the table. Straining to look over his shoulder, he sees Blondie approaching him, dressed in red leather and carrying a large plastic instrument in the shape of a phallus. In her other hand is a tub of body lotion. With an angelic smile she encourages him to relax. Looking around desperately for a source of salvation, he sees Herring standing beside Ben. Both are grinning. Then he recognises the surroundings, it's Herring's office. Ben turns to Herring and whispers, "Serves him right." They chuckle and Blondie joins in, as she lubricates the phallus. "Open wide," she says, "and I'm not talking about your mouth."

Soaking in sweat Martin wakes to the sound of his alarm. The details of the dream remain crystal clear in his mind.

20
THREE BANQUETS A DAY, OUR FAVOURITE DIET.

It's the one day of the year where everybody in the office looks slightly smarter. The men are a little better groomed than normal and the women's make-up is a little sharper. Everyone is wearing their best clothes. Suits are a little more tailored, skirts are shorter and trousers a little tighter. Attire is still work appropriate but would not look out of place in a formal social setting. The annual office party is held on the last Friday in August. No-one knows why, it has just always been done this way as long as anybody can remember. Jenkins in the Finance Department, one of the longest serving employees with seventeen years' service, postulated the theory that it was originally held to celebrate the publication of the accounts. Everyone outside the Finance department considers this highly unlikely. Whatever the reason, people let their hair down. Over the years, legendary risqué stories were born of other things being let down. Last year, discarded underwear was discovered when the photocopier was serviced a week after the party. The engineer from Xerox had to move the copier from the wall to access the internal electrics and found the offending item resting on the power cable near the socket.

"Looking forward to the party. Nice little taster before we go big in Ibiza mate," says Ben with a snigger, after he sits on the corner of Martin's desk.

"Rumour has it that they are going to lock the photocopier room this year," replies Martin, laughing.

"I've just checked out the conference area on the top floor. It's already been set up like a bloody night club. Should be a great night. What time is it?"

Looking at the bottom right of his screen, Martin says, "Four forty."

"Let's go to the Ship and Shovell for a couple of looseners. It doesn't kick off here until six."

"Good idea."

In the pub they chat and joke about the apocryphal events of previous parties.

"Have you seen that bird in marketing, Tessa. She looks hot today, all made up and have you seen that skirt she's wearing. Wow," says Ben, whistling in appreciation.

"Mate you have no chance."

"Dunno my old fruit. Rumour has it, that with a drink or two inside her, she's a wild one. Kev, from her section, reckons she's the photocopier girl and he's going for it this year."

"Kevin is a saddo who wouldn't have a clue. He couldn't pull a muscle, let alone Tessa."

"Fair point, so that leaves the way open for me, doesn't it?"

"Seriously, you're not much better than Kev. The two of you can have the last dance together, because it sure aint' gonna be with Tessa."

"Fuck off. You're one to talk. I'm not exactly looking at Casanova here," laughs Ben.

By quarter past six they arrive back at the office and take the elevator to the top floor. The music reverberates around the conference area which has been dimly lit but with flashing lights behind the DeeJay. It's early, most people are standing with a drink looking slightly uncomfortable and typically tribal, in huddles with their department colleagues. An hour passes; people have had a couple of drinks and the tribes begin to intermingle.

Herring sidles up to Martin who is standing on his own after Ben abandons him in pursuit of Tessa.

"Enjoying the party Mister Hazel."

"Yeah, it's okay." Determined not to encourage a long conversation, Martin doesn't offer any further comment. Herring shuffles uncomfortably.

"Meant to say Martin, that was a good report and, also, excellent work on the annual clear-out. I'm told there was a record number of bins filled."

Continuing to stare ahead at the group shuffling on the dancefloor, Martin replies in a tone devoid of any enthusiasm, "Cheers. Ronald did a great job."

"Good to hear," replies Herring, now feeling very awkward and struggling to find something else to say. "Okay then Martin, catch you later."

With no more than a cursory nod from Martin, Herring scuttles away.

Two hours, three overly long banal conversations with male colleagues and four drinks later Martin is not feeling the vibe and considers the possibility of leaving. Having lost the interest of Tessa, Sarah and a woman from the corporate suite whose name Martin cannot remember, Ben returns with his tail between his legs.

"I told you," says Martin.

"At least I gave it a go, mate. Not just stood here with a drink in my hand looking miserable, talking to the accounts team."

"I'm not feeling it. I'm thinking of calling it a night."

"Yer can't do that, it's too early. Tell you what, come with me to the toilets."

"Are you coming out of the closet? I'm not up for cottaging."

"Very funny mate. Just come with me."

In the toilets Ben checks the three cubicles to ensure they are unoccupied. Smirking, he reaches into his inside pocket and pulls about a small plastic bag which contains two small brown cubes.

"What the hell have you got there?"

"Choccy cake. One piece for me and one for you."

"What's in it?"

"It's a happy cake. Chocolate with a bit of Black Lebanon baked in."

"Dope?"

"Here just take a piece. It's not too strong but at least it will loosen you up."

They both pop a piece in their mouths, chew and then swallow.

"Chocolate with an herby taste is bloody disgusting," complains Martin.

"Stop whining and let's get back to the party".

The next three hours are lost to Martin. He has various conversations with colleagues he barely knows and vaguely remembers saying something to Herring' which he suspects may have been overly sarcastic. His conversation with Tessa is also a blur and all he recalls is her constant request to repeat what he has said because he's slurring. Rejoining Ben, who is sitting alone at one of the tables put aside for non-dancers, Martin flops onto the chair next to him.

"How y'doing, maaate," slurs Ben.

"Aaamm, starving," replies Martin.

"So, aaam I. Reckon we've both got the munchies."

Aware that there is a kitchen at the end of the floor, which is used by the corporate staff, Martin says, "Maaate, let's go and check out the kitchen for some grub."

"Geeenius idea, Marto, bloody genius."

Alone in the kitchen they open the fridge. There is a variety of food in containers labelled with the names of staff members who bring their own food in to work. They grab the containers and sit at the dining table. Thirty minutes later they are giggling in front of a pile of now empty boxes.

"Yer've got something on yer top lip," says Ben.

Wiping it off, Martin licks his finger. "It's the dressing of that potato salad."

"I'd liked that curry."

"Mate, I couldn't believe you ate that cold," says Martin. "Should've zapped it in the microwave."

"Couldn't be arsed, I was starving. It was okay, even if it was cold."

"Those falafels were tasty as well. I'm still a bit peckish," says Martin, rising from his seat. He opens the fridge door and brings back a plastic tub with a pink label on it."

"What's on the label?" asks Ben.

"It says, 'please don't eat, it's special food.' It smells okay and it's the only container left," replies Martin as he opens the lid and empties the contents into his mouth. "Tastes weird, but it does the job."

"Anything else left in the fridge?" asks Ben hopefully.

Looking at the pile of empty containers on the table, Martin shakes his head. "No mate. Like I said that special food was the last one. We'd better make ourselves scarce before we land in the shit."

"Good idea," slurs Ben.

With his journey home a hazy memory, Martin climbs into bed fully clothed. He dreams vividly, finding himself in a small theatre. A group of children dressed in rags are on stage performing their school's production of 'Oliver'. All their eyes are on Martin sitting alone in the middle of the front row, whilst they sing "Food, glorious food." In front of them, with his back to the audience, is the conductor, vigorously waving his baton. When the song ends, the children run off the stage leaving the conductor alone. He turns to face Martin, grinning. It's Sebastian. He points his baton at Martin and bursts into laughter. Martin can hear a phone ringing from the back of the auditorium.

He wakes, groans and reaches for his mobile. It takes a few seconds to realise it is not his alarm tone; he was too drunk and stoned to set it, but someone is calling him. Eyes half closed, he answers.

"Yeeesss," he says groggily.

"Wakey, wakey Martin."

He instantly recognises the caller's voice. "Not a great time to ring Sebastian."

"You'll be late for work."

"I'll call in with a sickie, along with half the workforce."

"Well, well, well Martin, you've had quite a night."

"You could say that. Look, I don't want to be rude but my head feels as though it is encased in cotton wool with one of your hellish imps tapping my forehead with a fucking ice pick."

"I fully sympathise. I just wanted to call you to pass on my thanks."

"For what?"

"Your little escapade last night has put me ahead once more."

"How so?"

"Gluttony. One of the seven sins. Defined as overindulgence and over consumption to the point of excess. It's an interesting one. The reason it was condemned as a sin, back in the annals of time, was because of the obscene gorging by those who were prosperous at the expense of the peasants who starved. You may recall you emptied the fridge and ate all the food that your co-workers had paid for, prepared and stored for a time when they are genuinely hungry."

"I was stoned."

"That may very well have been the case but, unfortunately for me, the personal use of low-level recreational drugs is not listed as a sin. We are however allowed to facilitate its supply as part of a grander plan to encourage your gluttony. Nevertheless, your excuses are irrelevant. The decision is in. It is clear to the adjudicator that you shovelled copious amounts of food into your sorry body with little or no regard for the needs of others. You were so intent on fulfilling your base needs, that you even ate poor old Amanda's food."

"Sorry, Amanda who?"

"She is a recent starter in Corporate services, but more to the point she's celiac."

"Sorry, a what?"

"Celiac. She suffers from a chronic autoimmune disorder triggered by eating gluten which, if consumed, attacks and damages the small intestine. The poor thing is also allergic to shellfish and peanuts as it happens. Still why should you care, you'd only already eaten a kilo of food before you decided to empty poor Amanda's container. You even ignored her pleading."

"I never heard her; she wasn't there, was she? There were only me and Ben in the kitchen."

"Tut, tut. The pink label Martin, which read, 'please don't eat, it's special food.' But what did you care, what thought did you give to others. You just went ahead and snaffled it down like a porker, despite your already bloated stomach. An open and shut case of gluttony, for which I thank you. Two one, to the bad guys."

"I still don't think it's fair."

"My dear Martin, you've clearly forgotten that you ate so much that you vomited in the train on your way home. Luckily there were only three other passengers, all of whom got off at the next stop to change to a carriage with a less offensive odour."

"I don't believe you."

"Once you are fully awake and in the land of the living, I suggest you examine the front of your shirt."

Lifting the bed sheet, he sees the evidence crusted onto his clothes.

"Anyway, the deal is done and we move on. I'll let you rest now Martin. Fear not, I'll be in touch in due course."

Once the line disconnects, Martin hastily types out a message to Herring informing him that he is not well and will not be in the office today. A minute later he has a reply expressing a lack of surprise after what Herring describes as 'last night's performance.' A further message pops up, this time from Ben. He was not going to make it into the office today, either.

Martin closes his eyes and drifts off back into sleep. This time it is uninterrupted and dream free.

The following day, Martin is back at his desk, head down, working hard and keeping a low profile. When he logged on, Herring had appeared. Between the small talk and enquiries as to how Martin was feeling, Herring had probed, in what he thought was a subtle and clever manner, to ascertain if Martin has any involvement in what the staff were calling 'KitchenGate'. There was no evidence to connect Martin, nor Ben for that matter, to the scene of the crime, but they were both clearly on the list of suspects. Martin expertly balanced a crafted expression of cluelessness and innocence. When Herring revealed what had happened, Martin looked surprised and showed concern for the poor victims. He was not sure, but on balance felt he had done enough to throw Herring off the scent.

Herring finally left him alone once Ben came across to Martin's desk and announced that he also wasn't feeling one hundred percent. Martin had a minor heart attack when Ben said that it must have been something they'd eaten. Seeing Herring's expression, Ben added that they had both grabbed a kebab before the party. He also confirmed that they both left relatively early. As Herring marched off, Martin silently prayed that no one saw them enter or leave the kitchen. There was no reason for any staff to go into that room, especially those who were not in Corporate Services.

At Marios Sandwich Bar, Martin and Ben de-briefed.

"They're all talking about 'KitchenGate," says Ben, through a mouthful of a ham and cheese croissant. Bits of the flaky pastry fall onto his lap.

"Yep. I got the third degree from Herring, but I held my ground. Thanks for coming over."

"Same, I got the third degree earlier from HR," replies Ben. "They've been all over it and I was asked if I'd seen anything. I told them I left quite early, long before the party finished."

"At least our stories are consistent."

Laughing, Ben says, "Luckily, they don't have CCTV on the floors. We'd have been buggered."

"How did you pull up today?" asks Martin.

"Surprisingly good. Passed that Tessa on the corridor, she snubbed me. I remember talking to her but no idea what I said."

Martin sniggers. "All I remember is that you were talking to her and she didn't exactly look impressed. It didn't take her long to rush off. I think I also chatted to her, but can't remember a thing I said."

"Plenty more fish Marto. I've moved on anyway. I quite fancy that new one upstairs in Corporate Services."

"You mean Amanda."

"You dirty dog Marto. Were you sniffing around her as well last night?"

"No, someone mentioned there was a new recruit in Corporate Services," lies Martin, recalling Sebastian revealing she's celiac.

"Well keep your hands off, the Benster is riding the love train into town and the first stop is Amanda's boudoir."

"I think in your case we're talking Thomas the Tank engine. If she has any taste at all, you've no chance."

21
DON'T LOOK BACK IN ANGER ... AT LEAST NOT TODAY.

After a few uneventful days at work, the KitchenGate drama has quietened down. With only forty-eight hours before he goes on annual leave, Martin is beginning to get that holiday feeling. Although initially dubious about the whole venture, the feeling of impending freedom from work and the drudgery of everyday life, has lightened his mood. His outlook has transformed from slightly negative to quite positive. If pushed, he would go as far to admit he is looking forward to the break.

The only potential roadblock to negotiate, before he leaves in good spirits, is the six-monthly team meeting with the Head of department, Basil Farmer. The previous meeting was the first held since Herring's promotion. That experience left Martin feeling that his testicles had retracted into his body, coupled with a powerful desire to punch Herring in the face.

The whole team attend along with Herring and his manager, Myles Dodson. Basil Farmer chairs the meeting. Nobody outside management understands the purpose of the session, but Martin gleaned, during his acting up period, that the intended goal is to bolster morale. The managerial echelons operate under the illusion that the troops will get a kick out of sharing a room with the higher orders and having an opportunity to interact with the great and the good. Martin is far more grounded and fully aware that team's morale gauge barely rises above 'apathetic.' Regarding their interest in the machinations of senior management, the needle might peak at the 'indifference' level on a good day.

For Herring and Dodson, it is an entirely different matter. Many believe Herring's meteoric rise to Assistant manager is largely attributable to zealous, dedicated toadying with a liberal helping of fawning, kow-towing, buttering up and currying favour. Herring and Dodson are birds of a feather and Dodson soaked up all the plaudits, acclaim and accolades that Herring could lavish upon him in the months prior to his surprise promotion. Generally, this behaviour is out of sight, therefore out of mind, of the team. Every six months it comes fore in an excruciating side show of virtue signalling, self-congratulation and mutual back patting. What makes Martin's testicles retract most, are the insincere attempts at self-deprecation. Dodson is the master and Herring comes a close second.

"Welcome gentlemen … and ladies," says Farmer, correcting himself in time. "Most of you were at the last meeting and I don't think we have any new faces."

"Just Ronald, over there," says Herring pointing to the far corner of the table. Ronald gives a self-conscious wave.

"Yes indeed, welcome to Ronald for the first time. Most of you will recall that I like to keep this meeting open and informal. A chance to air any thoughts on how we are performing or ideas on how we might do things better. All views are respected in this meeting, so please don't feel intimidated."

"We'll do our best to make sure they don't, won't we," says Dodson who is sitting next to Herring and pats him on the shoulder.

Herring gives a snort of amusement and nods enthusiastically saying, "We sure will Mister Dodson."

Dodson returns the snort after hearing himself addressed as Mister. They clearly share the faux formality joke.

"Yes, well. Good," says Farmer, not quite sure how to respond. He finds their propensity to ingratiate themselves annoying. "I'm sure everyone around the table is more than capable for speaking up and contributing."

Over the next hour the meeting is dominated by Dodson and Herring jockeying for position, holding the floor for prolonged periods and placing themselves in the best light, whatever the topic being discussed. Martin looks around the room and can see the majority are dis-engaged, bored and irritated. To his credit, Farmer attempts on occasion to draw in junior staff and invite them to comment but after the utterance of a sentence or two, Herring, Dodson or both, talk over them. Examining the paper provided by Dodson,

Farmer congratulates the whole team for their year-to-date performance which prompts half-hearted nods of acknowledgement around the table. With no one speaking up, Herring says, "Yes Mister Farmer, we like to run a tight ship here."

Martin visualises standing astride a prone Herring repeatedly stabbing him in the chest with a spear.

There is an audible sigh of relief around the table when Farmer eventually decides that the meeting has reached a natural conclusion. He thanks the team who quickly rise to leave before there is any change of mind. To consolidate his own authority, Dodson also calls out and thanks the team as they exit. It dies, unheard, swamped by the sound of relieved chatter amongst the departing team. Only Herring hears his boss, and says, "Cheers," and turns to Farmer who is gathering up his papers. "I'd like to thank you for your valuable time, Mister Farmer, it's great to have a senior manager who engages with the team." Farmer nods in acknowledgement as he passes.

Although the team disperse and return to their desks, Herring and Dodson walk side by side conferring. Both head straight to the kitchen to de-brief. Martin fancies a coffee but cannot face the prospect of joining them in the kitchen and makes a beeline back to his desk.

Seething, Martin taps on his keyboard. He enters data into his spreadsheet, whilst in his mind he replays the meeting and the constant game playing of Herring and Dodson. For the next few minutes, he sees red.

Oblivious of his surroundings, he is consumed by his anger.

Pulling up a spare chair, Ben joins him.

"Hey, mate, you okay. You've gone puce. Are you struggling with that spreadsheet?"

"No mate, it's fucking Herring and his sugar daddy. They are a couple of absolute cunts. They've spent the last hour taking credit for our work when they are both just above fucking useless."

"I know mate," says Ben.

"How do you know?"

"Just now. I went to the kitchen to make a coffee and the two of them were having a big conflab in the corner. They couldn't have crawled further up each other's arse if they tried. They're back patting and congratulating themselves because apparently Basil Farmer's impressed with the team's performance. The way they're talking, it's all down to them. Herring's telling Dodson that its hard work trying to keep the team focussed and in order. That it's a struggle to get you all to meet deadlines and you all require constant direction."

"Whaaat,"

"Yeah Marto, all that crap. Dodson is lapping it up, congratulating Herring. I almost wanted to puke, so I left the kitchen, coffee unmade."

"Wankers. I tell you what, I've had a gutful. I was close to walking out of the meeting. I've no idea what the rest of the team think, but they must be pissed off with that debacle." Martin kicks the leg of his desk in frustration.

Ben sees Martin's hands tighten up into fists. "You can't be surprised. It's half yearly report time. All the managers submit a summary of their team's performance. It's a time to bullshit and set themselves up for the end of year appraisals."

"Mate, your managers aren't like that," says Martin.

"True. I've got to admit I'd be tempted to resign if I had to deal with Herring and Dodson."

"I'd love to fuck them over."

With a vindictive smile, Ben says, "I know how you can. Hang back after everyone has gone and I'll show you how."

"Tell me now."

Tapping his nose as he walks away Ben whispers, "The walls have ears. Loose lips sink ships. Just hang on for half an hour."

Once the office has emptied, Ben calls Martin over. Pulling up the chair from the adjoining desk, Martin sits next to Ben who tells him to wait. Martin watches in silence as Ben taps away on his keyboard. Once he has finished, he gestures for Martin to look at the screen. A list of unfamiliar folders and sub-folders have been accessed.

"These look like Management folders. Aren't they restricted access?"

"Normally yes," replies Ben, grinning roguishly.

"So how come you're allowed access?"

"Admin error mate. You know the exercise that the IT Department did a couple of months ago. A sort of housekeeping project to tidy up all the rubbish that people keep because they are too scared to delete stuff."

"Yes, we had to review our own files and those of our teams."

"Bingo. If you remember they gave us temporary Systems Admin access so we could clear out stuff from other people's files."

Realising what has happened, Martin smiles. "Don't tell me they forgot to remove your Systems Admin status."

"Correcto mundo. What you are looking at here are all the confidential folders from Assistant manager to Head of Department which, in your case, is the trifecta of Herring, Dodson and Farmer."

"Wow."

"And your Uncle Ben has been doing a little unofficial research and I can tell you that the half yearly report has been submitted and there is no way those excellent results would have been achieved without the driving force of Herring and Dodson. Reading it, you are all clearly a bunch of barely competent muppets who had to be dragged across the line by the scruff of your necks. Have a read."

After clicking on the files, Ben moves aside to allow Martin to move closer so he can read the report comfortably. If he thought he was angry before he read the report, it increases by a notch after every page. Once he reads the conclusion and recommendations, Martin is exasperated. The main recommendations are about giving all the staff basic technical training to reduce their dependency on their poor overworked managers.

"For fucks sake. They even have the cheek to say that the managers need to be given space to manage and strategise. They claim that they're constantly drawn into basic tasks that should be easily completed by the team. Farmer must think we are an absolute bunch of idiots."

"Not yet," says Ben, "Look at the date and time stamp. They've only been sent this morning and I know for a fact that Farmer's copy is unread."

"What. How can you?"

"I'm a System Administrator mate. I can access their emails. Dodson got the report from Herring yesterday, reviewed it, signed it off. He only sent an email to Farmer this morning, to tell him that he had uploaded the report into Farmers folder for review. Farmer replied saying he would get around to it in the next couple of days."

"Oh!"

"Yes Oh! indeed Martin. I don't like to put ideas into your head, but there is scope here for a little retribution."

"Retribution?"

"Yes mate, or in layman's terms, scope for Herring and Dodson to take it up the proverbial."

"Lovely. You have such a subtle way with words. But what do you have in mind?"

"Delete the report from all their folders, so there is no copy. Maybe, whilst you are at it, delete a couple of other interesting files."

"They can probably get IT to recover them."

"Yes Marto, but it will cause hassle and angst and will take some time. And it will not exactly show Herring and Dodson in a good light. The reports would be late and Dodson did tell Farmer that he would drop the files into the folder by the deadline which, if we delete them, clearly didn't happen. Before the deletion you could do a couple of edits. Maybe an added comment or two from Dodson voicing concerns over Herring's competence."

"Jeez, you're an evil bastard."

"Mate, I can see that you're fuming. I've never seen you so angry. This is your perfect opportunity for revenge. You may not get another chance. At some point IT are going to realise that they forgot to remove my System Administrator access and correct their oversight. When they do, I'll just play dumb and say I didn't realise."

"Dodson will probably see the edits before it gets to Farmer."

"Possibly, but more likely there will be pure relief at recovering the reports and not having to re-write them. I think he'd just tell IT to get the files re-instated into the appropriate folders."

The argument and counter arguments flow back and forth like a moral tennis match. Ben firing aggressive top spin shots to act, Martin returning with defensive strokes of reasons why he shouldn't. Eventually Martin's anger dissipates and he makes a decision.

"No mate. Look, thanks for what you've done but I can't. I'd be no better than them if I did this sort of shit."

"Mate, you're a mug. But fair enough, it's your call."

Back in his flat Martin eats his dinner for one, cod in butter sauce, and watches the News. He barely takes in the report of a mining disaster somewhere in South America, with the events of the day tumbling around his mind. Should he or shouldn't he have. There was still time if he called Ben and went in early tomorrow. His thoughts are interrupted by the ringtone of his mobile.

"Well, well, well, Martin. If you want my opinion, you should have."

"Evening Sebastian, should have what?"

"I think you know Martin, and frankly your failure to act is a little disappointing. I'd have thought that you have a little more backbone than you appear to be showing."

"Can't say I'm sorry to disappoint."

"I'm sure you aren't. I'm afraid this makes it two all with everything to play for."

"What was it this time, Envy?"

"No. It was Wrath."

"Wrath?"

"Yes Wrath. You were angry, for you, extremely angry. Anger becomes a sin when it is unduly strong and when it creates the desire to impart excessive punishment in relation to the act against you. Had you followed your friend's advice I have to admit it would still have been a line ball as to whether this qualified. The adjudicator could've gone either way. Your anger needed to be unduly excessive and long lasting to qualify as Wrath. In your case the point is moot, because you chose not to act at all. You've wimped out and went home with your tail between your legs. That's one of the most annoying things about the other side. They give rewards to the likes of you for inaction and a lack of intestinal fortitude."

"Careful Sebby, you're beginning to sound a tad bitter," says Martin, deciding he's heard enough and wants to push back.

"Touche, Martin. Now that's the sort of attitude I'm looking for."

"So, Sebastian. Two all then."

"Yes. You've fallen to Greed and Gluttony. Excellent sins I must say. But unfortunately, not to Wrath and Sloth."

"Three to go then, Sebastian."

"Three indeed, Martin."

"I'd wish you luck, but for some reason I don't feel inclined to. I'll wait to hear from you."

"You won't have to wait long Martin. Remember we're holidaying together in the sunny Balearics. Make sure you pack your swimwear and bring that attitude with you. It makes my job much easier. Pride before the fall, and all that sort of thing."

In contrast to earlier exchanges, his conversation with Sebastian leaves him with a warm feeling. It also helps him resolve his should I, shouldn't I, dilemma.

He did the right thing and didn't fall foul to his anger. Better still, much better still, he is sure that he, ever so slightly, got underneath Sebastian's skin. It feels very, very satisfying. Bring on Ibiza, he's ready to party.

22
PACK YOUR BAGS AND LEAVE TONIGHT.

Sitting on the train with his small case between his legs, Martin takes the Piccadilly line westbound to Heathrow and has three stops to go until he reaches his destination. To get him into the mood, he has his earbuds in place, listening to a playlist of holidays songs. John Denver fades out having left on a jet plane and is replaced by one of Martin's favourites, Wham, Club Tropicana.

As the last chorus fades out, the train pulls into Heathrow and he follows the crowd into the terminal. Making his way to the agreed rendezvous, the Crown Rivers bar, Martin sees Ben sitting near the entrance and waves. Ben gives the thumbs up, points to a pint of lager on the table, and gestures for him to take a seat.

"There you are mate, first drink of the holiday," says Ben.

"Silver service indeed," replies Martin.

"Only about an hour until Boarding, so we can have a couple to lubricate the tonsils."

"Where are the others?"

"They've got an earlier flight, like I told you. They should be landing shortly," replies Ben, looking at his watch.

"Yeah, I forgot. Any news from your mate?"

"Sebastian? Yeah, he sent me a text yesterday. We'll meet him by the pool bar at his hotel tomorrow lunchtime. It's next to our apartment block."

"Yep, I remember."

Fifty minutes and two drinks later, the departures board shows that their flight is now ready. The plane takes off on time and the flight is smooth, landing five minutes early. They quickly make their way through passport control and out into the heat of the night. Outside it is evening and the night sky is black. The airport sign, Ibiza Eivissa, is lit up brightly, welcoming new arrivals. They take a taxi and arrive at their apartment block twenty minutes later. After they have finished checking in, the receptionist hands them the keys and explains that the other two guests have left them a note. She hands over an envelope which has the apartment logo in the corner. Ben takes it and they take the lift to the eighth floor and make their way to apartment 803.

The apartment is clean, neutrally decorated and has a living room, kitchenette and balcony. They find the two unoccupied bedrooms and dump their cases. Martin freshens up with a quick wash. When he enters the living room, he sees Ben on the balcony and joins him. Ben hands him a bottle of beer.

"What does the note say?" asks Martin.

"That they've left these beers in the fridge," he says holding up his bottle. "They're down in the bar, so after we've downed these, we'll go and join them, if you're up for it?"

"Sounds good," says Martin.

Martin's cool beer flows down easily as he takes in the vista from the balcony. Bright lights flicker everywhere, and music floats up to them from the town below. Thumping bass starts to reverberate through the air from a nearby club. They drain their bottles, leave them on the kitchen table and make their way down to the bar.

As they enter, Ben points to a table and says, "That's Jacko and Dave over there."

"Waaaayyyy, Jacko, Waaay Dave," shouts Ben as he approaches their table. They both turn and give the same greeting back. Ben introduces Martin.

"Right boys this is Martin. This, Martin, is Jacko." Martin gives the blond-haired man a handshake before Ben says, "and this sad old ginger, is Dave." More handshakes. Dave has longer hair tied back into a ponytail.

"Grab a seat and I'll get you a couple of beers," says Dave with a welcoming smile, before going to the bar.

"Welcome Martin," says Jacko. "So, you have the misfortune to work with this reprobate." He pats Ben on the shoulder and chuckles.

"Yes," replies Martin. "Have you all known each other for long?"

"Since school," says Ben, before Jacko can answer.

"Here's the beers, I'm a poet and I don't know it," says Dave, putting four bottles down on the table."

"So, what's the story here?" asks Ben.

Jacko shrugs. "Don't know mate, we've only been here a couple of hours ourselves. The bloody plane was delayed. I reckon we down these and have a trot through the town to check out the lay of the land."

"Good idea," agrees Ben. "Let's not go silly the first night."

"Yeah, just a few beers to get us warmed up," agrees Dave.

Waking with the headache from hell, Martin checks his mobile and sees the time is almost ten o'clock in the morning. He staggers into the living room but finds the apartment abandoned. Checking his phone, he sees a Whatsapp message from Ben, sent an hour ago. They have gone to a local café, exotically named Sid's Full English, to grab some breakfast. The mere thought of what Sid's would dish up makes Martin nauseous, so he opts for a shower. Grateful for his foresight when he packed, he swallows two paracetamol from the box in his toiletry bag and gets a bottle of water from the fridge. Sitting on the balcony soaking in the sunshine and drinking as much water as his stomach can accommodate, he feels vaguely human when he hears the other three enter the flat, laughing and joking.

"Marto," shouts Ben, slightly too loudly for Martin's comfort. "We've just had a superb full English from across the road. Eggs, bacon, mushrooms, black pudding, fried bread, the works. Shame you missed it but you were in the land of nod."

The list of food items makes Martin feel slightly queasy and Ben's loud voice causes his now dull throb of a headache to thump a little harder. "Sounds great, but not that hungry this morning," replies Martin.

"Not surprised mate, you were giving it large last night at the club."

"What club?"

"Pacha mate. That bird you were talking too was well up for it, but you disappeared off to the toilets for ages and she gave up waiting and buggered off. What were you doing mate?"

"I can't remember."

"Well to be fair you were totally wankered. You're not yet match fit. It's been a while since you've had a good session with the boys."

Jacko and Dave laugh and pat Martin on the back. Jacko says, "Right come on, let's get our shorts on and go poolside. The bar opens at eleven and I need a hair of the dog to get me going."

Dave nods in agreement.

"Yep, come on Marto, chop, chop," says Ben.

"You lot go ahead; I'll be down soon."

Martin wakes up with a start. He reaches for his phone and is surprised to see the time is eleven thirty. Intending to catch a quick nap to stave off the remnants of his hangover, he finds he has passed out for over an hour. Sinking two more glasses of water, he feels better and makes his way down to the pool where the group of three has grown to four. Their new companion is wearing Ray-Bans, a light blue Hugo Boss Polo shirt and white Louis Vitton linen shorts. By contrast, the other three look positively scruffy. They are all resting on a lounger with a cocktail drink in hand. Tapping the spare lounger next to him, the new companion invites Martin to join him.

"Well, here you are at last Martin," says Sebastian. "Big night last night, by all accounts."

Jacko and Dave laugh out loud. Ben holds up his glass which has a ruddy orange liquid at the bottom, which fades into a yellowy orange towards the top. A slice of pineapple is wedged onto the rim of the glass. "Order one of these mate, we're all having them. They're called Bahama mamas. They've got fruit in them so they're good for you." He gestures over to the barman at the poolside bar and holds up four fingers and his thumb. The barman nods in response. Martin gingerly sits on the lounger.

"So how are you feeling Martin? You look a trifle delicate." asks Sebastian.

"Fine," replies Martin, curtly.

"I hope you were a good boy last night."

"As far as I am aware, my behaviour was exemplary," replies Martin. He adds, "Do you know any different?"

"Not at all. We didn't set any test for you last night. The other side declared it unfair, given the long day you'd just had. All that travel, your fatigue and the drink had clearly gone straight to your head."

"Good on them."

"Good is what they do," smirks Sebastian.

"Are you planning to test me over here?"

"No necessarily. I think we'll just see how things pan out."

The barman places two drinks on the table next to them. Sebastian thanks and tips him.

Ben calls over.

"Hey Marto, Sebby thinks we should try a new club tonight. It's a bit more up market and he knows the owner. Reckons he can get us a table. Whaddya think?"

"I'm easy," replies Martin. "What's it called?"

"Chinois Ibiza," says Sebastian. "It's new and decorated in the style of 1920's Shanghai. There's a show on every night. You'll love it. My friend has kindly given me a VIP table for the evening."

"Well, it would be rude to refuse then," says Martin, shooting a suspicious glance at Sebastian who responds with a smile.

Addressing the group, Sebastian says. "Only one condition. You'll all need to be dressed a little smarter than your current attire. They have what they term, a classy casual dress code. Sportswear and open shoes are not allowed and you need to wear long trousers. Chinos or something similar will suffice."

"No problemo, Sebster," says Jacko.

"Ditto," says Dave.

They spend the rest of the day at the pool. The others sip on a steady supply of cocktails whilst Martin chooses soft drinks. After a relaxed rest on the lounger, with occasional dips in the pool, he feels like a new man by the time they all pack up to get ready for the night's entertainment.

By midnight Martin has a gentle buzz, having carefully managed his alcohol intake, and feels like a minor TV celebrity sitting at the VIP table. He has been more reserved than the others who, fuelled by alcohol and he suspects other recreational drugs, have been to and from the dancefloor which is a pumping mass off sweaty bodies. Occasionally, he catches women looking up to their table, presumably trying to work out the identity of the 'celebrities.' If he smiled when they caught his eye, the women would often look at each other, giggle and wave back at him.

The unexpected adoration boosts his ego and confidence. In the toilets, Ben gestures for him to go into a cubicle. He follows and watches Ben put out four lines of cocaine on top of the toilet cistern. Following Ben's lead he sniffs the powder, one line in each nostril and suddenly feels a buzz. Immediately he's alert and has a renewed burst of energy. Back at the table Sebastian is talking to the two women who had previously been smiling at Martin. Ben joins Jacko and Dave on the dancefloor whilst Martin sits back at the table.

"Hi Martin. Let me introduce you to these two lovely ladies. This is Candice and Cherry."

Wearing clothes that leave most of their bodies uncovered, the two women smile and offer their hands in greeting. Various thoughts enter Martin's mind, none of which he could share with Maureen. Bolstered by cocaine and alcohol, Martin oozes with social confidence and charm which grows and grows as the minutes pass. He leads the conversation and they hang on his every word. The more they laugh at his jokes, the greater his confidence and ego is boosted. Sebastian sits in the background, offers little in the way of conversation himself, giving Martin the limelight and undivided attention of the women.

"Don't mind me asking," says Candice, "but are you famous?"

"Not in the sense of being an entertainer or sportsman, but I am quite well known in my field," says Martin, oblivious of the raised eyebrow of Sebastian.

"Oh! what's your field?" asks Cherry.

"I don't really like to talk much about it, but let's say I'm much sought after."

"My, you sound really important and clever," purrs Candice.

"Some think so," replies Martin, giving them a rakish wink. Once more Sebastian's eyebrow raising goes unnoticed.

"I bet it's something like fashion, films or maybe you're a music producer."

"Quite warm," replies Martin, taking a sip of his Margarita.

"Does it involve travelling all around the world?" asks Cherry.

"A little bit," says Martin, then adds, "to be honest quite a bit. I'm in quite high demand."

And so, the conversation flows and progresses. Molehills develop into mountains. By the time the club closes at five in the morning, Candice and Cherry are both firmly of the view that Martin is a billionaire, jet-setting, troubleshooter of some undisclosed enterprise. Imagining the possibilities, Candice hints at going back to Martin's place. Despite his intoxication, Martin knows that his cover would be blown as soon as they set eyes on his small, shared apartment. It does not take a genius to recognise that it is far nearer the budget category of holiday accommodation than a luxury retreat for the discerning billionaire.

Once they realise that they are flogging a dead horse and Martin has no intention of inviting them to his penthouse for a nightcap, they leave disappointed.

"Quite a performance Martin," says Sebastian as they leave. "We'll have a little chat about it tomorrow."

23
YOUNG MAN PUT YOUR PRIDE ON THE SHELF.

Sitting poolside, the worse for wear, Martin is dozing. Ben, Jack and Dave have gone exploring the town, leaving him in a much-welcomed state of solitary peace. Sensing a presence, he opens his eyes to find Sebastian on the lounger next to him. The barman delivers two large multi-coloured drinks and sets them on a small table between the loungers. Condensation from the cold drinks runs down the side of the glass.

"Thought you could use a pick me up, Martin. Don't worry, they are non-alcoholic. Mocktails, they call them Hangover Busters."

"Cheers. I thought you'd be out with the others."

"No thank you. Frankly I find their conversation, how can I put it, one dimensional. Besides which, we have a minor matter to discuss."

Martin sits up and takes a drink from the mocktail. It is both refreshing and delicious.

"Mmm, nice. Thanks for the drink. So, what do we have to discuss?"

"The usual topic."

"Well, if you are here to tell me I have committed the sin of Lust, you're wrong. I didn't lay hands of Candice or Cherry. In fact, they left the club before we did. Unless of course you are here to tell me that I passed the test and you are now three two down."

"Actually, no Martin. We weren't testing lust this time. This time it was pride."

"Really, Pride. To be honest I never fully understood that one."

"Yes Pride, often referred to as hubris by the ancient Greeks. They were a clever old civilisation but with a rather bizarre perspective on Gods. Zeus, Poseidon and the like."

"So, what exactly is it?" asks Martin.

"Pride is regarded by the other side as an anti-God state, where the nature of the ego and self are directly opposed to God's principles."

"Yep Sebastian, still not with you."

"It's an excessive love of oneself and a distorted sense of self-importance which, frankly, you demonstrated brilliantly last night. By the time you'd finished with them, those poor young women were left with the firm impression that you are some fabulously wealthy, highly intelligent, globetrotting superhero."

Wincing internally, Martin replays the evening in his mind and recalls parts of his conversation. He struggles to manufacture any sort of defensible objection, so stays silent.

"So, you see Martin, the adjudication is in, and it is another point for the bads guys. It is three two but three to me, not the other lot. I did try to get two points for this one but rules are rules."

"I'm not sure I follow you."

"Pride is considered, by those upstairs, to be the root of all sins because it displaces God from the centre of one's life. All gobbledy gook to me, but if that's their stance on the matter, I suggested that pride should be a double pointer being the root of all evil. Of course, on the occasions that I lose this one, I keep quiet."

"I see. Well, I suppose that it's fair enough. I did go on a bit about stuff. I suppose I can't argue the case that I was drunk and high as a kite."

"Not this time Martin. Agency and free-will, I'm sure you remember. You had a choice. It's a shame you didn't take those lovely ladies back to yours. I could have got that double pointer I was asking for by adding lust to the game."

"Mate, if they had come back with me, I think they'd have cottoned on to the fact that all the pride stuff I was spouting was a load of bollocks."

"A good point Martin. And I shouldn't be greedy. After all, greed is a deadly sin as well. As you know."

"I still think you tricked me on that one."

"Now, don't be a bad loser."

"You're only one ahead at the moment," chuckles Martin.

"Yes, all to play for and still two and a half weeks to go. Plenty of time, my friend. And there is that famous quotation."

"What's that."

"Pride comes before the fall. Or to quote the Bible more accurately, pride goes before destruction, and a haughty spirit before a fall. And on that note, I'll shoot off."

"Are you out with us tonight?" Against his better judgement Martin is beginning to warm to Sebastian.

"No Martin, when I say shoot off, I mean off the island. My work here is done and I tend to have a full agenda, as you can no doubt imagine."

"What will the others say. They're under the impression you're here for a couple of days until we all leave."

"As nice as it is to be wanted, duty calls. Just tell them I had a fun time and wish them happy holidays."

"What do you mean he's gone?" asked Ben. It is early evening and they are only one beer in.

"Off the island Ben. He muttered something about being called away on business. Anyway, what did you all get up to today?"

"Had a few drinks, a bit of lunch and a kip. Nothing too heavy with the night ahead. By the way, we bumped into those two birds you were talking to last night. I haven't a clue what you've told them, but they seem to think you are a cross between James Bond and Richard fucking Branson."

"Just gave them a bit of chat," replies Martin, enjoying the kudos. That pride feeling was coming back again.

"All I can say is that it was close, but we didn't give the game away. Unless they read the look of shock and surprise on my face," laughs Ben.

"Some of us have it, some don't," says Martin. Immediately Sebastian's voice echoes in his mind. *Beware of that pride Martin. It comes before the fall.*

That evening they ended up back in Pacha, deciding that, without Sebastian's generosity, Chinois Ibiza is a little too pricey for their pockets. To Martin's relief there is no sign of Candice or Cherry. It is likely, he thinks, that they are in Chinois busily hunting new prey, having drawn a blank the previous night. The alcohol and drug fuelled session in Pacha leaks into the following day which blends into the final evening. With a degree of relief, Martin wakes realising it is the morning of their departure. He is looking forward to getting home, and more importantly, a good night's sleep.

"Tell me all about it then, did you enjoy your holiday?" asks Maureen, sipping a cup of instant coffee. She came round to Ben's flat with an Indian takeaway.

"It was good, just a restful few days, lazing around the pool. A few drinks, good food and a bit of banter with the boys. Got plenty of sleep."

"You don't look as though you got much rest, your eyes are hanging out of your head," replies Maureen munching on a bhaji.

"Probably just all the travel back. Ibiza is a fair distance away. Maybe I've got a bit of jet lag".

Eyeing him sceptically, she says, "You can't get jet lag from a European holiday. There's hardly any time difference. Well, if you found that tiring, I'd better not book us a holiday to America next year. The flight's twice as long and it's a different time zone."

"No, I'd be up for going to America."

"Good, maybe next year then."

They finish their meal in silence. Martin takes the containers and puts them in the bin, whilst Maureen sits on the sofa, enjoying her glass of wine. When he has finished tidying up, he joins her on the sofa with a bottle of beer in his hand. She makes small talk. He yawns, then glances across guiltily. Her expression changes, but it is not one of irritation. She gives him her familiar, come to bed look. "I hope you are not too tired," she purrs. "I've bought my overnight bag."

"Have you now," says Martin, grinning.

"Let's have an early night then," she whispers, suggestively.

Manufacturing an expression of enthusiasm, when his whole body is telling him otherwise, Martin smiles. Like it or not, he is going to have to perform and that night he does. When she rolls over with a satisfied sigh, she tells him she is immensely proud of him. It was quite a performance considering his apparent travel exhaustion. *Yeah, I'm quite proud of myself*, thinks Martin.

Before he drifts into sleep, Martin hears Sebastian's voice echo through his mind. *Beware of that pride Martin. It comes before the fall.*

24
I REMEMBER YOU WERE INCREDIBLE.

"**M**orning Mister Hazel." Engrossed in his spreadsheet, Martin does not hear anyone approach his desk. He looks up to see Herring accompanied by a tall man with dark wavy hair and piercing blue eyes.

"Let me introduce you to our latest recruit, Andy Phillips. He's joined us at your grade, but let me warn you, he's come with a reputation directly from our competitors, whose name we never utter." Herring sniggers at his own joke. "Andy trailblazed at the firm whose name we never utter, and we head hunted him. He's assigned to the team on the second floor, but I'm already fearful of him taking my job. Ha, ha."

Andy smiles and holds out his hand, which Martin shakes. "Hi Martin, pleased to meet you, and don't believe the publicity. I'm looking forward to working with you and have heard good things about the work you do. I understand our teams are going to join forces on the Mayfield project next month."

"Yes Andy. Nice to meet you too. If you need anything whilst you are settling in just give me a call and, if I can help, I will."

"Very kind Martin."

Herring gives a light cough. "Yes well, that's excellent. Andy joined us whilst you were sunning yourself in Spain and I have to say he's settled in quickly. He's already caught the eye of Basil Farmer. We'll let you get on Martin and I'll continue the tour with Andy."

Once they leave the floor, Ben comes across and sits on the corner of Martin's table.

"I see you've met the new superstar. I was introduced earlier. Everyone is talking about him. He's only our age but he's already got this amazing reputation around the sector and apparently destined for big things."

"He seems nice enough."

"Yeah, I know. You may not be so charitable when he takes the next spot in the promotion queue. He could be your assistant manager by the end of the year."

During the morning, Martin loses counts of the number of people around the office who gossip about the new starter. His focus, on the spreadsheet he is working on, wanes during the morning to the point where he has come to a halt. Happy to be in Mario's taking a break over a minted lamb roll, he chats to Ben.

"If anybody else mentions what a superstar our latest recruit is, I'll slit my wrists."

"I know," says Ben. "It's bad enough going on about his skills, but when Tessa from Marketing started drooling over him, that was the last straw. I was trying to chat her up and all I got was a sickly smile from her as he passed by, followed by her whispering, 'isn't he dishy', whilst her tongue followed him along the floor."

"Maybe she thinks you're gay," says Martin, with a chuckle. "Y'know, feels she can confide and gossip with you about the office hunks."

"Hilarious, bloody hilarious. You're wasted here; you should be on stage at the local comedy club."

"Did you agree with Tessa?"

"About what?" asks Ben.

"About him being dishy."

"You're having a good laugh but aren't you a bit worried about the situation?" asks Ben.

"No, I don't fancy him."

"You keep making jokes, but you might end up laughing on the other side of your face. He could be the one who takes your promotion spot. Hardly been here five minutes and gets promoted, whilst you've been working your arse off for the last twelve months."

"Not worth worrying about," lies Martin. The new arrival has caused him some concern but he is trying to put it to one side. He adds, "I'll just have to keep my head down and hope for the best."

Back in the office, Martin re-focusses and has a productive afternoon. At the end of the day Ben suggests a quick, post work, pint. Martin declines, explaining that he has a prior engagement.

"Oh yeah, with who?" asks Ben, a little put out that he has been snubbed once again.

"Now don't get jealous. I promised Maureen I would drop in to her work event. They are celebrating twenty-five years in business or something like that. Partners are invited and she wants me there."

"If you're under the thumb, then I'll have to see if Andy is up for a drink," jokes Ben.

"Now I'm jealous."

Eighties anthems are being pumped out by the Deejay. Martin is standing against a wall at the side of the room nursing a beer, whilst Maureen dances with a male colleague to her favourite A-ha song, 'Take on me'. The song finishes, they laugh and hug before walking off the dance floor.

She introduces her colleague. "Martin, this is Andrew, he works in accounts."

"Hi Andrew."

"Hi Martin," responds Andrew. "Maureen's told me all about you."

"That must've been a riveting conversation," says Martin. A worried expression crosses Andrew's face.

"Don't mind him, Andrew. It's his sense of humour."

"Yeah, ignore me, Andrew. I'm just joking."

"Oh! okay. Er, I'll leave you two to catch up and get myself a drink."

They watch Andrew as he walks away. Once he is out of earshot, Maureen says, "That was a bit curt, wasn't it?"

"Sorry, didn't mean anything by it. A joke gone wrong. His name triggered it probably."

"Andrew, what's wrong with the name Andrew?"

"Nothing really. It's just I've had Andy this and Andy that, all day. We've got this new starter called Andy. Apparently, he's a superstar and everyone worships at the altar of Andy. Ben thinks he'll get in before me when the promotion Board comes up. If Andy is half as good as everyone seems to think, then Ben could well be right."

"Oh, that's a bit of a shame."

"I know, and to cap it all, Andy seems like a nice bloke."

Laughing, Maureen says, "I thought for a minute you were jealous about my Andrew and I quite liked it. But all the while it was another one."

Playing along, Martin says, "Maybe I am a bit jealous about yours as well."

She pecks him on the cheek and says, "Well no need, you're the one that I want, ooh ooh ooh. That's Oliver Newton John, if you didn't get it."

"I did."

Two days later, Martin takes the train home. Work is becoming beyond tiresome. The Andy love train is running stronger than ever and Martin feels that the next person who heaps praise on the golden boy in front of him, runs the risk of instant execution. Before he left the office, Herring stood over him giving an impromptu lecture about the marvellous work Andy has done resurrecting a halted project. It seems that the hitherto disastrous project is now on track and will meet the client's deadline. *Bully for Andy*, thinks Martin.

A message notification beeps on his phone. He reads a text from Maureen. She's unable to come over to the flat because her friend is leaving for another job and all her close colleagues are going for a meal to wish her goodbye. Martin types a reply. He tells her to enjoy herself and asks who else is going. She replies at once with the names Sandra, Lindy, Jessica and Andrew. He stares at the last name. Does he feel annoyed or perhaps just surprised, as Andrew is the only male in the group. Maybe he does feel just a tinge of jealousy.

Dismissing the thought, he pulls out the novel he's been reading. Only two chapters to go and he will be released from the obligation of finishing what he started.

Starting the final page, he is distracted by a jolt because the driver is heavy on the brakes. This causes him to look up from his page as the train limps into the station. The sign on the wall of the station shows that they are crawling into Archway, which triggers a thought. He has not seen Blondie for some time.

On cue, he looks out of the window and sees her on the platform passing his carriage. She must have been seated further up the train. As he tracks her progress, he notices that she is accompanied by a tall dark-haired man, who puts his arm around her shoulder as they walk. Squinting, he cannot quite believe his eyes. Surely not. Straining to get a clear view, he only manages a passing glimpse before they disappear out of sight down the exit tunnel. Although he would not bet his mortgage on it, he ponders the possibility that the man in question could be Andy, I'm so bloody perfect, Phillips.

Waiting for Ben to arrive, Martin is in the Ship and Shovell. He felt guilty at blowing Ben away the previous three nights and agreed to meet for a drink after work. Whilst checking a text from Ben telling him he has been delayed, his phone rings. It's Maureen.

"Hi love, how did the leaving do go last night?"

"It was good. A nice restaurant, but it turned out to be a late night, so I'm exhausted."

"Really, were you okay getting home on the tube that late."

"Yes, I was with Andrew, he gets off the same stop as me."

"Oh! really!", exclaims Martin, with mock surprise.

"Stop that. There's nothing going on between us. Jealousy doesn't suit you."

"Oh! So, you say. You two seem to be getting on like a house on fire."

"Just stop it. I didn't comment on your little boys' trip to party island. Did I? God knows what went on over there," replies Maureen, shifting defence to attack. "Okay then, I'll see you Friday. Love you."

As the call ends, Ben enters the pub. Martin waves and points to the glass of beer on the table.

"How's it going mate?" says Ben, picking up the glass and taking a drink.

"Good mate, what about you?" asks Martin.

"I know you don't want to hear this, but the 'Elect Andy for President' campaign is still going strong. I don't fancy your chances when promotion time comes up. It is fucking relentless."

"Yes, same. It's becoming boring."

"Are you concerned mate. I'd be really pissed off and a bit jealous."

"A bit, I've just had a gutful of listening to it."

"I meant to tell you," says Ben, "I happened to see him in the tube station the other day. Get this, I saw him go on your line. He must live somewhere along the Northern line as well. Imagine if he lives in Finchley Central. That would be a major pisser. Adding insult to injury."

This new revelation takes Martin back to his recent tube journey. Perhaps it was Andy who was with Blondie. What are the chances. Not only a career nemesis but an unrequited love nemesis. Surely not.

Behind him, a familiar voice greets them. Martin swings round on his stool.

"Well hello gentlemen. Long time no see," says Sebastian, haughtily.

"Sebster, how are you?" replies Ben.

"Mind if I join you two?"

"Not at all," says Martin. "Take a pew."

Sitting down, Sebastian says, "An odd phrase that. Taking a pew."

"I suppose so. Wouldn't be your style, would it Seb, being a church reference and all," says Martin.

"Indeed, it wouldn't Martin."

The exchange goes above Ben's head, who asks "What brings you here Seb?"

"Just passing through on my way home. Thought I might catch you two reprobates in here."

Their conversation is light, reminiscing about the Ibiza trip. Ben excuses himself for a toilet break. Once he sees Ben enter the restroom, Sebastian turns to Martin.

"So, Martin, how are things at work? I hear you have a new colleague."

"I won't even ask how you know that. But for the record you would hate him. He is Mister fucking Perfect."

"You're quite right, not my type at all. But things are not always as they seem. You can't always judge a book by its cover. How do you feel about this new imposition?"

"Don't know really. Annoyed at the incessant hero worshipping."

"A bit jealous?"

Martin ponders the question, before answering. "Maybe a bit, but I'm probably more pissed off constantly hearing about how good he is."

"Understandable. I called in for a reason. I'd like you to come to my office again for a little chat. Can you do that tomorrow?"

"To be honest it's a bit of a pain. But I can take a longer lunch hour I suppose."

"I won't take too much of your time Martin. From your office it shouldn't take too long to get to Mayfair and you'll be back behind your desk within the hour. I'll even have a little light lunch for you. See you at one o'clock."

"Okay, I'll be there."

"Splendid. Right, I'll pootle off. This priest is taking up a lot of my energy."

"What about Ben."

"Just tell him I got a call and had to leave urgently."

Having told Herring that he might take a little longer than an hour for lunch, Martin leaves the office for his appointment. He takes the Bakerloo line to Piccadilly Circus, and then one stop along the Piccadilly line to Green Park. Less than twenty minutes after leaving his office, he rings the bell of Sebastian's Mayfair pied de terre. Harry answers the door and shows Martin directly into the office, where Sebastian waits. On the desk there is a small plate of sandwiches and a carafe of freshly squeezed orange juice. Sebastian gestures for Martin to help himself.

"Not your usual prawn or minted lamb Martin. They are Cromer crab and lettuce; delicious I might say."

Taking a bite, Martin is pleasantly surprised. He pours himself a glass of orange juice.

"So, Martin, I have called you here today to discuss the latest test."

Reaching for another sandwich, the first having barely touched the sides, Martin waits for Sebastian to continue.

"You may or may not have realised that you've been subjected to another test."

"To be honest I wasn't sure. Too pre-occupied with stuff at work," replies Martin.

"Those things pre-occupying you were part of the test. Namely Mister Phillips. Though he is only part of the test."

"What were you testing?"

"Envy Martin. Good old envy. Often described as a sad or resentful covetousness towards the traits or possessions of another person."

"So, you were trying to make me envious of Andy Phillips."

"Indeed, and I have to say despite my best and concerted efforts, I wasn't successful."

"Full disclosure, I did feel a bit jealous."

"Oh! we realise that Martin, but nothing like enough to qualify. Having a vague or minor feeling doesn't constitute envy. You see there are three stages, the first of which is trying to lower another person's reputation. In that respect you didn't even make a mild attempt to dishonour Mister Phillips. The second stage, which is joy at another's misfortune, didn't even come into play as you hadn't sought to undermine him in the first place. As for the third stage, which is hatred, you didn't even get close."

"I did get pissed off."

"Irritation isn't hatred, Martin. But there is more. I tried to make you jealous and envious with Maureen's little escapades with another Andrew. Her colleague. But that failed as well. You trust her implicitly, and rightly so."

"Is that it then?"

"Not quite, I even tried to make you envious of Mister Phillips through the Blond object of your unrequited love."

"So, he was with her in the tube station," says Martin.

"Indeed, he was, but you held fast."

"Bully for me."

"Yes. Bully for you, Martin. The result of this is, despite my best efforts, you passed the test."

"Three all then," says Martin, with relish.

"Three all it is, with one left."

Scowling, Martin says, "That's all very well, but with your interference and game playing you've left me with the likes of Phillips to endure."

"We'll see about that. Call me vindictive, as well as a bad loser, but I expect more effort from those I use. Mister Phillips did not pass muster, a bit too nice for his own good. I feel the need to act."

"Underneath that smooth exterior, you're a nasty bastard. Aren't you Sebastian?"

"Always Martin, always."

The following morning Martin had barely logged in when Ben rushed over to his desk.

"Hey Marto." Wide eyed and animated, Ben looked fit to burst.

"Jeez mate, calm down. You look like you're gonna have a heart attack."

"Have the heard the news?"

"Clearly not," replies Martin.

"The Golden Boy has gone. Phillips. The rumour is he's been sacked."

"Sacked, you're kidding me. For what?"

"Agnes in Marketing says her mate in HR told her that it was gross misconduct."

"No way, he's way too nice."

"Yep, he's nice alright and an animal lover too."

"So?"

"So, the IT lot found he had a load of animal porno on his work laptop. The rumour is that he's got a thing about Llamas. Agnes says she was told he was paid off in his previous role which is why we were able to head hunt him. There's a non-disclosure agreement with his last employer."

"I can't believe it." Seeing Herring striding across the open plan towards him, Martin says, "you'd better shush now Ben, Herring's on his way over."

As Herring arrives, Ben leaves.

"Morning Mister Hazel."

"Morning Herring," replies Martin.

"Just letting you know that Mister Phillips will not be working with you on the joint project next month."

"Really, why not?"

"Actually, he won't be working on any project. He's left us."

"Oh! that's a shame. He's a bit of a star, isn't he? And he was only here five minutes. Is there some sort of personal problem he's got to deal with."

"A star you say. More of a falling star. But the reasons are confidential. For the ears of management only. I'm sure you understand. I'm not allowed to say anything to junior staff members."

"No worries. If it's management in confidence, I fully understand. It's a shame though. He is well liked and had a fair bit of charisma. A sort of animal magnetism."

Listening to the conversation from his desk, Ben lets out a loud snort. Herring swings round to look at him and turns back to find Martin's expression hadn't changed. Poker faced, Martin says, "I did think when I asked him about why he left his last job, that he looked a bit sheepish. I hope he didn't pull the wool over management's eyes."

Martin expression remains deadpan.

Another loud snort from Ben echoes across the room.

Searching for something appropriate to say, Herring struggles to respond. "Er, well, yes, yes. I suppose you're right. Let's leave it at that shall we. In the meantime, you'll have to lead the project alone. Supervise both teams until we find a replacement."

"No worries," says Martin.

After watching Herring walk back to his office, Martin looks over to Ben who is sniggering so hard that he has tears in his eyes. With a smile and a twinkle in his eye, Martin returns to his spreadsheet.

He has a fleeting thought of, '*Well done, thanks Sebastian.*'

To his surprise, he hears the timbre of Sebastians voice in his mind. '*And well done to you, Martin. You were very funny; there's hope for you yet.*'

25

ONCE I HAD A LOVE AND IT WAS A GAS.

O n the Friday, Martin receives a text from Sebastian. There is a week to go before the contract ends and its customary to conduct a debrief. They agree to meet at the Black Cat Café on Saturday morning.

Martin wakes up with a feeling of excitement and anticipation. Maureen is in the shower singing an old hit by Blondie. He shouts for her to leave the water running, telling her he will jump in after she is done.

They sit together at the breakfast table, drinking orange juice.

"That was a pleasant evening," says Maureen.

"Yeah. It was nice," replies Martin.

"What have you got on today?" she asks.

"Not a lot. Once you've gone to your class, I'm going to meet up with Sebastian for a coffee. He's one of the blokes I was in Ibiza with."

"What's he like?"

"He's okay. Has a wicked sense of humour but quite sophisticated."

"That's nice. Actually, I think it's good you've got a new friend. I sometimes have my doubts about Ben. His sole interest seems to be getting drunk and chasing after women. At his age it's all a bit sad in my opinion."

"Maybe," says Martin. "Or maybe he's looking for love." Hearing Maureen's opinion on Ben, he's pleased he didn't tell her he's out on the town with him tonight. Against his better judgement he had agreed to be Ben's wingman on a trip to Infernos, a new nightclub in Barnet. His usual offsiders, Jacko and Dave, were otherwise engaged.

"You're a better person than me Martin. Or possibly you're just a bit naive."

"You could be right."

"Okay. Time for me to toddle off. I've got a lot on this weekend so I'll see you next week. Maybe Wednesday, if that suits you."

"Yep. Let's lock that in. We can go to the wine bar."

"Excellent, see you." She pecks him on the cheek.

The door slams shut, marking her breezy exit from the flat.

As Maureen makes her way to her Pilates class, Martin walks to the café and finds a spare table. Shortly after the two coffees he ordered are delivered to his table, Sebastian enters the café and joins him dressed in his usual casual chic. Black polo shirt, chinos and loafers. In contrast Martin is dressed in outdated jeans and a shapeless tee-shirt that has been through the washing machine too many times.

"I have to say Martin; I've found this project very entertaining."

"Glad to be of service."

Stroking his goatee, Sebastian gives Martin an appraising look. "I also think that you've developed in this process."

"How so?" asks Martin.

"Less timid, a bit more edge and your sarcasm and humour are way higher up the scale than when we started. There's more of a spring in your step so to speak."

"I'm not sure that I should feel happy about being complimented by the devil."

"So finally, you believe I am the devil."

"Devil, demon, whatever. I don't care. As long as I get my money."

"There goes that greed thing again Martin. It seems that a long time has passed since you committed the first sin. Unfortunately, after that promising start, your performance has been a little mixed, I have to say."

"Let's not dwell on the past Sebastian. So, where are we at. Six sins down and a week to go. Does the money get deposited immediately after the period closes?" asks Martin, theatrically rubbing his hands together.

"Don't worry Martin, you'll get the money. You won't be kept hanging on. The other side wouldn't allow it and they insist on playing by the rules."

"Right then, are we done? Is this all you wanted to tell me?"

"Pretty much. We'll not be meeting face to face again until the contract ends which, as you know, is next Friday, late afternoon. So, you'll need to leave that day free. Are you able to take a day off work?"

"No worries. For five million I'll take the whole year off."

"That's the spirit. Well, as that's settled, I'll be off and see you next Friday. I'll pay for the coffees on the way out. Until then, be good, or preferably, be bad." Sebastian chuckles at his own joke and rises from his seat.

"Hang on Sebastian. Where do we meet next Friday?"

His question is met with a mischievous grin. "It will all become clear during the week. It's not goodbye, it's au revoir."

After finishing his coffee, Martin gets up to leave but the server calls him over.

"Excuse me sir, you need to pay for the coffees."

"Oh! sorry. My friend said he would pay on the way out. He must have forgotten."

Back in his flat, Martin opens his laptop and logs on to work remotely. He fills in a leave request form and emails it to Herring. A stickler for the rules, Herring would complain if he wasn't given the required notice of three working days per leave day requested. After he logs off and closes the laptop, his phone beeps. It's a message from Ben telling him to meet at eight o'clock in the Three Hammers, a pub near Infernos. He responds with the thumb's up emoji.

Looking around the flat, he tuts and decides it needs a good clean. The next hour is spent dusting, wiping and vacuuming. Once he is finished, he inspects his own work and gives it the seal of approval before he is suddenly overcome with fatigue. It's two thirty so he decides to have a power nap, to set him up for a long evening.

A car in the street outside the flat issues a large shrieking noise. The owner has set off his car alarm accidentally. Martin wakes with a start, realises the alarm is outside the flat, rubs his eyes and checks his phone. He does a double take, unable to believe the time. The clock shows six thirty. His power nap had lasted four hours and needs to get a move on. He makes a coffee to revive himself and clear his foggy head, then jumps into the shower. Despite a delay on the tube line and a long walk from High Barnet tube station, he enters the Three Hammers with five minutes to spare. Ben arrived early and is already halfway through his first pint. There is a full pint glass next to him, waiting to be claimed by Martin.

"Man, I'm buzzing tonight. I've been on a lean run recently. Tonight's the night I'm gonna break my duck."

Martin laughs in response. "Mate, your whole life's been a lean run."

"Fuck off. I'm serious, I've got to pull tonight."

"Mate, you couldn't pull a muscle."

"Fuck off again, Martin. You're my wingman and I'm relying on you to focus on your role. We'll be hunting in pairs and you'll need to keep the ugly one busy."

"Taking a different perspective, in other words, that of the female victims you select, what if they think you're the ugly one. What do you want me to do then?"

'We'll cross that unlikely bridge when we get to it," laughs Ben.

"Jeez, that was expensive," complains Martin, bringing back two drinks to their table.

They arrived at the club early and though the music is pumping there's only a few customers standing at the bar and a group of five women shuffling half-heartedly on the dancefloor.

"Mate, it's a night club, you always get scalped with the price of drinks. That's why we loaded up at the Three Hammers. Don't moan. We've got a table near the dancefloor so we're in prime position."

"It's pretty bloody empty."

"We're early mate. Don't fret yourself, it'll soon fill up after the pubs close."

An hour later the club is packed and the dancefloor is a pumping mass. All seats are occupied and it's standing room only around the dancefloor, except for the two unoccupied chairs at their table. Ben is focussed on the crowd bobbing and gyrating to the music whilst Martin returns from the bar balancing four drinks in his hands. Having queued patiently whilst trying and failing to catch the eyes of one of the bar staff, he decides it's prudent to double up on the order when he finally gets served. Gingerly, he places the drinks on the table, relieved there is no spillage.

A female voice catches his attention as he is sitting down, so he looks up and nearly knocks one of the glasses of beer over.

"Excuse me, are these other two seats taken?" asks Blondie, who is accompanied by her friend. Immediately Martin recognises the friend. She was with Blondie when he followed them through Archway a month ago.

"Er, no, please help yourself," says Martin, nudging Ben. Ben drags his eyes away from the dancefloor.

"You were ages mate," says Ben. Martin replies with a slight nod in the direction of Blondie and her friend, who are pulling out the unoccupied seats. Slightly perturbed at being stared at by Ben as she places her wine glass on the table, Blondie says, "I'm sorry, but the place is packed and these are the only free seats." Ben continues to stare. Glancing over to her friend for support, she starts to babble nervously. "We're both desperate to rest our legs, aren't we Helen? I hope you don't mind. At first, we thought they were taken by two of your friends but when no-one claimed them, we thought we'd ask."

Seeing his friend stare, Martin elbows him. "We don't mind, do we Ben?"

"Er, no, of course not."

"Please feel free to ignore Ben," jokes Martin to lighten the exchange, "he's only got limited social skills." He turns to Blondie's friend and says, "Hi Helen, pleased to meet you," and then holds out his hand for Blondie to shake.

Blondie gives a polite laugh and says, "Oh! I'm sorry, my name's Katie."

At last, a name to the face, thinks Martin.

The seating arrangements work out perfectly. Katie occupies the seat nearest Martin and Helen is nearest to Ben, who having recovered from his initial shock, is now in lothario charm mode. Their conversation is light and easy as they get to know each other. Helen's body language favours Ben, crossing her legs towards him and laughing at all his quips. Katie is more reserved but is comfortable talking to Martin whilst the other pair are getting on like a house on fire. Ben buys a round of drinks and he is soon pounding the dancefloor with

Helen whilst Martin and Katie remain seated, watching their friends.

Three dances later, Ben and Helen are still going strong. Occasionally Ben leans in to say something and Helen reacts by throwing her head back and laughing. Although the conversation with Katie is relaxed, Martin does not suggest a dance until she takes the initiative. Across the sound system the Deejays voice booms.

"Allllllriiight everybody, it's midnight and time for our signature tune at Infernos."

When the introduction to the music starts, Katie immediately recognises it. "Hey, Martin, it's an oldie but one of my favourites. Come on let's go."

She grabs his hand and leads him to the dancefloor as the Deejay introduces the song.

"YEAAAHHH," shouts the Deejay, "It'ssss Disco Inferno by the Trammps."

The first verse of song pumps through the speakers.

"Burn, baby, burn. Burn, baby, burn.

Burn, baby, burn. Burn, baby, burn.

Burning."

A combination of the alcohol and the beat of the seventies disco music make Martin's dancing less awkward than usual. Across the floor Ben and Helen are gyrating their bodies around each other in time with the music.

All four stay on the dancefloor for the next three songs before returning to their table.

Helen flops down in her chair giggling. "I am absolutely exhausted," she declares.

"Shall I get another round," gasps Ben, breathing heavily from the exertion.

"Not for us," says Katie. She looks over to Helen. "We need to go Helen. We've got an early start tomorrow and at this rate we won't be in bed before two o'clock."

Ben and Helen exchange glances, and she says, "I really better go Ben, but I've had an amazing time." She makes a contrived pout of disappointment.

"Me too," replies Ben, trying to appear cool. "How about we all meet up next Friday?"

"Yeah, that would be great."

"I don't mean to be the killjoy," says Katie, "but we can't next Friday. We've got to be at the airport early on Saturday morning."

"Oh! shit, of course," says Helen. "Sorry Ben but we have a girl's week in Menorca. We're going with two other old friends from school."

Feeling guilty, Katie says, "We could get together before we go away. How about next Thursday?"

"Yeah," comes Ben's quick response, before realising that his cool demeanour has slipped.

"Suits me," says Helen.

"What about you?" asks Katie, looking directly into Martin's eyes. Seeing she is also keen to meet, Martin looks over to Ben, whose expression shows he expects nothing less than a positive response.

"Er, yeah. Sure. That would be good."

"That's settled then. How about meeting at the Three Hammers at eight," suggests Ben.

"No, that place is a bit rough. Let's meet somewhere a bit nicer," says Katie. "How about St. John's Tavern, it's in Archway. Have you ever been there?"

"Er, I don't think so," lies Martin.

"Sounds good," says Ben.

"We go there lots. It's a lovely place, I'll book a table for four," says Helen. It's a gastro pub. Let's meet at seven."

They leave the club together and wait on the street corner away from the main entrance of the club. Two bouncers are having an altercation with three drunks and they don't want to get drawn into the drama. Katie orders an Uber whilst Ben chats to Helen, and Martin looks at his phone. He is silently praying that there is no message from Maureen which will escalate the mild feeling of guilt that he is already feeling. There are no unread messages.

The car arrives and Katie jumps in. Helen hesitates and stands on her tiptoes to give Ben a peck on his cheek before getting in the back seat next to her friend. Once the Uber turns round the corner, Ben gives a fist pump and shouts, "GET IN."

Martin laughs. "For you that was a successful night. Dare I say probably the most successful of your sad women pulling career thanks to, yours truly, the wingman extraordinaire."

Smirking, Ben retorts. "Not only for me mate. You've played it cool, but out of nowhere you've connected with Blondie after all these weeks." Ben pats himself on the chest. "And, my friend, you've got yours truly here to thank for that."

"I think me and Katie are just the extras. Chaperones for the sex hungry desperate couple."

"Come off it, mate. I saw the way she looked at you. She's keen."

"No way."

"One hundred percent and you've got a few days to think on what you are going to do about it."

26
DON'T KNOW WHEN I'LL BE BACK AGAIN.

"**I**'ve approved and sent your leave request to HR," says Herring, standing over Martin who is sitting at his desk.

"Thanks."

Herring waits for further elaboration, but none is forthcoming. Undeterred, he says, "I have to say I'm surprised at your request. You've only just come back off holiday and with Phillips leaving we're under pressure. You've got a lot on at the moment."

Martin wants to respond by saying if that's the case when doesn't he just fuck off and let him get on with his work. But he doesn't.

"It's only a day, no big deal."

"Anyone would think you're looking elsewhere. Going for a job interview. Disappearing off and leaving us in the lurch."

Martin considers Herring's comment and crafts a truthful response with care. He does not want to dishonest but neither does he want to share his plans knowing that once he gets the five million, Herring would not see him for dust.

"I can assure you that I am not going for a job interview. Nor have I applied for any jobs." He's going to add that he is happy working at the company but pulls back from making that statement to avoid breaking his private undertaking to be honest.

"Well, I'm glad to hear it. I know you're disappointed about not getting your promotion but in the coming months that may be rectified. One never knows. We've got a lot on and there is an opportunity to shine."

Looks like he's beginning to panic with Phillips leaving and all the increased responsibility and work that's falling on our teams, thinks Martin, relishing his boss's discomfort.

"Good point, I'd best get on then," replies Martin, enjoying the opportunity to dismiss Herring from his presence.

Waiting for Herring return to his office, Ben rises from his desk and comes over to Martin. "That was hilarious mate, you sent him away like a teacher dismissing a naughty schoolboy."

"I've had a bit of a gutful of him and this place to be honest. Frankly, it wouldn't worry me if I was sacked or made redundant. I'd welcome the break."

"That's not going to happen, is it? You're Herring's main man. Without you he'd be paddleless, up a creek. Moving on to more important matters … just checking you're still okay for tomorrow."

"Yeah, yeah, don't worry yourself. I won't let you down. I've got to get through tonight first. I'm out with Maureen.

"You're turning into a regular Casanova. That Ibiza thrip obviously did you some good," says Ben, chuckling on his walk back to his desk.

Refreshed from his shower, Martin sits on the edge of his bed checking messages on his phone. A text from Maureen tells him to meet her at On Cloud Wine at 7.30pm. She is running a bit late. Checking the time, Ben sees he has an hour to spare before he needs to leave the flat. He decides to have a quick nap and sets his alarm to alert him. Half an hour later he is woken by the shrill alarm. He's surprised that he managed to fall asleep and that the time had passed so quickly. After allowing himself ten more minutes dozing, he gets dressed and leaves to go to the wine bar.

There are only a handful of customers and a lot of spare tables, so Martin looks around the bar for the best place to sit. Not expecting her to have arrived, he almost misses Maureen sitting at a table near the window. She waves at him and he joins her. There is a glass of red wine waiting for him.

"You look as though you've been drugged Martin. I was waving and waving and waving, but you didn't see me. Sometimes I think you take me for granted."

"Sorry love. Believe it or not I passed out on the bed after my shower."

"Really. Was that due to your big weekend clubbing with your besty."

Martin's heartbeat quickens slightly, from guilt. Trying not to sound defensive he says, "It wasn't a late night and quite uneventful really. I was glad to get home to be honest. No, it's nothing to do with that, more about what's going on at work. It's full on and the golden boy they recruited, Andrew Phillips, left under a cloud, leaving yours truly in the lurch. Herring is panicking."

"Well, that's a good thing. Perhaps he'll value you more."

"Perhaps pigs will fly."

"Okay, enough about your work. Let's talk about Lanzarote. Everything is booked and two weeks from now we'll be sitting in a Spanish wine bar eating tapas."

Pleased that the conversation had moved on to safer ground, Martin consciously builds up his enthusiasm. "Yeah, really, really looking forward to it. I love Spanish food."

"Me too. All the nice restaurants will be in the streets behind those overlooking the sea."

"Yep. If you want to look at the sea whilst you're eating, then it will be burgers, kebabs, pizzas or fish and chips," says Martin.

"Restaurants with a Union Jack on the sign," adds Maureen, running with the theme.

"A pint of bitter and karaoke 'til late."

Maureen laughs. "Listen to the two of us. A pair of snobs."

"Not me. I'll be happy with a good kebab on the odd night out."

"Can't wait," says Maureen, blowing Martin a kiss.

Martin sings, "We'll be leaving on a jet plane …"

Throwing her head back Maureen laughs. "You never get the words right when you attempt to sing."

"Whaddya mean by 'attempt'. John Denver, eat your heart out."

"It's not, we'll be leaving, it's, 'cause I'm leaving on a jet plane."

"Intentional mistake, I was being romantic and used 'we'll be leaving.'"

After a pleasant evening, Maureen stays over at Martin's flat. It had been quite like old times. When he kisses her goodbye in the morning, he has a tinge of guilt when he thinks about his arrangement in the evening.

The journey into work is uneventful. Unusually for him in recent weeks, Martin does not feel the need see Blondie, aka Katie, on his way into work. It has the potential to be an awkward encounter outside the social environment. Having seen her at close quarters in the flesh and spoken to her for most of the evening last Saturday, her allure has grown. Not only that, but he also danced with her at close quarters and arranged a date, even if it is under the pretence that it is all for the benefit of Ben and Helen. Despite a nice evening with Maureen, he's struggling to get Katie out of his mind, especially with the evening ahead.

A series of client meetings during the morning makes the first half of the day race by. Ben emails him suggesting they meet in Mario's at half past one for a quick sandwich. He wants to discuss tactics for the evening ahead.

"Tactics, mate," says Martin through a mouthful of prawn sandwich.

"Yes mate, tactics. What do we do if Helen and I are, y'know, getting on well."

"I suppose you either go back to your place or hers and make sweet love. What do you think will happen?"

"Yeah, I know that you muppet. But you're gonna have to stay with Katie, you can't just bugger off halfway through the evening or that could stymie my chances."

"Of course I won't do that. The person most likely to mess up your chances is you. Just make sure she doesn't get to know you too well,"

Ben tuts. "Hilarious mate, fucking hilarious."

Patting Ben on the shoulder, Martin says, "You can rely on me, don't fret. Just concentrate on your own game. We both know it needs quite a bit of work to get it up to speed."

"Mate, I was on fire the other night. Helen couldn't get enough of me."

"Then you've nothing to worry about," says Martin as he pops the last of his sandwich into his mouth. "Right. I've got to get back. There's a lot on and I'm off tomorrow."

"Yeah, you said that this morning. How come you're taking the day off?" asks Ben.

"Oh! just a few personal things to sort out," replies Martin, being purposely vague. "Come on let's get back," he adds, to cut off any further probing from Ben. He need not have worried; Ben is focussed entirely on the evening ahead.

"Yep, let's go. I want to leave early today. Do you want to go for a drink before we meet up?"

"Nah! But maybe we could get there early and have a drink at the bar before they arrive," suggests Martin.

"Good idea mate, let's get there half an hour before."

27

SOMETHING CALLED LOVE, WELL THAT'S LIKE HYPNOTIZING CHICKENS.

Both arrive at St. John's Tavern a few minutes before their agreed time. With the reservation not until seven, they are invited to wait at the bar. They place themselves on the end nearest the entrance so their dates would see them as soon as they arrive and by six fifty are into their second drink of the evening.

Two couples leave the table that Helen had reserved. Once it is cleared and reset, Martin and Ben are shown to the table just as the two women arrive.

Helen calls to them as she approaches the table. Katie follows her close behind.

"Perfect timing. You just beat us to it."

"We were just a bit early, so had a quick drink at the bar," replies Martin. Ben was not going to admit they came earlier, thinking it appears uncool, but Martin's admission stymies that strategy,

A flurry of slightly awkward hugs and cheek pecking precedes seating themselves at the table. For the first twenty minutes the conversation is polite, steering clear of any topics that could remotely be at risk of controversy. Once they have all disposed of their second bottle of wine and Ben has ordered a third, everyone has loosened up. Martin is silently impressed with his friend, who is showing a side to his personality that has hitherto been well hidden. Ben is proving to be both charming and witty. Martin supposes that they've never been in the scenario they find themselves now, a double date, and this may explain the apparent transformation. Their joint social ventures are generally single gender affairs focussing on alcohol and laddish banter.

Once the main course is cleared Ben and Helen both excuse themselves to visit the restrooms, leaving Martin alone with Katie at the table.

"I hope you don't feel too awkward Martin. I know you've been dragged into this at Ben's request. Helen is at fault as well. I don't know why they didn't just bite the bullet and go on a date alone."

"It's no problem for me Katie, but don't feel as though you have to hang around on my behalf."

"No, don't get me wrong Martin. I am pleased to be here and get a chance to learn more about you. I really enjoyed your company at the nightclub. I had a great time and was glad this date was set up. But if you need to get off, the same applies."

'Oh! not at all Katie. I was also keen to meet up again. I am just a little self-conscious that you've been pressed ganged into being Helen's chaperone."

Katie bursts out laughing. "Chaperone! I can assure you the last thing Helen needs is a chaperone. She knows her mind and I think she is quite keen on seeing more of Ben. Talking of which …" Katie looks up and points. Martin sees they are both walking back to the table.

As she sits down, Helen is giggling at something Ben has said. She addresses Martin.

"Your friend is quite the comedian, Martin."

"Including him, that's now two people that think that's the case," replies Ben, quite surprised at the speed of his own wit. Katie bursts out laughing.

"Looks like I'm not the only comedian here," says Ben, slightly miffed, but hiding it well.

"Ben says he knows of a late-night bar nearby, I think we should all go there," says Helen.

Katie looks across to Martin for a steer on his thoughts. Martin nods and says, "I'm happy to try it but you don't need to feel obliged to babysit me, Katie."

"No, I think that would be good," she replies.

"It's five minutes' walk down the Junction Road towards Tufnell Park."

They pay the bill and walk into the unseasonably warm evening. Ben and Helen stroll a few metres ahead, chatting, laughing and leaning into each other as they make their way towards the bar.

"They're getting on like a house on fire," says Martin, before he realises that Katie had unconsciously hooked her arm around his, as they follow behind.

The bar is small, dimly lit with an intimate atmosphere, bolstered by the quiet, easy listening music floating around the room. Andy Williams is crooning 'Can't take my eyes off you,' and an older couple sitting at a nearby table, sing along and smile at each other.

Helen looks at them and says, "Isn't that sweet. I wonder if I'll be that romantic at that age."

"You're not that romantic at this age," jokes Katie.

"Sod off Katie," replies Helen, chuckling.

More drinks than they intended to have later, the barman calls time. All four are drunk and all inhibitions dissolved. They laugh, joke and banter easily as, once more, they emerge into the evening which now has a slight chill in the air.

They gather a few yards outside the door of the bar. Helen turns to Katie. "Ben has invited me back to his for a night cap, so I'll see you tomorrow. It's a couple of tube stops away so we'd better get going before the last train."

Katie looks at the time on her phone. "You'd better get a move on or you'll miss the last train. What about you Martin?"

"Yeah. I suppose I'd better get off as well or I'll miss it."

"You're welcome to come to mine for a nightcap. My flat is only a couple of streets away from here. You can get an Uber home after."

Looking across at Ben and Helen, he sees them both smirking. Ben claps his hands and says, "Right then, we'd better get a shift on Helen or we will miss the train. You'd better see Katie home Martin. You can't let a woman roam the streets alone at this time of night."

Watching Ben and Helen trot off towards the tube station, Martin turns to Katie. "Well, if you're sure, then let's go before you get accosted."

Katie laughs and they walk arm in arm leaving the main road to weave through side streets. Eventually they arrive at a Georgian house converted into three flats. Katie leads him down narrow steps to the basement flat.

Decorated and furnished in light colours to counter the darkness of a flat below ground level, Martin notices that there are no photographs. Whilst everything down to the small ornaments on the shelves are tasteful, the neutrality of the interior design does not give the place a homely feel. It is almost as if the flat has been staged for a sale, rather than for comfort.

Sitting on the cream sofa, the room sways slightly, Martin has drunk more than he thought.

Katie brings in two whisky glasses, each with a small measure and joins him on the sofa. The whiskey is of high quality and its smoothness makes it slip down easily.

"Are you okay Martin?" asks Katie.

"Yah, I'm good, just slightly woozy after all the alcohol.

"Me too. You know it's late and you're welcome to stay the night. Would you like to?"

He looks into her eyes. *She's gorgeous*, he thinks.

She gets up and walks towards the bedroom. Martin stands and starts to follow.

A disembodies voice cuts through the air. Although the speaker is not shouting, his words resonate around the flat. The voice is loud and commanding.

"MARTIN, LISTEN TO ME. AT THE COUNT OF THREE I WILL CLICK MY FINGERS. THEN YOU WILL OPEN YOUR EYES AND REMEMBER NOTHING THAT HAPPENED TODAY.

ONE … TWO … THREE …"

28
JUST ABOUT
A YEAR AGO.

Ten months earlier, Martin arrives at the door of Sebastian's Mayfair pied de terre and is greeted by Harry. He is shown to Sebastian's office where he finds his host ensconced behind his desk. Two other men are waiting, both sitting on chairs at the side of the room. Sebastian points to the chair directly opposite him on the other side of his desk and Martin takes a seat.

"Good morning, Martin. I think you know both these gentleman. Mister Hopkins, who we appointed to represent your interests and Mister Cohen, our own legal representative. Both have been through the contract and have discussed the contents with you and are happy that the terms are fair and legally binding. Also, I understand that Mister Hopkins has discussed it with you at length and he's satisfied that you have a full understanding of the conditions."

"Yes, that is correct," replies Martin.

"Throughout the exercise, Mister Hopkins has been employed to monitor what transpires and, given you will be ignorant of what is happening, he will advocate for you, if he deems it necessary." Sebastian gives the solicitor a nod. Hopkins subconsciously strokes his bald head, before nodding back.

"So, where do I sign?" asks Martin, impatient to conclude proceedings.

"Before you sign, I want to give you a final opportunity to ask any further questions."

"No, I'm quite clear and satisfied. If I win, I get five hundred thousand pounds. If I lose, I get one hundred thousand for taking part."

Mister Hopkin's speaks up. "For absolute clarity Martin, can you confirm that you are content to abide by the decision of the panel on each test. I can guarantee that the process for their selection is unbiased and that all five panellists were selected and agreed by Mister Cohen and myself."

"Yes, I am happy."

Sebastian says, "Finally, those closely involved in the program, who are your friends and colleagues, including your partner Maureen, are fully on board and have no reservations."

"Yes, they all are."

Pointing to papers on the desk, Sebastian says, "Well then, please sign both copies in front of you at the places indicated by the yellow tabs."

Martin signs and pushes the documents back across the desk towards Sebastian, who smiles. "Thank you, Martin. Let me be the first to congratulate you. There were over one thousand candidates who applied and I examined twenty shortlisted candidates before selecting you. So well done and thank you for agreeing to take part."

"No problem, I can't wait to get started. When will that be?"

"In the coming months. For it to work, we will not be giving any notice nor signalling the start."

"What about the others?"

"They have been told all they need to know at the group briefing last week. When the project starts, they will be notified. I have to say, they are a good bunch of people and all of them, including Maureen, are excited at the prospect."

"So am I."

"And, Martin, so are we."

Hopkins gives a quiet cough, to gain the attention of the others. "I'd just like to make sure that Martin is clear that when the project starts, he will not be cognisant of the terms of this agreement until the end. That is right, is it not Mister Benedict?"

"It is indeed. I am sure Martin is fully aware. Isn't that right Martin?" asks Sebastian.

"Yes. Don't worry Mister Hopkins, I fully understand."

"Okay, everybody, I believe our business is concluded. And Martin …"

"Yes."

"We'll meet in due course. Although as far as you'll be concerned, next time we'll be meeting for the first time. When we do, I won't be Sebastian Benedict, I'll be Sebastian Balfour."

29
ON WITH THE SHOW, OOH I'LL TOP THE BILL.

Outside of the cinema, the white art deco façade houses a large pink bird. The Phoenix is one of a dying breed of enterprises which strains to keep itself independent from the chains that now dominate the scene for film goers. It is purposely chosen, by the Director, to premiere a much-anticipated show from the latest phenomenon to hit the world of magic and mentalism. Like the building itself, the show, consisting of seven one-hour episodes, endeavours to be different from the norm. For the Premiere, the highlights have been put together in a ninety-minute special before the series becomes available on Netflix. A select few have been invited, including all the participants and, of course, Martin.

The opening credits play eerie music whilst the head and shoulders of Sebastian Benedict, alias Balfour, fill the screen. The smiling clean-shaven face of the showman slowly transforms from a welcoming open expression to a sinister glare as black facial hair in the form of a goatee beard, gradually appears. When the music ends, Sebastian's expression conveys evil mischief and his eyes have a red hue. The face fades out and the title of the show appears.

SPEAK OF THE DEVIL.

When the title fades away, the first scene shows Sebastian sitting in a room that looks as though it has been lifted from a Victorian Gentlemen's Club. In his maroon, padded, leather chesterfield chair, Sebastian sits in a relaxed pose. A Victorian fireplace is behind, to his right. He addresses the camera.

"Welcome to my twilight world where fact, fiction, truth and lies overlap to create, for some, a new reality. In my last series I tackled the world of espionage. A world full of glamour and myth. I evaluated whether an innocent person could be used, through mind control, to assassinate a selected target. Was it fact, or the overactive imagination of conspiracy theorists, that people could be brainwashed, hypnotised if you will, to commit a heinous act such as murder."

The film cuts to the final scene of the previous series where the unsuspecting protagonist points a gun at his target and fires it. The weapon has been engineered to issue a loud noise which sounds like a gun but does not fire a bullet. The subject then drops the gun and flees. Sebastian returns to the screen.

In this series we will examine the issues of religious belief and morality. Can a man who is an ordinary decent law-abiding citizen and an atheist, be persuaded that the Devil exists. But it doesn't end there. Those who believe in the Devil, believe that he can tempt and set traps to lead good Christians to do evil. To commit what the religion regards as immoral acts. I believe it can be done and to ensure we have fair play, I've invited a special guest to watch my every move and adjudicate.

Let me welcome award-winning investigative journalist, Gavin Brockman."

The camera pans to another chesterfield chair, previously out of shot, opposite Sebastian. A grey haired, slim man, with piercing blue eyes nods at Sebastian.

"Welcome Gavin."

"Thank you, Sebastian. Happy to be involved."

"Now Gavin. You're an award-winning journo, with a reputation for hard edged inciteful investigative journalism. You aren't going to risk your reputation by being part of some parlour trick scam just to titillate the viewers. Am I right?"

"I'm here to fill the brief you gave me, which is to ensure, to the best of my knowledge and observation, that everything is genuine."

"You will be also chairing the panel which determines whether a sin has been committed for the sake of the exercise."

"I am. It is probably going to be subjective to some degree and it is agreed I will have the final say if the jury is split. I 've been invited in from the outset and involved in every stage of the selection process. I am one hundred per cent certain that the subject of the program is not a plant."

"A plant?"

"Yes. In other words, someone you know, who has been selected to act out a role and your wishes. I witnessed the exercise of interviewing applicants and the final choice of the candidate. I am fully satisfied that Mister Hazel is a genuine applicant with no prior knowledge of you or anyone involved in the production."

"Thank you, Gavin. Any questions for me?"

"Yes Sebastian. You do not describe yourself as a magician. What are you and what techniques do you employ?"

"Great question. I think I would describe myself as a psychological illusionist. I use a wide range of techniques. Certainly, I am trained in conjuring skills such as misdirection, but for these sorts of exercises I use memory techniques, hypnosis, body language reading, cognitive psychology, cold reading, subliminal techniques, neuro-linguistic programming and ideomotor suggestion techniques."

"I've heard of most of those, but one or two sound more like a foreign language. I don't want to get into a psychology lecture but accepting you use techniques with some sort of scientific basis, do you use other non-psychological techniques."

"What do you have in mind?" asks Sebastian.

"Well … paid actors for example."

"There are some paid actors in the show. You could argue I am one of them. Afterall, I am purporting to be the Devil. But to answer your question there are a handful. Katie and Helen for example, are actors. Not to mention Andrew Phillips of course, who took time out from a busy filming schedule to make an appearance in the second half of the film. But those in the show who are friends and work colleagues are all genuine. And yes, most are fully briefed and totally up to speed with what we are doing but they all react to what Martin's says or does. They do not guide him into situations at my behest nor do they lie or mislead with the obvious exception that they know what is going on."

"So how did you choose Martin?"

"Over a thousand applicants filled in a questionnaire. This enabled psychological profiling. A long list of potential subjects was invited to the studio and were assessed for their suitability, or rather susceptibility, to hypnotic suggestion. Martin stood out as the ideal candidate."

Gavin laughs. "Are you saying Martin is stupid?"

"Not at all, in fact the propensity to be hypnotised is often linked to good concentration and intellectual curiosity. It's not a weakness but rather a brain-based ability that involves a focused state of attention and the ability to tune out distractions."

"Anything else we need to know before we start the show?"

"Not much. Some of the filming and sound can be of a lower quality. We often use hidden cameras and microphones. Martin was made fully aware prior to the start that this would be the case and friends and work colleagues have all co-operated to make filming possible. I should also say that nothing Martin did is illegal. In fact, viewers will see at one point Martin takes marijuana. He did not. What he consumed contained no drugs but I had, during hypnotic suggestion, convinced him that when offered the cake, it did. I also programmed the effects he would feel once he ate the cake."

"Are you telling me that the hypnosis of Martin lasted several weeks?"

"Not really. Viewers will see that I appear many times as the supposed Devil. During those interactions I took the opportunity to top up and program new ideas prior to setting up a temptation scenario. Another good example is Katie. She is obviously an attractive woman but Martin's obsession with her is all down to my suggestion which I constantly re-enforced during our meetings. The same applies to his boss, Mister Herring. In the show he appears a buffoon but that is a combination of him acting as we directed and Martin's skewed perception re-enforced by his friend Ben, who we also recruited to help. I am told that John, that's Mister Herring, is highly respected in the company and in real life is Martin's mentor. As viewers will notice Mister Herring is clearly much older than Martin but through Martin's eyes, after my programming, he physically appears much younger."

"That's all I have for the moment Sebastian."

Sebastian turns to face the camera. "Thanks Gavin. One final comment from me. There's an old saying, don't judge a book by its cover. Please don't judge Martin and his actions. Remember, a lot of his behaviour is probably attributed to my hypnotic suggestion and the battery of other techniques I employ. Hypnosis is a powerful tool and there was quite an army of people, so called colleagues and friends, conspiring against him."

The audience bursts into laughter.

"Without further ado, let's get on with the show and see what happened."

The show begins and quickly runs through the events prior to the tests. Martin is seen with other candidates being hypnotised and assessed. It is the first time Martin has seen himself in a hypnotic state and can't quite believe how deeply he falls under Sebastians control. A few scenes introduce the main conspirators and Martin looks across the front row each time one of his party is featured. John Herring gives him a wicked smile and thumb's up when he appears in the show for the first time and uncharacteristically acts stupid, immature and clueless. Maureen chuckles when Martin gives her a reproving glance after she dupes him. Ben likewise. At the beginning, when he is filmed on a tube journey to work, he recognises 'baldy man'. He cannot believe that 'baldy man' is his solicitor, Mister Hopkins. How hypnotised could he have been not to realise?

When the scene where Sebastian tricks him into committing his first sin finishes, Martin turns to Sebastian who is sitting next to him, and sniggers, "I still think that it was unfair. Getting me on greed because I wanted the money. I mean tell me, who would have turned that down." Sebastian laughs in response.

Next up is a series of work scenes where he is filmed at meetings. There is also a hidden camera in the basement where he is tested on Sloth. Martin smiles. He came out well on this one. Secretly filmed in the pub, later that day, he gives a cheer when he decides to go back to work to help Ronald. He is less impressed by the scene where he helps Ben empty the fridge of his colleagues' food. Most of the audience are in tears laughing. Laughter still echoes around the cinema as the audience leave their seats for the intermission.

In the foyer, the audience's chatter gets louder as the free champagne goes down. Herring approaches Martin.

"Well done, Martin, you're soon to be a Netflix star."

"I don't know what to say John. I'm embarrassed at my behaviour."

"Don't be silly Martin, the whole thing was a blast and frankly my partner is excited to have a husband on Netflix. But tell me one thing. What did I look like twenty years younger?"

Martin laughs. "I don't know what to say, It's weird. Whenever I was talking to you at work it all seemed a bit surreal. I must admit that Sebastian's hypnotic suggestion of a younger you didn't portray you in the best light. At the risk of crawling to you, I have to say you didn't look anywhere near as good looking as you probably did twenty years ago."

Herring guffaws and says, "I'll need to process that to work out if I've been insulted or you're propositioning me. Anyway, I'll leave you alone, it looks like Ben wants a word."

"Jeez mate, Martin Hazel, worldwide reality star," announces Ben.

"Listen mate. You were great and it must have taken up a fair bit of time babysitting my project. What with Ibiza and the rest."

"Let me put you straight my friend. If you recall, I let you have the Ibiza apartment for free. Did I not?"

"Yes," replies Martin.

"Unfortunately, I can't now claim generosity. Our whole trip. That's Jacko, Dave and me, was paid for by the TV company. A sort of thank you. So don't feel too guilty on our behalf."

"What everything?"

"Yep. Flights, accommodation and they even picked up the incidentals on the hotel bill."

"Bloody hell. I didn't realise."

Maureen sidles up besides Martin and puts her arm around him. Ben says, "Catch you later mate, I'll leave you to chat with the love of your life."

Martin gives Maureen a peck on her cheek. "I was telling Ben that I appreciated the time he put in. Apparently, there was something in it for him. I should have guessed."

"Not just him. You're a hundred thousand pounds better off and you were a hair's breadth of getting the half million. If only you'd been able to keep your little fella in your pants."

Martin laughs, "I think, as you no doubt recall, the scene was stopped long before the critical moment. The case for the defence rests on the fact I was hypnotised by Sebastian, with a strong mental suggestion to follow through."

Raising an eyebrow, Maureen replies, "Well I'll guess we'll never know. But Ben isn't the only one who got a thankyou gift."

"Really?"

"Yes, you know our week in Lanzarote?"

"Yes. You're not going to tell me that the Lanzarote trip is paid for by the TV company."

"Actually Martin, no it isn't. We were never going for a week in Lanzarote. But … we are going to spend fourteen days in the Seychelles, all expenses paid." She hugs him and he lifts her off the ground and swings her around.

"That is bloody amazing."

A bells rings and one of the ushers announces that the second half will begin in five minutes. Once the audience are settled, the projectionist starts the show. Various scenes are shown in the office when Sebastian does his utmost to engineer a reaction of Wrath but fails. Maureen leans into Martin and whispers in his ear that she cannot believe he didn't react after all the buttons they pressed. She is far less impressed when the scenes in Ibiza appear on the screen. "My God, I never knew you are so full of shit," she whispers, with a furrowed brow.

After failing the Pride test, the scenes switch back to the office where Martin is tested for Envy. Again, Maureen whispers in his ear. "I can't believe you didn't recognise Andrew Phillps; he's on the BBC all the time. He's very dishy. Shame he's not here." When Sebastian tells Martin he has passed the Envy test in the final scene of that section, Maureen leans over once again. "Well done you, Andrew Phillips is good looking enough to make any man feel a bit jealous." She quietly chuckles into his ear.

In the final scene, filmed in rented flat which Martin believed at the time to be Katie's home, Martin squirms in his chair. He keeps his eyes glued to the screen to avoid eye contact with Maureen. The scene finishes with Sebastian intervening, having hidden in the ensuite. As Martin enters the bedroom. Sebastian's instruction is heard, closing off the scene.

"MARTIN, LISTEN TO ME. AT THE COUNT OF THREE I WILL CLICK MY FINGERS. THEN YOU WILL OPEN YOUR EYES AND REMEMBER NOTHING THAT HAPPENED TODAY. ONE … TWO … THREE …"

The final piece in the film reverts to the setting where Gavin is interviewing Sebastian.

"That last scene could have got a bit tricky," says Gavin, smirking into the camera.

"It was all under control Gavin. I also want to re-iterate that Martin is highly suggestible, which is why he was selected. I'm sure if I had not intervened, the outcomes in many of the scenarios are likely to be quite different. The point of the exercise is to prove that with a range of techniques, it's possible to make someone believe and behave out of their ordinary. They can be made to believe and do things that they would not do in normal circumstances."

"Even believe in the Devil?" asks Gavin.

"Yes, even that."

"Well, to conclude, Sebastian, I have to say what you did was highly impressive. Some would describe it as devilish."

The credits roll and are greeted by rapturous applause.

One year later, Martin and Maureen buy a house together in Muswell Hill using the hundred-thousand-pound fee for appearing in the show (as well as income from TV appearances including a reality couples show) for a deposit.

Two years later, Ben gets engaged to Helen. After six months, Helen breaks off the engagement and moves in with a B-list actor who has a regular part in a C-List soap opera.

Three years later, Martin and Maureen have a baby boy. They call him Sebastian.

Four years later, John Herring is made a partner of the company.

Five years later, Martin gets his second successive promotion and is now a Senior Manager. He no longer sees 'Baldy man' nor 'Blondie' nor the Devil on his way to work. He is still an atheist but occasionally borders on agnostic.

The end